EAGLES of a DIFFERENT FEATHER

The United States and Mexican responses to the demands within and without World War II. An intriguing novel revealing hidden truths of an ambivalent ally, incorporating fictional characters and imagined scenarios.

By Joaquin Hawkins

Book design: Mike Riley Ajijic Books Publishing.
www.ajijicbooks.com

First printing September 2018

Contents

ACKNOWLEDGMENTS

I must pay a sincere tribute to a certain Mike Riley of Riberas del Pilar of Lake Chapala, Jalisco, Mexico. Mike is a talented publication designer and more. He understands computers and the publishing world better than I do and without his patience and expertise *Eagles* would never have made it into publication. His neutral eyes and savvy brought all aspects of the manuscript together in a final ready form to publish this book. Mike's in-put was of paramount importance!

I also must pay tribute to Patrick Winn of Ajijic, Jalisco, Mexico. He was the first to tune me into the historical happenings of Japanese-Mexican internments of World War ll, a fact never known to so many, including myself. This mere introduction to nigh-lost history prompted further investigations and the more I discovered the more my imagination entertained kernels of thought that resulted in this novel.

So, to both individuals I am grateful for the inspiration to stay the course and for the assistance to cross the finish line.

Of the novels I have written it is most definite that without my wife Efigenia's encouragement nothing would have proceeded forth from the keyboard. Her love of books, readings of books with educational merit and degrees in Comparative Literature Studies of the World seemingly have put her on a higher stage than me. For her to promote my talents is indeed gratifying, yet humbling.

Forward

'Birds of a feather flock together,' so the saying goes. But, they do not necessarily soar at the same heights. There are yet determinate differences.

The Great Seal of the United States bears in the center a bald eagle with wings spread out. It has fast-held within its beak a scroll bearing the national motto; e pluribus unum, Latin for *out of many, one*; a proclamation of national unity. The left foot has firmly gripped in its talons thirteen arrows signifying the original thirteen states, and within the talons of the right foot is firmly clutched an olive branch, representing the national desire for peace. The combined representation is that of a national commitment to peace, but an ever-readiness if war is thrust upon the nation. To emphasize the strong commitment to peace the face of the eagle is focused upon the olive branch, but with the arrows of war in standby mode.

The Mexican flag bears an eagle in its center, perched upon the prophetic cactus of Aztec legend, firmly holding within its beak a serpent. The symbolism represents the Aztec prophecy as to when and where they could end their nomadic wanderings. When and where such a scene was witnessed would be deemed the sought-after divine revelation as to make that place their permanent home. This occurred at the site where the Conquering Castilian hordes would build Mexico City. The Aztec's Tenotchtitlan would become an engineering marvel of canals and waterways hyphenating what seemingly appeared to be a magnificent city floating in a lake. It left Hernando Cortez and his fellow Spaniards breathless before its awesome beauty! It would become the richest center within the Aztec world, thriving at the expense of others they had conquered until their foretold doom came true at the manifestation of the Castilian Conquistadores and their allies they made along the way from Veracruz, those indigenous peoples so consumed with hatred for the enslaving Aztecs.

Both eagles are paramount in representing both countries. There have been periods when both have opposed each other with screams and talons. As much as the United States has promoted peace among the nations, the vortex of war has all too often pulled the country in. The American eagle has had to soar abroad far more than has been wanted. The Mexican eagle, on the other hand, has been content to fly over its domestic domain instead. That all changed, however, when Nazi Germany decided to torpedo and sink neutral Mexican shipping in the Gulf of Mexico. Germany believed that cargos were destined for the United States and its war effort against them and the Axis Powers. Mexico thus stepped upon the world's stage May, 1942 to play a latent part in World War ll. The Mexican eagle thus allied with the American in a joint war effort against the Axis Powers, with a focus on Japan in the South Pacific. *The characters of this novel are fictional, composites of actual persons who lived the ordeals. They are products in print of my imagination, of those living through factual events of their day. It is my hope that light shed upon obscured historical truth will impart to readers an appreciation of what Mexico experienced, and the contribution that somewhat reluctant ally had rendered to the cause of bringing peace back to the Asian Pacific, and too the United States and Mexico herself.

Joaquin Andre Hawkins

Chapter 1

A Day Unlike Any Other

January 1942 had begun well enough in the Mexican border town of Ciudad Juarez in the state of Chihuahua. It had been a flaming red and pink sunrise with the chill of the winter's evening bidding adios. For Haru Yamashita it was like any other morning for him and his Mexican wife Rocio. They had risen up to have their customary early breakfast of quesadillas with guacamole and cups of tea. Rocio had already tended to the needs of their two young children, Kenji Carlos six years of age and Kasue Maria, four. Rocio was expecting their third child. It was a typical morning as so many others had been. It was still a couple of hours yet before Haru and Rocio would open the doors of their general store unto their community. The local Mexican community placed a lot of value upon them and their store of *aborrotes* where they offered whatever the community seemingly needed. To the Mexicans Haru, the son of Japanese immigrant parents who had become naturalized Mexican citizens shortly after the Mexican Revolution, they saw no foreigner in him. He was as Mexican as they, and true by birth he was. They had even tabbed him "Mano", short for hermano, brother. Haru was quick to pick up on the Spanish language as he grew, even though his folks talked in Japanese within the home. Outside they had become conversant in Spanish, with the Mexicans, as they worked to establish their little business. The Yamashita family had homogenized well into Mexican society and they had won the respect of their neighbors. Rocio's family frequented visits with them.

Sipping his black tea from a small porcelain cup, Haru sat on a high-backed chair at the back door of their house, yet garbbed in a robe and slippers. Their store, *Abarrotes de Yam,* was in the frontal portion of their house, the windowpanes facing street-ward. He sat in the mellow glow of the early morning sun reading a local newspaper of the after events in the United States in the wake of Japan's attack upon Pearl Harbor the previous month. He had a troubled demeanor, vividly displayed by his furrowed brow and intent stare at the newsprint. He had a sense of shame of his ancestry as he had first learned of the accounts of all the death and destruction caused by Japan. And yet, there was no backlash by his Mexican neighbors, despite the fear mongering that Americans held for any one hinting of Japanese ancestry. Reports he had heard said that a racial backlash was being felt across the country, mainly focused upon those Japanese Americans on the U.S. west coast, in the states of Washington, Oregon, California, and even Arizona; as understandably Hawaii also. What would the American government do he wondered? They had been in a state of declared war against Japan since Pearl Harbor. It was a good thing, he reasoned, that he was in neutral Mexico. Nothing should happen to his family there. He looked up into the colorful sky of various hues of blazing colors to delight the eye when the newsprint was so vexing. As if by reflex he sipped some more tea, then stretched and yawned in the dawning light. Yes, Mexico was not paranoid he mused. He sighed a sigh of relief and remained silent for some time. He would read several lines of newsprint only to pause and stare off into the fiery sunrise; then after a few moments would resume and repeat as before. The only sounds audible were some early morn songbirds in the trees, harbingers crooning at the dawning light. He marveled at their melodies, which were now rudely interrupted by the sudden squeal of brakes out on the street, echoing over the rooftops and through the store's environs behind him. He could hear the gruff barks of commands followed by the trampling of heavy boots. Behind Haru, inside the house he suddenly heard many sharp voices and heavy heeled feet. His jaw dropped, wondering what was happening as he suddenly faced the door behind him. He hurriedly stood up and entered the back door.

"By order of *La Secretaria de Gobernacion* you will come with us for registration and detainment," commanded a soldier of bearing to the masses. He wore the insignia of a captain and conveyed an arrogant, all-business air about himself. A close-cropped, pencil-thin mustache lined his upper firm lip. He depicted the stereotypical image of a spit and polish military man, but overly-scented with an orange blossom after shave-cologne so early in the season. A dozen years prior he had been a newly brevetted lieutenant in the army of President Plutarco Elias Calles. He had taken an active part in carrying out the edicts of the President's to put an end to the religious clerics of the Catholic Church, those far right winged conservative radicals who zealously bore arms against the liberal federal government, a secular body they had deemed anti-Catholic, opposed to the Church. The Catholic hierarchy gave these warriors their blessing as they deemed them the Church's faithful, willing to defend and die against a secular foe, even perceived atheists. The *Cristero War* they waged from 1926 – 1929. It was seen as a war of State versus Mother Church. Only when the government had made enough concessions to appease the Catholic Hieracrhy did the Church withdraw her support for the *Cristero* rebels, and the war concluded in 1929. The Catholic Church, however, remained defiant of the government, yet - hating the rule of President Benito Juarez who in the previous century had stripped the Church of its worldly wealth, the lands, and had redistributed them to the nation's people. They continued to grimace at how the new 1917 Constitution arising from the ashes of the Revolution of Pancho Villa and Emiliano Zapata and countless others had further endorsed the infidel Juarez. Having lost the war they yet-harbored a yearning to throw off the yoke of the anti-Catholic government. The captain carried out his orders with his own zeal and commitment.

"Sergeant Alvarez! This man, take!" barked Captain Eusabio Hernandez, pointing at Haru. He simulataneously scoured with a keen eye the floor spaces between the shelves and aisles, looking for any others who he, the government, would deem a risk.

"Sir?" inquired the hesitant sergeant. "What about these children?"

The captain eyed both the six and four year old. "They look Japanese, don't they? They go too! A babe today is an enemy tomorrow!"

The sergeant looked bewildered, as if the orders pained him beyond belief, too absurd to carry out.

"Yes, sir." He did an about face and barked out his own orders to rank and file soldiers in hesitation.

Haru's and Rocio's cherub-faced children appeared to be more Japanese than indigenous Mexicans and the soldiers separated them from a bewildered and pleading Rocio and placed hands upon Haru and forcibly led the three partially dressed internees to a truck awaiting the human cargo out front. Rocio was beside herself, in disbelief, unable to grasp the moment. Her braided hair was tightly twisted, as if reflecting her wrought soul. But, as she came to her senses, seeing her young children taken in tow for the front door and her husband ushered that way too, her son and daughter began crying. She spurred to action! She screamed out in Spanish, "What the hell are you doing? What is this? You can't just break in here and do this! Where are you taking my family?"

The brazened captain brushed her pleas aside as if trying to avoid a pesky mosquito. "Orders are from Mexico City, that every one of Japanese descent is to be rounded up, registered, relocated elsewhere and detained. These orders come from the top! They are not our doing!" He sidestepped her, issuing more orders.

"But, but, where, where are you taking them? How long will you detain my family?"

"The train station," answered the captain. "They shall be held there until the appropriate time to put them on a train."

"Train? What damned train? A train for where?" screamed Rocio.

"No orders for that yet. My bet is Mexico City. That is where the orders came from and that is probably where they'll be resettled. You can inquire at the station more about that later today. All we know is our orders, to bring them in and others will take over from there."

Train Station, thought Rocio. Mexico City! Resettled? She hastened behind them cradling her expectant belly, still pleading in vain, crying out after Haru.

"Keep Kenji and Kasue close to you, my dear!"

Haru turned her way as he was pushed through the door

outside, the look upon his face haunted Rocio, an expression of shock. She followed in close pursuit. Standing in the doorway, facing the idling truck, she saw her two crying children handed up into the back to other soldiers who placed them on benches. Haru, with soldiers at his heels, climbed up to join his children and others.

Rocio heard across the street a commotion, of screams and cries like theirs had been. It was the Nakamura family, friends who owned a butcher shop. Rather than only part of the family, they all were taken; grandparents, parents, children, all destined for the same trainstation as Rocio's loved ones were. She watched in horror as the truck now hastened away, the driver jamming the gears as if the clutch was not engaging, sounds of metal upon metal. A cloud of noxious exhaust spewed from behind and those sitting closest to the tailgate coughed. Rocio and other bystanders stared after it with faces frozen in time, an interlude when minds tried grasping what had just happened.

Why would the government do this? Mexico was not at war with Japan? Not like the Americans! President Camacho must be acting out what Roosevelt had encouraged him to do! Yes, that must be it! He would never have taken it upon himself to do such a horrible thing as this! He will come to his senses, and believing this offered some pacification. They'll be back, probably before the end of the day.

Rocio hurried back inside their store and home, slamming the door on a world no longer understood. A loose windowpane rattled, mimicking her nerves. Her thoughts were anything but business that day, a day which had dawnwd with beauty and suddenly a dreaded darkness enveloped them.

"Rocio!" called out a voice. "Where are you?" It was Señora Guerrero her neighbor, eagerly there to inquire and assist. A woman with a large round face and bosom, her salt and pepper hair was still wet from an interrupted shampoo. She wiped away some suds from wincing her eyes.

"Lucia," cried Rocio. "The government has gone mad! They are arresting all people of Japanese ancestry for registration and relocation. They've taken Haru and my kids, the Nakamuras across the street and others too! What threat are we? I cannot believe this is happening!"

Lucia Guerrero was not alone. Other Mexican neighbors hurriedly entered. Lucia's husband still had the remnants of shaving cream on his face and Señora Garcia's hair was still wet from an early morn shampoo, a towel wrapped around her head. They all came to inquire further from what they had heard, the screams and shouts, came to offer support.

Señor Guerrero, Lucia's husband, had taken a cloth to hurriedly wipe the shaving lather from his partially-shaven face, hastened shirtless behind his wife Lucia, cried out, "Rocio! Be ready in about five minutes! I'll take you to the train station to find out more about all of this business. Don't worry! We'll probably be coming back with them all. Five minutes!" Then he hurried home to put on a shirt and ready himself.

At the train station they beheld throngs of people milling about as innocent sheep in a fold anticipating something bad to about happen. Soldiers stood guard on their perimeters. This was feeling more like a concentration camp, something they were reading about in the papers of what was happening in Europe. But, this was Mexico! This should not be happening!

"Who is in charge here?" asked an angry Rocio of a boyish, timid guard, more fit to be a schoolboy than a rifle-carrying soldier. He pointed to a man by the station's ticketing window, on his way up to a boarding platform to survey all those below. He was issuing orders to subordinates of how to carry out the registration process. Any attempt to communicate with him was in vain. Exasperated Rocio and others were pleading for answers. Then a Señor Padilla, the man in over-all charge, took notice and delegated to one of his minions to address those people, to appease them somehow, to just keep them out of the way. They had important business at hand and these people were distractions.

A mousey- looking man of no apparent value, certainly of no mestizo lineage, cautiously stepped forward to the edge of the platform to do as ordered, pacify Rocio and others to do as he was instructed. "Listen, people, these Japanese pose threats to Mexico. By orders of the President we are to register them all, and while the threat remains, they will be removed from these northern, border-states and from the Pacific Coast, and will be relocated to places far removed from these vulnerable areas. Those here at this station will be placed on an express train for Mexico City this evening. Don't worry! This is just until the dangers pass. They'll be taught new trades to do while away. When they return they will have more education and talents. So, it is not all bad! This is just a temporary thing. So, do not despair! This is for the good of Mexico!"

"Sir, you do not look Mexican either. What is your ancestry, German?" inquired an angry voice. "Why are not you and your kind rounded up like this? These are family and friends, our good neighbors! Not livestock destined for the slaughterhouse! They are Mexican citizens! We are not at war with Japan. Look at the United States. They have been at war since December 8th and have not done anything stupid like this! This makes Mexico look like scared jackrabbits."

The man held his tongue, had no answer. He uttered not a word of self-justification before the waves of indignation battering him. More disgruntled voices arose from the thronging mix before him.

"Like I said," he finally emitted in an agitated voice. Some signs of perspiration glistened above his upper lip, further wetted by his drippy nose in the cold air. He could taste the salty mix seeping into his mouth and drew a hand across his nostrils to clean way the discomfort. "The train is due to depart at 6:00 pm. If you have any food or clothing to give to them bring it here well before. It will need to be inspected first! That is all!" Then he beat a hasty retreat in order to avoid any more pointed queries.

Rocio began to cup a hand about her belly while drawing about her shoulders with the other the shawl she had hastened on. Wrought nerves added unto her discomforts. 6:00 pm tonight and her loved ones and neighbors would be railed many kilometers south to the Federal District? Well, she reasoned, Señor Guerrero could drive her back home and she could gather up some things and perhaps he could bring her back later in the day. The throng of people began to disburse, not allowed access to family and friends being detained. They cast disparaging looks at the soldiers and authorities, looking beyond them unto their loved ones, milling about like unfortunates in a stockyard.

"Come Rocio," summoned Enrique Guerrero "Let's go back home, get some things together for them. The train will get cold on its way to Mexico City. They'll need warm clothes. Come."

Rocio Yamashita walked inside the environs of her home, suddenly feeling anything but a welcoming domain. Her stressed mind regarded her echoing steps upon the tiled floor as being harsher than her children's laughter and cries. She pondered what things to gather up to take to Haru and the kids. Heavy coats and a bag of food were necessary. From 12:00 noon throughout the afternoon hours neighbors came by in support and offers of help. She now had about an hour of being alone with her troubled thoughts, aware of the occasional pain in her belly. Even the fetus seemed troubled.

Japan! She frowned as she contemplated family photos on a wall. "Damn you for all of this!" she cried. She plead within her soul, why have you done what you have done! You bastards are responsible for all of this! Damn you for Pearl Harbor! You cowards! You devils! You are the cause for all of this! We are Mexican citizens! Damn you! I am sure my husband and others feel a shame now. Her condemning thoughts were hyphenated by the sound of a car's horn. Guerrero was there ready to take her to the station. She was soon on her way to a hastened hello and a labored good bye to her loved ones. She clutched the suitcase of jackets, shoes, various other clothing and bag of food at her side. Her mind and heart were racing, pained, and adding to her woes was an increasing discomfort in her belly.

The station came into view and already a train was primed at the loading docks, the belly of its engine belching black smoke. An occasional chug, chug could be heard, like some drunkard slowly gulping another beer. It was a scene readied for a departure, that of a cruel and forced separation of Mexican citizens all for a misguided sense of national security. Rocio nervously searched for her Haru and children in the guarded throngs.

"Señora," hailed a soldier. "Those things are for detainees?" If so, they must be taken to that desk over there to be examined."

Rocio looked the way he was pointing and she and Señor Guerrero pursued that way.

"Mama, Mama," she heard a familiar cry. It was Kasue calling out for her mother. Rocio's blood raced. *Yes my child. I am here,* muttered the mother. Then she nervously scoured the faces for those she knew so well. Where? Where are they? she pined. Then she beheld her Haru standing apart from the others. He held Kasue in his arms, their daughter's arms were outstretched for her mother, and his son Kenji clung to his father's side. There was an apparent great gulf separating them, enforced by soldiers.

"These things are for family?" asked a voice. Rocio nodded an affirmative. "Set them on this table so we can examine them!"

There was a sudden whistle, summoning the people to be centralized. They were being herded into groups to be ushered to their respective rail cars shortly. The same voice asked the recipients' names and confiscated the items. "They'll be issued to them as they are assigned their cars."

A voice over a loudspeaker was heard to begin the loading. It was a slow movement of shuffling feet and swaying bodies as they trudged forward to step aboard. Rocio saw her loved ones step upward into a car and then disappeared. The somber face of her Haru reappeared alongside a windowpane staring out at her. The faces of her children were pressed up hard against the window with hopes of seeing mama. The whistle blew once again and the train suddenly lurched forward a little, the cars straining against one another as the engine began pulling them along for the ordeal through the night. Rocio felt torn asunder as her loves slowly railed away, she running after their car for one last glimpse. Tears were streaming down her face. In her mad dash for one final look she suddenly tripped over some crates at the end of the platform, stumbled and fell over the end of the planking, striking the hard ground of rocks and tufts of dried grasses and cacti. She hit with a sickening thud out of view from Haru and the children, but witnessed by Señor Guerrero and others on the platform. Enrique rushed forward through the teeming crowds of tearful people, hastening to Rocio's needs. He had seen her disappear from view as she cascaded over the edge. He raced to the edge and wasted no time jumping down to join some others who had done the same moments before to rally unto her. She lay unconscious. Something else was of dire concern, her baby!

Thoughts of the train chugging away were no longer of a concern for Enrique Guerrero and the others about Rocio. "Doctor! We need a doctor!" he shouted, thinking how fortunate it was that Haru and the children did not see her fall.

"I saw Doctor Raygoza in the station," spoke up a porter. "I'll run to see if he is still there!" He hurried away, crawling up some pilings to the platform and running for the lobby, hoping the doctor had not caught a taxi and departed. He saw him ready to exit the front doors.

"Doctor! Doctor Raygoza! Please wait! There is an emergency out back. A lady fell off the platform and looks like she could be hurt bad. Please! Hurry!"

Doctor Hector Raygoza was a stalwart personality in Ciudad Juarez. People would clamor unto him for a ripped hangnail to more serious cases. He was returning home from a Christening, the baptismal of a baby he had delivered months before, the first born of a couple he had known for many years. He still had thoughts of their little Alicia in mind as he stood briefly on the edge of the landing, peering down upon the prone figure of Rocio. His experiences as a doctor during the days of Villa and the Revolution served him well in the post years.

"Oh my Lord!" he exclaimed. "She's with child!" Now, he too was soon upon the ground as space was made for him to render his medical assistance.

A brief examination was all he needed to know, that she needed a hospital. He was aware of her bloodied brow. But, what mattered most was that she was expectant. "Porter," he called out, looking at the various faces around him.

"Yes?" answered the young man.

"Have an ambulance get here, sooner the better!" emphasized Dr. Raygoza. He did not have his stethoscope with him. But, he did feel her belly and put an ear to her stomach to listen to the fetus.

The last wails of the locomotive engine could be slightly heard far off in the distance and as it droned away the siren of an approaching ambulance replaced it. Dr. Raygoza wondered about the baby, would it wail or not.

Rocio was now semi-conscious, in pain. Her head throbbed and her abdomen hurt. She was gingerly placed upon a stretcher and was carried to the ambulance.

"Doctor?" asked Enrique. "What do you think? What about her baby?"

Doctor Raygoza never wanted to assume too much. "We'll know more once we can get her to the hospital. That's all I can say just now! Excuse me." He hopped into the back of the ambulance with her for the ride to a hospital of questionable facilities.

For Enrique Guerrero there was no question what he would now do. He would hasten to his car and drive to the hospital himself so he could learn more, offer support.

Rocio lay in bed. Her bandaged head throbbed. She was tearful. Her thoughts were plagued with the day's events, of her forced separation from her husband and children. And now, she had been informed that she had suffered a miscarriage. How painful that would have been for Haru to know! Now, it was a painful loss that she would have to bear without him. She had suffered the breakup of her family, and now the loss of their baby was insult to injury.

Her tear-stained cheeks and blurred eyes were turned towards the window. She stared that way as if into apparent oblivion, no longer sobbing. She was mum, lost in pained thoughts.

"Haru! Haru!" she moaned. "I am so sorry, so, so sorry," she pined as if guilty for the miscarriage. Her last view of her family was in the train car's window, they straining to catch one last glimpse of wife and mother. Another tear streaked her cheek as she envisioned them disappearing into the night.

For Haru Yamashita, he clutched at his two children as the train clicked and clacked on a southerly course through the night. It was an express train, no unnecessary transfers or stops. It was as though the federal government was racing to get them and other Japanese Mexicans away from the border and west coast, so they could be controlled and observed. *Well, my dear, my life and love, take care of yourself and the baby,* he grieved. He reasoned that sound reason would return, that they would be headed north again and the family would be together once more, even with a new addition. He closed his eyes and began to drift off into a restless slumber. His last considerations were that it indeed had been *a day unlike any other* they had known. He swallowed hard, convinced life had to get better.

Chapter 2

A New Social Order, a New Ally

The black iron locomotive huffed and puffed, did a long sigh as it came to a stop mid-morning at the far end of the landing at Mexico City's train station. The depot was busier than usual for it teemed with the curious on-lookers and media, and would swell even more when the prisoners would disembark the train. Soldiers had formed lines, prepared to keep them physically separated from the public and its prying eyes. Haru sat with his Kenji and Kasue on either side of him. Their eyes were reddened, teary from numerous yawns. Haru could hear a mix of chatter working its way through his car; that of Japanese and Spanish he had once tabbed in humor as Japanish. There was an armed soldier at both ends of their car, as in all the others also. When the cars jerked a final time to a complete stop they barked some commands for Haru and all the others to rise up and get off the train. The response was slow and the order was repeated. Slowly, movements here and there indicated there was an obedient response. Haru lowered his head and whispered to his children.

"Kenji, Kasue, stay close to me! Hold onto my pants if you lose hold of my hands. There is going to be a lot of people out there. We must stay together! Tell me! Do you understand this? I have to know that you do! You have to know what I am saying!"

"Yes, Papa. I understand," said his six-year old son, Kenji. The young boy looked nervously up and down the fast-filling aisle. "I guess we have to go."

Haru followed his son's gaze. "Yes, it's time. "What about you, Kasue? Do you understand what I told you? You must stay close to my legs! Do not let anyone else force you away from me! We must stay together!"

His four year-old daughter did not reply, just looked big-eyed at the goings-on all about her. Rather than trying to reason with her, Haru decided to take her up in his arms, firmly hung onto his little girl.

"Kenji, I cannot hold your hand because I need to carry Kasue. I have an idea. You have a belt around that jacket. Let me have it."

Haru slid the cloth belt through the loops until it was free. "Give me your hand." Kenji held up his hand and his father tied an end around his wrist, and the other end Haru tied around his own belt.

"There! We should not get separated now! Now, it is time. Lets go."

There was a momentary break of passersby in the aisle and Haru Yamashita stood up, stretched his sinews and then stepped in the aisle, led the way up the passageway, to the exit of the car and the step down to the landing. Kasue rested well in his arms and Kenji was in tow like some puppy dog.

At first view upon stepping off the train Haru saw many like themselves being guided between the lines of armed soldiers. He had no idea there were so many Japanese decendents in Mexico's border states! Were they Japanese or Mexican citizens, he wondered? Why were they a race singled out, and not those of German or Italian parentage, those totalitarian countries at war with the free peoples of the world? Why was any of this happening at all since Mexico was not at war with anyone? *His* country was neutral after all! It must have been the Americans coercing President Camacho to move out those of Japanese heritage, get them away from the border. Yes, that must be it he reasoned! The Americans see a bogeyman in all Japanese, fear they will do some sort of spying or espionage on them, suspecting anything and everything after Pearl Harbor! Well, maybe I can understand them. They were so surprised at Pearl Harbor! That must have made them paranoid about anything or anyone Japanese.

"Listen everyone!" shouted a tall and angular soldier in a nasal tone; an apparent lieutenant. His throat was elongated and his Adam's apple protruded more than his Romanesque nose, like some knot on a skinny tree trunk. He pointed to a grouping of military trucks and buses parked at the far end of the tiled landing. "Those vehicles are for you. These soldiers will guide you there. Follow them! Do not lag behind or stray! We still have a ways to go."

There were seemingly hundreds like them, milling about and then being ushered along. Haru looked into the eyes of the individual youthful soldiers carrying out their orders. Rather than having granite - like features, unfeeling and calloused, he surmised that many had a reluctance in doing what they were ordered to do. Japanese - Mexicans had assimilated well into Mexican society. They were widely appreciated in the Mexican communities they had chosen to live in. A good number of these young soldiers saw no national threat in Haru or the others, and the look in their eyes suggested as much. President Camacho had over-reacted he thought and apparently so did many of their armed escorts. His thoughts were reinforced when a boyish private offered him a smile. He cautiously held out to Kasue a cookie, looking unto Haru if it was OK, hopeful a sergeant or officer never saw him. Haru was surprised, but slightly bowed his head in thanks. Kasue took the cookie. Haru carried young Kasue, she staring over his shoulder at the kind soldier, munching the cookie as they were hurried-on in the flow of the ushered people unto the waiting vehicles to taxi them to prison or wherever.

The buses and trucks had been idling a long time. The stench of diesel exhaust hung over them all that cold winter's morning. They had spent the night lulled by the rhythmic clickety-clacks of the train's iron wheels upon the serpentine rails. Now it was the black exhausts of spent diesel that nauseated them as each vehicle began to drive away, leaving those near the tailgates coughing and choking on the exhausts. None had been to Mexico City before. But, this is where President Camacho and the Federal Government were and this is where the orders came to wreck their lives! They watched the passing street scenes of the country's largest city. There were posh zones and not. All in all, the nations capital looked a wealthy place. How were they to fit into it, they wondered?

Their transport ended at a soccer stadium. It was to serve as a temporary solution to their forced relocation. The vehicles drove inside the stadium and those fortunate with a window view beheld perhaps 100 canvas tents pitched, more in the process, in military fashion. This was in preparation for their arrival and any others soon due. This had a feeling of some liberality, not of incarceration, no cells with bars, and no hint of any thing like feared deportation. They began to unload from the buses and trucks. The same nasal toned tall man shouted out.

"These are your temporary homes. The tents are actually spacious enough for half a dozen people. There are extra blankets on the cots because we know it is winter and it gets cold at night. I do not know just how temporary this will be. The government is still figuring out something more permanent. Just be patient! You all will be assigned a tent. Once that is done we will summon you all together for some basic instructions while here. There should be some food too, maybe."

It seemed to Haru and all the other adults that the government had rushed into this relocation process without much forethought. They were not prepared to house and furnish the logistics to all the people they had ordered rounded up, registered, detained, and relocated. The federals, the state and municipal authorities all acted as though in unison of thought. But, the average citizenry of the country cared not for these policies, saw it an affront to fellow Mexicans regardless of what their past heritage was. They were Mexicans now and deserved better than this! President Camacho had embarked upon a road of racial paranoia, having neutral Mexico behave like some belligerent nation. Perhaps Japan would declare war on them? Did their fellow Mexican citizens care about their ordeal? Haru's mind recalled the young soldier's smiling eyes and his offered cookie. Perhaps?

The tent assigned to Haru and his children also now housed their former neighbors in Ciudad Juarez, the Nakamuras. The soldier had said that the tents could accommodate half a dozen people. Well, their number now tallied ten. But, they were good neighbors in Ciudad Juarez and would prove to be here too, upon this soccer field, maybe even beyond. They had never considered ever becoming *Capitalinos, Chilangos,* slang terms representative of persons of Mexico City. But, here they were and here they would be for who knows how long? They might as well adapt the best way they can. They could do nothing more.

Within Mexico City is the University Autonoma, a vast school with huge enrollments. Student Felipe Alonzo Gurza was a major in Social Sciences. His aim had been to study in depth the indigenous peoples of Mexico, trace their heritages back as far as he could, even pre-Colombian, pre-Conquest. He had, however, been intrigued with the newspapers that exposed the Camacho Administration's relocation plan, of uprooting Mexican citizens of Japanese heritage and wreaking havoc upon their families unjustly. The government seemed to have no plan at all. Gurza's mind was on track to write his thesis for his master's degree with a focus upon indigenous Mexicans. But, the persistent thoughts of those unfortunate Japanese – Mexicans had robbed him of concentration. These intrusions could only be addressed by putting his thesis considerations on hold. He had to inquire himself about their ill fate. His major in Social Studies encouraged him to investigate their plight. The journalists he had read had only written partial truths, never disclosing that those prisoners of the state were Mexican citizens, that only their past parentage was Japanese. Like millions of people in the Americas, the majority were descendents of immigrants, just like those who were supporting and reporting on the internments of President Camacho. Felipe Gurza, the learned and inquisitive student, now attempted to learn for himself what the full truth was, based upon fact and not irrational political-racial fears. He concluded the matter, to go to that soccer stadium and speak to whoever was in charge.

Francisco Durcal de Valenzuela was the commandant overseeing the logistics and security of those interned within the soccer stadium. He was an older man, perhaps even too old from a past era, now delegated the responsibilities that perhaps a younger one should have had. When an aide informed him that a student from the university wished to see him he at first balked.

"What does an idealistic student really know about life's

realities?" he asked the aide. "Tell him I have no time for his nonsense!"

"Yes, sir," replied the aide as he turned to leave. But, suddenly the commandant halted him.

"Wait!" The aide paused, waiting to hear more but Valenzuela held off. Then he added,

"Show him in. I'll see what the young pup has to say. Then he will hear what I have in reply. In my years I have gained more wisdom than what any liberal college student has. There is something to be said about maturity, sergeant, something that cannot be learned in a classroom only."

"Yes, sir. I will show him in promptly!" replied his aide. Then he made for the door. Scarce a minute had passed when the door opened again and the sergeant escorted inside the youthful student.

"Sir, thank you for seeing me," greeted Gurza of the commandant. "My name is Felipe Gurza. I am a Social Studies major at the University Autonoma. I have come with the request to observe, maybe even interview, the internees. I have been following the newspapers and what they say about the incarcerations, that these people are actually Mexican citizens, not foreign threats. Would you permit me to do this?"

"Is this some sort of class project of yours? Did some exalted professor put you up to this?" asked a suspicious and condescending Valenzuela, his bushy eyebrows secluding his cold stare. "Social Studies? Haven't you any better subjects to study. These people are sort of like contraband. Even if they pose no threat, are innocent of all suspicion, they are just unfortunates in life, in the wrong place at the wrong time in history. There have always been people like them and they simply continue that line of unfortunate souls. In their case, they can fault their homeland for putting them here. Japan has caused it all, not us!"

"Homeland? Sir, I believe for a good many, maybe even the majority, this is their homeland. They are Mexican citizens as well as you and I. That is what I hope to find out, with your permission of course."

The aged commandant scrutinized Gurza with his dimmed eyes before saying more. He rubbed the stubble upon his nigh-double chin, then ran his hand to the back of his head, as if a new headache was coming on.

"How is it that you young folks at that university seem to think you have a better grasp on how to see and do things than we who have experienced more of life than any of you? You seem to think you have a greater enlightenment than anyone else, disregard the wisdom which my generation has gained along the way. You folks do not give us enough credibility in acting as we have. Japan is known as a very segregated culture. They care not for anyone that is not Japanese. You think these Japanese-Mexicans are innocent? They have tried to blend in well with our society and when they have us all fooled, then their true loyalties will be discovered. This internment will reveal their true natures."

Gurza remained silent before the commandant's bias criticism, wondering how to respond. He began to speak when Valenzuela held up a hand to silence him. He stood up from his desk, turned away, faced some tall windowpanes, made several steps to the sill and stared outward at the tented soccer field below.

"You know, I was man in my late sixties when Villa and Zapata and all the others led the Revolution against the government. That was a terrible time for Mexico! But, we came through it. We were scathed and bloodied for sure. But, we survived somehow. Then those contemptible far right wing fanatics of the Church and their Catholic dogma of ultra conservatism saw us in government service as secular atheists, of liberal extremes. They hated President Benito Juarez for stripping the Church of its stranglehold upon the people, and still hate anything of government! That hate came to a head as so called Christians bore arms against the government. Did you ever study in school the Cristeros War?"

"Some," replied Gurza.

"What a sham that was! If I remember rightfully, Jesus Himself told the Catholics' first pope, that was Peter, that His Kingdom is not of this world, but if it was His servants would fight. Since He has gone back to heaven, if one is convinced to believe all of that, then why in the hell did these fanatic religious nuts take up arms and wage a war against the government when their Lord and Savior told them not to?"

Young Felipe had no comment.

"Well, in 1929 that war ended. The government caved in, compromised their position with the Church brass. When the Church leaders came to an understanding, agreed to terms, they ended their support for their religious warriors and those rebels gave up the fight. Picked up their toys and went home. Now look at our world!" Valenzuela paused, with his hands folded behind his back as he rocked upon his heels, his back still towards Felipe Gurza. Then he turned about and faced the student.

"You know, those Catholics never gave up really when that war ended. They just sort of re-grouped. Back in '37, they formed their *Union Nacional Sinarquista*, up in Leon, Guanajuato I think. They wrote their "Manifesto" which basically condemned anything of President Cardenas then, and surely anything of President Camacho today. Young man, I do not suppose you are one of those Sinarquistas, are you? They would be first in line to condemn the government for this internment!"

"No, sir. I am not. I know of students on campus who speak about them. But, I am not part of any organization nor do I have any specific leanings politically. I am interested in only truth. To find the truth requires going places and doing things, often solo, that may be a challenge. That is why I am here." He stared at the commandant, a challenge before him, wondering if what he had said resonated with Valenzuela in any detectable way.

"You know, when orders came down for all of these political arrests I and others thought it too much of an undertaking. The citizens of Mexico do not necessarily support this edict. I, for one, do not fault the government's reasoning. But, the numbers, the logistics, are all daunting." He smirked. "Yes, that is a good word, 'daunting'! It says it all!"

"Sir, if I may. You can shadow me with some soldiers. Just allow me to get up close to observe the prisoners, and if the occasion allows converse with some. Then I'll be gone. I have a thesis to write this year and I am troubled about what the topic will be. Perhaps elements of this I can incorporate into it."

"Tell me, young man, what aspects of this would satisfy your collegiate ideals? You probably perceive that I am one who does not give a lot of credence to classroom studies. Life is learned outside that environment. These creases upon my face are the records of my journeys in life. These stooped shoulders indicate the responsibilities and burdens I have carried. You too will come to this point some day. Hopefully you will not just get old but will increase in knowledge and wisdom also. I would like to think that I have, compared to when I was your age."

"I want to know these people as people, see if there are justified fears for them being spies and saboteurs. Or, what I suspect, that this internment is an over-reaction due to racial fears of the Japanese. What Japan has done to China and that part of the world, and now that cowardly attack on Pearl Harbor, surely exacerbates those fears! Truth! That is what I am after, sir. I am no journalist. But, I feel myself a writer and I have no idea if or what I may write pertaining to any of this. My goal has been Social Studies, and the more I understand society and all of its components, I believe that will lead me to wisdom."

Commandant Valenzuela hailed his aide. The door opened.

"Sergeant Torres," informed the commandant. "This young man has the right to observe close hand the prisoners and if he so wishes, and an opportunity rises, he shall also have the right to converse with them. However, wherever he goes I want two armed soldiers to accompany him! That is all."

Both men exchanged salutes. The aide did his smartly, did an about-face and departed. Valenzuela seemed bored with such formalities, watched the man open and close the door, his thoughts ricocheting from decade to decade in his past, of places and people he had known. He rubbed his chin in momentary contemplation, offering a cynic's smirk.

"Well, Mr. Gurza, you have what you came for. Go and solve the world's cares. When you come to know truth be prepared to suffer for it. It usually costs something. There is always a price to pay for knowledge. The trick is to recognize it when it stares you in the face, be able to understand it. If you can rightly discern between truth and falsehood, you will be on your way to being wise. Good day to you now."

Initially, Felipe Gurza had been intimidated by the old man's manner. He had come across as condescending. Perhaps he was, even a bigot of sorts. But, perhaps too beneath his crusty veneer of cracks and creases he retained some element of humanity. If not, why would he have granted him this permission? Perhaps he just wanted youth to stumble and fall, learn to get up again, learn true life, and thus qualify his own assertions.

Commandant Valenzuela returned to his window, studying the youthful, purposeful gait of Gurza striding with two soldiers in the direction of the internees' tents. He studied the man's form, perfect posture and a self-assured demeanor. He surmised that Gurza was maybe more mature than his years numbered. No, he concluded. This Gurza fellow was no lemming, no Sinarquista puppet. He seemed to have a life of his own with no strings attached. He stroked his chin again in contemplation and reluctantly turned to face his desk once more. Duties, he thought. Yes, they never let up. He sat down to a stack of papers and ledgers. Yes, the registrations! Now we have a record of who is who out there. He began to thumb through the leaflets until he settled to read a certain page, at least content that his superiors felt he was not obsolete, fit only to be put out to pasture.

Felipe Gurza had walked the secured perimeter of the compound, with his escort close to his heels. He could not help but feel sorrow for the people, so uprooted and displaced, recipients of a biased government afraid of shadows and innuendos, not truth. He stopped and observed various children bundled up in warm jackets that cold wintry day. They paid him no mind as they busied themselves with childish improvised games. He noticed a young boy and girl apart from others, just outside the entrance to their tent. A man, perhaps his own age, perhaps a bit older, had come outside and called to them.

"Kenji Carlos, Kasue Maria, there are some crackers in here. Would you like to have some?"

They were quick to respond. They had had those crackers before and liked them a lot. The man held the tent flap back for them to scurry inside. Must be the father, surmised Gurza. He strongly considered the names the man called out. They were

Japanese and Spanish. Yes, this seemed indicative that they had merged with Mexican culture; that Mexico was indeed their new national identity despite what their ancestral heritage was. He had never heard before a person's name being both Japanese and Spanish! Yes, they were intriguing. He studied the man again as he exited the tent solo. Haru's thoughts were far away, wondering about his Rocio and the baby. But, those soft memories faded when he took notice of Gurza's stare. It was unsettling. Their eyes locked upon each other, wondering about who was who. Haru slightly turned his face to the tent flap, concerned about his children. The distant stranger troubled him.

Felipe Gurza turned to his soldier escorts, said he would like to talk to the man by the tent. They hesitated at first but knew their orders and agreed to accompany him to the lone Japanese man.

Haru was uneasy at the approach of this young looking man accompanied by soldiers. What did they want, he wondered? Why me? There are plenty of others here to focus on! Felipe Gurza's features became clearer. He watched with intrigue, but with some concern too, at the youthful man's approach.

Felipe considered that he was roughly his own age or maybe a year or two give or take. He had soft hazel eyes and jet-black hair with a slight natural wave on his crown. He stood about six feet surmised Haru and had a slender but strong frame garbed in modest attire. He was a man that groomed himself well. There was nothing intimidating about this man coming his way. But, why? What was on this fellow's mind? Who was he?

"Hello, my name is Felipe Gurza. I would like to talk with you, if you are willing," introduced a hopeful Gurza.

Haru did not know how to reply. Should he say yes or no, or simply tell Felipe to go away. He studied Felipe's pleasant demeanor; something that had been so alien to them all in the compound since their apprehension and confinement. What did this fellow want to talk about, wondered Haru. Why me?

"Don't you know I am your *enemy?*" asked Haru with a tone of sarcasm. "What could you possibly want to talk to me about? You think I am a personal friend of Emperor Hirohito?"

"No. Not at all!" replied Gurza. "I want to inquire what truth is. We cannot believe the newspapers or what the government says. The government wants to control the people and newspapers want to sell their news, be it true or not. I'm here to find out things on my own. Can we talk?"

Haru was hesitant to trust him. He certainly had reason to mistrust anyone not of his heritage. Just then Kenji and Kasue came outside with cracker crumbs on their faces and jackets. Seeing Gurza and the soldiers prompted them to suddenly cower alongside their father. Haru looked down at them, had a faint smile, placed tender hands along side their heads.

"We need a better future for Mexicans as they," admitted Gurza. "We need to start somehow with this goal in mind! You agree?"

Haru nodded his head yes, instructed his children to return inside the tent. They slipped behind him and the entry flap fell shut. Haru and Felipe stood face-to -face, soul analyzing soul. After a pause that seemed more than just that Haru spoke.

"Well, Mr. Gurza, I am not going anywhere and I seem to have plenty of time. I am sorry our home furnishings are so sparse. I cannot extend a hearty welcome. But, then again whatever you want to talk about may not be something that I will be so welcoming to discuss. But, there are some boxes behind the tent we can sit on." Haru led Felipe behind the tent, the soldiers in tow. Now, what does this fellow want, wondered Haru? They sat down, waiting for whomever to speak first. It was an awkward few moments, eye studying eye and body language. Questions of *why* and *how come* laced through their mutual silent thoughts. Felipe cleared his throat.

Chapter 3

"Interviewing the Enemy"

W as it just a chance meeting, wondered Gurza, he singling out this lone individual? Was this prisoner a true Mexican just as he was? Would this man be truthful? Felipe Gurza was no experienced journalist, given to know how to conduct an interview, how to initiate a conversation with a complete stranger under such trying circumstances, with someone convicted by the government for being guilty of nothing more than what ancestry he bore in his blood. They seemed to be at an impasse, sitting upon the crates face to face not knowing how to begin. Haru sat on the edge of his wobbly crate, wondering what Gurza would have to say, or maybe he should say something first? The nearby soldiers made him nervous.

"Thank you for agreeing to talk with me," said Gurza suddenly, breaking the stilled air between them.

"My name is Felipe Gurza. I am no investigative journalist. I have nothing to do with the government or with anyone responsible for you being in this deplorable place. I am a Social Studies major at the Universidad Autonoma here in Mexico City. I am in the process of concluding what I'll write my thesis about. I have been captivated by the injustice and ordeals you have been subjected to by the government. I am not alone in this. There are comments on campus and in the classes, all over the city itself. We know this is a grave injustice done and I, for one, am hoping by talking to you that I can make it known to the entire nation, perhaps even beyond. The more I know and understand, which to me is an illegal act of the Camacho regime, the more I might be able to do on your behalf. I do not guarantee anything. Like I say, I am not some high-profile writer. I am not the press or some heralded author. But, I have the drive to get at truth and the commandant of this hastily set up compound has given me permission to come here." Gurza cast a half-way look at his accompanying guards sitting on their respective crates, rifles straddling their laps. "Of course he has imposed some things, like being shadowed by these fellows."

Gurza ceased briefly, looking for some sort of registry upon Haru's face for what he had said. Seeing none he asked, "Are you willing to work with me? Tell me who and where you are from? How the government came and arrested you and others and brought you here? I am not interested in writing exposes and gossip. I want fact, truth. Are you willing to grant me this?"

Haru Yamashita was as Mexican as Felipe Gurza, born and bred upon these native soils, but not of Catholic leanings. Of course, Felipe Gurza was a mestizo, being of indigenous and European blood ancestry, unlike Haru's oriental ties. He thought long upon Gurza's words. It did not appeal to him that well, that he was maybe a classroom test rat of sorts, a curious object of theoretical study. But, despite some hesitation, beyond his reasoning, his mouth uttered a single word, *yes*. As soon as he had spoken he wondered why he had said that, why he had agreed. But, there was something about this student sitting opposite him, something intangible for him to identify with. Gurza was his approximate same age he surmised. There was something about this man that he was drawn to, perhaps his peaceful demeanor. Whatever it was his zest for truth was appealing and if his pen and voice would speak out on their behalf, perhaps something good would come of it all.

"Thank you! Thank you very much! I know I must appear to be a mystery to you. Perhaps you even are suspicious of me. I hope, if that is so, that you will see I pose no threat." Gurza opened a ledger and with pen in hand was primed to begin his interview.

"May I ask who you are and where you are from?"

"I am Haru Pedro Yamashita, of Ciudad Juarez, Chihuahua," admitted the internee, adding that the *Pedro* came from his parents adopting the new culure of Mexico.

"How is it that you came to live there?" inquired Gurza.

"My folks . They had lived on the Pacific Coast when they first came to Mexico. But, things did not work out there and they had some hard decisions to make. That is when they sought residency, even citizenship. To make a long story short, they moved to Chihuahua in 1912, not a good time at all! I recall my folks saying there were so many problems with Francisco Madero being President, that there were a lot of problems up in Chihuahua. They used to talk with locals and they would accuse Madero of being either too liberal or too conservative. I know from history that he wanted an open democracy, admired the United States and wanted Mexico to have the same peaceful transitions of government changes, valid elections, free press, and the right to organize labor and the right to strike. I read once that at a banquet in Ciudad Juarez that even Pancho Villa tried to warn Madero that he was being used, being made a fool, that he was too naïve to see what was happening. Well, Madero wouldn't listen and that cost him. I was born in Ciudad Juarez in 1913 just after Madero was assassinated."

"A sordid history of Mexico's for sure," commented Gurza. "But, please tell me, why did your father and mother first come to Mexico? Certainly there were better places to go. Mexico was in such turmoil then. Why Mexico? You said they were first on the Pacific Coast? Where?"

"My father and mother were from some obscure, coastal fishing village in Japan. I really do not remember what they said the name was. They never really talked about it that much, like they wanted to forget it. I really don't know much at all about Japan. But, my father, somehow, had a great opportunity to be trained in the fisheries in Tokyo at the Imperial Fisheries Institute. I understand he was well respected. He told me years later that there was a commission sent by the institute to look for marketing opportunities abroad, and that led them to Los Angeles, California. There they met the people from the International Fisheries Company. They were important because the Mexican government had granted them the exclusive rights to establish fisheries and canneries on Baja California. Well, they entered into a loose collaboration of sorts. That American company established a lobster cannery on Santa Margarita Island on Magdalena Bay. That is on the west coast of lower Baja. They hired my father for his expertise to supervise operations there. But, that was not enough and the business venture failed in 1912. My folks had to move on, find something else to do. I know they had it tough. Foreign land and culture! I could have understood if they had decided to return to Japan. But, that fishing village they did not like to talk about. There had been a cholera epidemic and they had no one or anything there anymore. But, there was something about Mexico that appealed more to them. They became naturalized Mexicans and I am the family's first generation of native-born Mexicans, my children the next."

"It is a long way from there to Ciudad Juarez," commented Gurza. "How did that happen?"

"We have family, cousins, just across the border in El Paso, Texas. I know they had tried to convince my folks to move up that way, and if they did they could help them somehow. Santa Margarita Island and Magdalena Bay are like the ends of the earth, so remote and desolate. Again, to make a long story short, they did. Our cousins spoke Spanish and English well, even enough Japanese to get by. They helped them get a little house and general store combination in Ciudad. Father and mother worked hard to make a go of it. They succeeded, were well received by the local Mexican community. They valued their status and life in their new homeland and were proud of that.

"What about them now?" asked Gurza. "I have not seen your apparent father and mother here with you."

Haru's brow lowered, darkened with sorrow. "You know, they escaped that cholera in Japan. But, it got them here five years ago. We had it in Ciudad Juarez one summer and it killed them both." There was a trace of a tear in the corner of an eye.

"I am sorry for you," soothed Gurza. "That must have been very hard to take. I can see that memory is still painful, like a wound that never healed."

Haru said nothing, just absorbed Gurza's manner. Yes, there

was something in the man's spirit that seemed genuine. That made conversing incrementally easier, freedom to open up some more about his personal life.

"I took over the store after they passed in '37. For the past five years things have been fine with us. We are doing well enough economically and we have great neighbors! The only bad thing that has happened since is that craziness of Pearl Harbor and the racism against us in the U.S. and now here too, apparently. My cousins in El Paso have not been allowed to come see us anymore, and we were not able to go see them. It is not a good time to be a Japanese immigrant in either country. And yet, what have we done? We are deemed guilty just because of our race."

"Your wife?" inquired Gurza. He paused, wondering if he dared say more. "Was she a victim also of cholera?"

Haru looked down at his feet, kicked at a tuft of grass of the soccer field. He grimaced. "My wife is not Japanese. She is Mexican as you, with some Yaqui ancestry. When they came to arrest me they left her behind. Visibly she is not an oriental and they perceived she posed no threat. She is home in Ciudad Juarez, expecting our third child."

"That has to be tough on all of you, you, her, the children!" commented Gurza. "How are you coping?"

"That is an interesting word, *coping*. I do not know how to answer you. Am I coping? I feel numb in many ways and if numbness helps to cope with insanity then that is a good thing. I hope my Rocio and baby are well back home. All I can do is see that my Kenji and Kasue here with me are well; do the best I can."

"What happened when they arrested you? You care to share this with me?" asked Gurza.

"I was sitting outside reading a newspaper, enjoying the sunrise when soldiers suddenly entered our store. When they saw me, and our children, they took us, forced us outside and into some trucks. We saw other Japanese-Mexicans like us being rounded up like cattle. I recognized some neighbors. A lot of people were crying, some in shock. They took us to the train station where we were registered like criminals. Eventually we were crowded onto a miners' train and taken to Coahuila. Once there they transferred us to an all night express to here. Then, when we arrived they bused us all over to this stadium and here we have been since. That is about it."

"Any thing said about what is next? Is this home or will they be moving you?"

"This is supposed to be just temporary. It feels like a prison, really; all the soldiers standing guard. These tents get cold at night. We hear coughing. We know people are getting sick. There are not enough blankets or even food or water. It is a miserable place!"

"It seems like Presidente Camacho over-reacted, like some jackrabbit, scampering out of fear. It is like they had not given any of this much thought at all, not even how to address all the relocations and logistics. Just lunacy!" exclaimed Gurza.

"I suspect they will put us into some sort of forced labor. After all we are prisoners. It will cost little for this workforce and there are no unions to deal with.," commented a sarcastic Haru.

"Your children, how are they doing? What are their ages?"

"Kenji is six and Kasue is four. I think they see this all as some sort of camping venture. I see them having fun while ignorant of what the reality is. There is something safe in their childish innocence. It is my job, to ease them through this as much as is possible. I pray for wisdom."

They had talked about thirty minutes. Signs of the soldier-guards becoming impatient were indicative it was time to leave. Gurza saw a faint motion of the muzzles of their rifles motion to him, suggesting, let's go.

"Think you'd like to carry on this conversation some more?" asked Gurza as he stood up.

"For what purpose?" added an inquisitive, yet doubtful Haru. "We are nobodies! Our voices are not heard! I fail to see what worth I have to warrant your interest. But, if you return some day and we are still here, yes I'll talk with you."

"Public opinion is divided about all of this. There are those who swallow every word the government says. But, there are many also who believe what was done is totally wrong, even criminal. There is much talk that this world war does not involve us.

Mexico is neutral and intends to remain so. That being the case, your incarceration is seen by many as unconstitutional, something unjustifiable. Pressure is mounting against Camacho. I will return if I am permitted to. And, if I can somehow bring you some things I will."

"Actually, we have observed the soldiers. They are not that cruel really. When they know their superiors are not observing them some are even cordial, even compassionate. They do not have much to offer. But, they will offer us cookies, chocolate, something to read. But, as soon as an officer appears they change, assume their soldierly posture and character. I believe you when you say there are Mexicans opposing Camacho and these incarcerations. But, I doubt they will effect changes in his hard-line policies towards us."

"I must go! I see the soldiers getting fidgety. But, and I say but, if the commandant allows me again I will return to see you. Your story is intriguing! I would like to learn more. But, if you please, no more formalities! Call me Felipe!" They parted from behind the tents, the soldiers side-stepped Felipe, allowed him to pass and then followed him. Just before disappearing from view Felipe turned and gave Haru a brief wave of his hand, and then was gone.

Haru remained sitting on the wooden crate, perplexed in the wake of Gurza's departure. He was perplexed as he contemplated the rather strange encounter. It had felt as though he and this stranger had just befriended each other. How did that happen? 'Felipe', is it now, he queried? Was this Felipe Gurza real, genuinely honest? Or, perhaps he was some subtle plant of the authorities, to spy on them, especially himself? He shook off his cautious suspicions. After all, this fellow would probably never return any way. He was not worth it to trouble his mind about any more. Besides, it was time to seek out his children. There were no mysteries about them. He rose up and went their way.

Chapter 4

"In Pursuit of Truth and Logic"

"What!" exclaimed Commandant Valenzuela. "You mean to tell me you want permission to continue to do this nonsense? I surely thought you meant just this once!" He stood in awe, staring at Gurza.

"I really believed your curiosity would have been satisfied, that mingling with those foreigners just a bit would have been more than enough to quench any idealistic curiosity you may have. You liberals at the university you think you have all the answers to life. I know your kind! I don't fault you personally that much though. You're just a victim of that institutional thinking. You are just naïve, haven't experienced life enough to know what is what! I give you credit, however, for getting out of that classroom, getting away from professors who profess knowing it all, getting off that campus and experience reality. Learning life is more than simply turning the pages in some textbook and discussion. You must look in the eye that which is real, like staring down a jaguar, not flinching at all! You will find that when you have done that, and over time, by the time you either lose your hair or grow silver-haired like me, your views on life, those youthful ideologies and lofty ideals you now entertain will have greatly modified."

Valenzuela looked upon Gurza, a young man he was torn asunder to fully understand. He had a subdued admiration for him for getting out into the world, to learn life firsthand. On the other hand he resented his schooling and the products hailing from those arrogant realms of higher education. He did not appreciate those graduates he had encountered in the past, telling him how things should be, critical of him and how he was too old now, had no more relevance. They had implied, and even in some cases literally told him, he and his generation were obsolete, of no further value, to step aside and let a new generation of learned people assume the reins of leadership. But, this student before him, at least initially, was unlike any other he had encountered. He was respectful. There was a mystique about Gurza that troubled him, and yet intrigued him also. Any other student he would have run off; but not this young man. He felt obliged to give him license, to loosen the leash and let him have his way, at least in part.

"Very well. No more than thirty minutes at a time, AND, no more than three times per week. You will continue to have the soldiers with you and if you learn of ANYTHING that may be of security's interest you are obliged to inform me immediately! Understood?"

"Yes, sir," replied a respectful Gurza. "That is more than I had hoped. Thank you very much sir!"

Valenzuela noticed protruding from his vest pocket what appeared to be a note pad. "You taking notes?" he asked, pointing to the ledger in his pocket.

"Yes, sir," answered Felipe, briefly raising his hand halfway to it then dropping it to his side. "I met a most-interesting man down there from Ciudad Juarez. He has an interesting past to know and understand, and how he adapts to all of these forced changes will be what I hope to follow. This is why I came to see you. This will take time. I perhaps will need several of these notebooks and plenty of pencils."

"Tell me, Mr. Gurza. After you have several of those books filled with your scribblings what do you intend to do with them all? Will you be sharing this at school with all those liberals or do you have some other motive, some purpose you have yet disclosed to me?"

"As I said before, I hope to use all I learn to enlighten others. Maybe in my thesis, maybe if I appeal to the right people, maybe even be published. I do not intend to share this in class with anyone. This will be my work and mine alone!'"

"If what you write is anti-government I forewarn you that can lead to trouble. You will find that getting such controversial material published in Mexico could be difficult. In the United States, however, that is entirely something else. Their publishing industry is huge, free to print whatever. That is a consideration. I do not advocate going up there. But, I do caution you that whatever you write here could very well have serious consequences of one sort or another. Your thesis may be rejected. Publishers may refuse you out of fear. You could be wasting your time in all of this. You best consider everything before you get too involved."

"I am aware of all of this, sir. You think me naïve, perhaps even foolish. Maybe so; when you were my age you too had to learn and earn your way through life, just as I intend to do. You, sir, still are in your own way," said Felipe, casting a look to the window, imagining beyond the pane the tented soccer field below. "Waste of time? Regardless of what I learn, all has merit one kind or another. I may or may not use any information I gain for some educational purpose at school, or in the publishing world. It depends if and how I am inspired. If anything, this experience will at least make me able to converse intelligently, will have valid views of my own."

"Very well. Just the same, it might prove worth your while to let me review your notes before you go public with anything. Just a safeguard, mind you."

There was no way that Felipe Gurza was going to follow that advice! He was convinced that Valenzuela would delete whatever he had written. He was opposed to censorship and any review of Valenzuela's he perceived that that would be the end result; even confiscation of his ledgers was a possibility. Felipe just smiled, stood up from his chair. "If there is nothing else I must be going."

"No, Mr. Gurza. That is all. I suppose you have other things to do also, like maybe a young lady waits for you?"

It was a personal prod, to reveal something of himself, of his life outside those stadium walls. "In a manner of speaking. My mother has lunch waiting for me! I never risk missing any of her cooking!"

"Ah," sighed Valenzuela. "Yes, mothers." He thought of his own long ago, long dead now, how she had worked her fingers to the bone to put the barest of victuals upon a tin plate for him and his brothers.

"Go and enjoy! All too soon those joys are gone. When they are here it is best to enjoy every aspect of them. I suppose you'll be here again tomorrow?

"No, sir. The day after I'll be here. I have a commitment I must keep tomorrow." He had heard of a meeting off campus, one of the local radical groups, that of the Sinarquistas. There was a real firebrand, a former priest from the Cristero War days, that spewed-out revolutionary ideals. He had a following with some on campus. Leaflets were handed out at the risk of retribution. It was a political cauldron boiling with intrigue and mischief, something he wished to observe personally. He dared not venture the nature of his commitment on the morrow's evening, something that Valenzuela would soundly condemn and fault him for even considering attending.

"Very well. You best hurry to your mother and that meal she has for you. See me when you return," said the commandant.

Felipe Gurza strode the open floor for the door, feeling Valenzuela's eyes upon his departure. He shut the door behind him and continued his walk away. Yes, tomorrow he thought. The Sinarquista meeting! This ultra-conservative movement of radicals, those far right-winged Catholics that had fought in the Cristero War, those who strongly opposed the 'atheistic', secular government of the liberals, was nothing ideologically that appealed to him. But, they represented a growing number of dissatisfied and disillusioned Catholics, those who believed in conservative values and the restored 'rights' of the Church, which the Federal Government had stripped away under the past presidency of Benito Juarez in the previous century. Those policies were still in effect and were being carried out by administrations since, albeit the Mexican Revolution had interfered. He was a Social Studies major, and just as he was commencing a research into the interned Japanese-Mexicans, he would attend and listen inconspicuously to what the Sinarquista dogma was. There was talk of the former priest, Ignacio Lopez Contreras, of him speaking. Who was this man, wondered Felipe? He heard that he was a fiery speaker; that he was charged with a certain intoxicating energy that inspired people. But, who was he really? He heard that Contreras was once a priest. Felipe was intrigued why he was no more. What happened? His inquisitive mind would not tone down. He looked forward to attending the meeting, an anti-government one at that! Would the Federal Police show up? Perhaps he could slip in unnoticed and out the same. What would be would be. He, a liberal-minded student living for enlightenment, would seemingly be so out of place at a Sinarquista meeting. No one would suspect who he was, just keep mum and draw no attention his way; get in, observe, get out and be gone!

Felipe could detect the aromas from his mother's kitchen even before the door had been opened. His stomach rumbled an echo in anticipation of being wooed and satisfied.

"Home for lunch?" greeted Horacio, their limping servant of many years closing the door behind them.

"Yes. I'll be here a couple of hours," replied Felipe. This was a repeat as many times before. Horacio had watched him grow from childhood into adolescence, and now into a fine young man with a keen mind, a curious intellect, just like his father's had been. He surely recognized those traits for he had been a close friend of his father's since the Revolution, a time that rent apart both their lives. They had had a mutual fascination with the revolutionary, Emiliano Zapata, the peon general in Morelos. The world of the rural Zapatistas, those who followed Zapata into battles against the Federal Army, was vastly different from those urban dwellers within the nation's capital. There was something about the handsome, charismatic leader dressed as a Jaliscience charro, his piercing black eyes and flowing, ebony mustache. His army of farmers, garbed in simple, pajama-like white pants and shirts, topped with floppy sombreros, were devoted to the one who rose up from among them. They would follow him to the very gates of hell, for he had never forgotten his roots or them. He was in this struggle for them, not himself. He led their army against the Federals and the rich hacendados who denied the farming peasants the lands needed to grow their crops and live. The rich grew richer at the expense of the needy people.

At first the Zapatistas had armed themselves with the implements of farming; shovels, picks, axes. But, that was remedied as they procured weapons from those they defeated and elsewhere somehow. The Zapatistas in the south were every bit as formidable a foe as *La Cucaracha, Pancho* Villa, had been in the north. The Federal Government had had a two front war to contend with. Intrigue and youthful curiosity had drawn Horacio Benevides and Rodolfo Gurza, Felipe's father, out of the city, in search of the Zapatistas in the steep-hilled and deep-gullied terrain of the state of Morelos. Whether for naïve ideals or a thirst for adventure, they had been swallowed up into the vortex of that civil war.

Felipe heard Horacio shut the door, shutting out the troubled world behind him, and enveloping him were the symbols of the material successes his father had garnered for them all. The Revolution did not solve all of the nation's woes, although a new constitution was adopted in 1917. Many had remained in poverty, and there were those like his father and Horacio, who somehow had made lives for themselves in the aftermath. Prosperity had been Rodolfo's, whereas for Horacio, he had suffered a mangled leg from a cannon's blast in the revolution, a wound that would hamper him for the remainder of his life.

"How's the leg today?" asked Felipe, cognizant of the gains and losses suffered in that futile war, and of how his father had gained a worldly education with the Zapatistas and a formal one at the university in the city post revolution. As Rodolfo Gurza had met with success he and his wife, Elisabeth Esperanza Gurza, reflected that in their privileged living status. Horacio, on the other hand, had gone his own way for a time, faced a number of calamities. When learned of, Rodolfo and Elisabeth had immediately rallied to him, and in all essence, he became part of their household as he had moved into the large house, had his own room and facilities of substance, and eventually on his own assumed the role of a servant. To him it was not a demeaning demotion. He was honored to be their close friend, even a confidante of Doctor

Gurza's. He was often referred to as *Uncle* Horacio as he helped nurture their son Felipe.

"It is like it has been, good days and bad," replied Horacio. "As you know, this time of the year, when cold sets in, it pains me more. Never you mind though. Your mother is in the kitchen. You probably can tell!" He leaned his head backwards, sniffing the aromas.

"Yes, her trademark! Loves to create her kitchen delights!" They walked the way of the dining room, Felipe in a manly stride and Horacio with his accompanying limp. Their footsteps echoed upon the tiled floor. They stirred and briefly moved large, potted ferns on either side of the passageway by their passing. High above their heads hung a crystal chandelier, one that cast a welcoming light into this world at night. During the day the skylights fulfilled the needs. They had not gone that far when the passageway turned a right angle, entering a small, enclosed plaza. This courtyard often served as a retreat for the Gurzas. Stone frogs spewed forth streams of water in a fountain. There were benches and tables placed along the perimeters for relaxation, contemplation. Rodolfo Gurza had often availed himself of these tranquil environs, cradling in his lap a book of one sort or another. He had come through the Revolution with the Zapatistas, troubled over humanity and just how cruel its tendencies are. He had become cynical about the Church's answers to life, witnessing too much hypocrisy and contradictions within that purported sanctuary of hope. No, he had opted for a life in studies, in the world of the Political Sciences at first. But that was later changed to medical science. That, of course, had nurtured within him the zeal to contemplate health matters, and he thrilled with philosophy, apart from what clerics asserted. There were glaring contradictions in what Christ had said and the practices and rhetoric of the Church. Mass had held no appeal for him anymore. In fact, he was convinced, as others were, that he was no Catholic at all; a Christian yes, however! Dr. Gurza was his own man. The war had taught him about what following others could, would cost. The mutual realization of that had held-fast his and Horacio's friendship all those years since.

They passed through the courtyard and followed their noses like some street dog looking for a morsel. This led them to an open entryway, opening up unto a large kitchen where Felipe beheld his mother enthralled with her culinary creations.

"Good afternoon, mother. Smells like heaven," commented Felipe. His stomach rumbled again.

Elisabeth Gurza heard the growl. "Horacio, is the table set?" she asked.

"Yes. All is ready," he replied. "May I?" he asked her, as if to pick up a serving tray of breads.

"Yes, please. Here, Felipe, you can carry this and I'll take this pot here," she instructed.

It had been a pleasant hour of fine food, enjoyed with his mother and 'uncle.' Horacio had risen and returned with a pot of coffee, left again, and then returned with a small platter of sweet breads. Then they settled back some into their chairs. Questions of the past and present ensued in between sips and nibbles.

"Elisabeth," spoke Horacio. "Those days in Morelos with the Zapatistas....well there were times we thought we would never eat again. And, when we were fortunate enough to do so, it was old beans and moldy tortillas usually. Food like this was never even dreamed of." There was silence. Felipe and his mother perceived Horacio's thoughts as he stared in contemplation into his cup of coffee, swirling it to mix with the cream he had just poured. Yes, they knew he was thinking of those turbulent days, even with an air of nostalgia when he considered his best friend ever, the deceased Rodolfo Gurza.

"How is it that you and father never talked about those days openly before us?" inquired Felipe. "He seemed to want to avoid those memories, maybe even tried forgetting all. If I had questions he would give me only brief answers, always told me to think on better things, to devote my mind and pursuits to a higher calling."

"He had his reasons," replied Horacio. "For me I have never been able to forget it." He patted his leg, recalling how he had been catapulted backwards as an artillery shell had exploded nearby; how he thought it had blown away his leg. It was thought that his leg had been so mangled that it had to be amputated. But, thanks to a gifted and persistent doctor, that was never the case. It had required many months to recover enough to warrant any therapies, exercises to strengthen the bones and rebuild his muscle tissue. Horacio was forever grateful to that doctor and an inspiration for Rodolfo to pursue medicine, with hopes of being a doctor himself. It had pained them both to hear a few weeks later of the doctor himself being killed in a subsequent battle.

"Before we met," said Elisabeth, "as you know, your father befriended that rich Englishman, Tristan Hill. He proved a godsend to Rodolfo, as a benefactor. Without him your father would never have afforded going to medical school. We would never have had this!" she said, waving her hand above her head in circles, referring to the inherited estate. "When he became an actual, licensed doctor he paid a moving tribute to that doctor that saved your Uncle Horacio's leg. The dead can inspire the living and that was the case with your father."

"I sometimes wonder how different life would have been for us all, at least most certainly me," admitted Horacio, "if Rodolfo had not happened upon that scene, when those thieves had attacked and nearly killed Mr. Hill, and how he had beaten them off and saved the man. We have much to be grateful for, for that grateful Englishman and for what Rodolfo was able to accomplish with his support. Here we are in the present, looking back at people who have made our lives possible. You know, I can still see my bloodied form on the ground and the intent face of Doctor Ramirez hovering over me. He had had the most striking face, baby smooth without the hint of any whiskers. It was a calming face, but stained in the blood of others. I can be doing anything during the day and somehow, even after all of these years, his image comes to mind. I never knew Mr. Hill. I guess all the rich, English petroleum people are not all that bad. Usually it seems outsiders come to Mexico just to plunder our natural resources, take and disappear. Well, that one, for a change, when he invested in Rodolfo, it was in Mexico really. As I felt about Ramirez, Rodolfo felt about Hill."

"It's too bad Mr. Hill died in that derailed train wreck outside Poza Rica. The English capitalists are busy as bees in Veracruz, after Mexico's petroleum. But Hill was different in most ways. It's too bad he never saw Rodolfo graduate and become a doctor," lamented Elisabeth. "I met him a month or so before the graduation, when Mr. Hill was getting ready to go up to some new well prospects on that doomed train. That was a horrible, needless tragedy! I should think that it doesn't take much to inspect and maintain the rails. But, these big international companies just want to invest a little and take out as much profits as they can! Take the wealth back to where they come from. That is capitalism for you!"

"Think that Mr. Hill would have been proud of father?" asked Felipe. "Think he would have been at his graduation? He must have been quite the man! Think of it! He must not have had any family back home. If he had he surely would not have left father and you all of that money in his will! Honestly! Not in the wildest of fantasies would this ever have been entertained! Never! But, it happened, is evident all around us."

They remained silent for a few minutes, each bouncing such considerations around in their minds like some tennis ball. Then Elisabeth spoke.

"Well now, tell us Felipe! We have not seen much of you today. Where have you been since there was no class? You certainly must have been up to something. You came with quite the appetite! Anything you care to share with us? We are sort of tired about this war news from the United States and Europe. Thank goodness that Mexico is neutral, wise to keep out of all of that nasty business. Besides, we are not as rich as the Allies are. We are better off staying aloof, unattached."

"Indeed?" emitted a surprised Felipe. "Are you aware what President Camacho has been doing? He acts as though we are at war, at least with Japan. You know about how he has issued orders to arrest all Japanese-Mexicans, whether they are Mexican citizens or not? Why? Does he have some innate fear of them? Hell, what about those in Mexico of German or Italian ancestries? What about the German colony right here in Mexico City? He hasn't issued orders to corral them like cattle, as he has the Japanese Mexicans! You know what is happening up north in the border-states, even on the Pacific Coast? Right here in our beloved

Mexico City Camacho has interned hundreds in a soccer stadium. We have to speak up and say how wrong this is!"

"Is this one of your liberal crusades at school, my son?" inquired his mother. "I should think the president knows best. After all, just what do we know? I am sure he knows what dangers there are. I myself feel uneasy about Orientals, any one from that side of the world actually. They look different and have their own customs; customs that are not compatible with ours."

"What!" cried out Felipe; comments he never anticipated from his mother. "Are you serious? Father would have been shocked by that! These are innocent people, mother! They have done nothing wrong! They are thought to be guilty of something even though there are no claims or proof they have done anything wrong. Camacho really must be reacting to the United States' declaration of war, thinking maybe by doing this he would put Mexico in the good graces of the Americans. They are at war! We are not! What our president has done is like some frightened rabbit, scampering about to do something that he hopes will be seen by the United States in a positive light."

"Dear! Do not misunderstand me!" she responded emphatically. "I am not a heartless bigot! Wars do not last forever. When this one is over they will return home and life will return as normal for them. This is actually for their own good. President Camacho is protecting them."

"Protecting them from what?" asked an incredulous Felipe. "We Mexicans have nothing to fear from them. Most are Mexican citizens anyway I bet. Camacho acts like Japan is about to invade us, that all of these people would be eager to help them! This is so far from the truth, mother! How much of truth can you handle?"

He had a ring of a challenge in his voice. She had never encountered him so before. "That is quite a pointed question, like you are thrusting a spear at me! Why do you ask me like that? Is this how you act after going to the university? Do you see in me some sort of adversary now? I am your mother!"

"I know. I know this well. I love you. That is why it pained me to have you say those things. If you knew what I know you would change your mind for sure! I guarantee it!"

There was silence around the dining table. Felipe held his tongue. Elisabeth and Horacio were perplexed at what he claimed he knew, and they hadn't. Elisabeth's left fingertips tapped the table's surface, just alongside her saucer with the breadcrumbs. Her wedding ring she still wore, even after her Rodolfo's death in a car wreck five years before, when upon a stormy evening when the taxi he was in had spun out of control, hydroplaned on the pavement and careened down an embankment, killing the driver and her husband. The ring had not lost any of the sparkle. The glistening reflections of light caught her eye; prompting her to wonder of Rodolfo. What would he have said in response to his son? Would he have been in agreement with him? Or, would he have reprimanded him verbally?

"Share with us what you know and we'll see what happens. We are not opposed to change. That is what life is all about, my son. We change our views and with the times as we learn more things. Don't cut us off from what you do at school and what you learn there or anywhere else. Include us and we will not be in the dark, not knowing what is shaping you in this life. You challenged me and this is my response. Agreed?"

His mother could be a feisty one and this was just such an occasion. He had thrown down his gauntlet and she had picked it up, accepting it. He wondered how to answer. Perhaps Commandant Valenzuela would allow her to accompany him next time? Perhaps. He would ask.

"Very well, I'll see what can be done," he said. "I have something to do tomorrow evening. But, the next day, maybe you can go with me, assist me in my research."

"Research? What kind of research?" she prodded.

"Just research. You'll know more later. After all, too much truth all at once can suffocate you. Be patient and you'll see what I mean."

She arched her eyebrows; puzzled with the mystery he had presented her with. Even Horacio seemed at a loss.

"You have a deal! Just let me know when you think I am mature enough to be presented truth, "she said with a slight smile. "Now, any one for another concha?" She held up the platter with a few remaining sweet breads.

For young idealistic Felipe, his quest for truth had taken him to the internment camp of what he perceived to be an unjustifiable confinement, a total disruption of families. He had beheld the offended and persecuted and it shamed him that his Mexico was guilty of the deeds. Where was the logic in all of this? How could Camacho justify his atrocities? In his reasoning he saw his government over reacting to an undefined enemy that had yet proved a threat to his country. And now, he was confronted with the challenge to convince his mother, even 'uncle', of just how reprehensible the government had proven itself to be, like some dictator imposing his will upon a select few of the citizenry. Well, two days hence and perhaps she would see and experience what he had. Meanwhile, he had that late afternoon a meeting with some fellow students, a study group he had attended numerous times. But, lingering in his back thoughts was the meeting the next day, that of the Sinarquistas. He had not divulged to anyone that he would be attending that rebellious group's gathering. He thought of that flier blowing across the campus that he had picked up, read of the meeting. His inquisitive mind convinced him he would go and investigate. Although the study group beckoned him now the Sinarquistas haunted his thoughts. Tomorrow would come soon enough!

Chapter 5

"A Speech Fosters a Quest"

Ignacio Lopez Contreras was a clone of hardliner Salvador Abascal, the leader of the National Synarchist Union (Union Nacional Sinarquista) from 1940 – 1941. He had relinquished that post as he was bound for Baja California Sur to set up a Sinarquista colony in the remoteness of Magdalena Bay. Replacing him was the moderate man that Contreras resented, Manuel Torres Bueno. Contreras had absorbed all the rhetoric of Abascal, swallowing all the bait the former leader had fed his followers, even siding with the Axis Powers against the free and liberal countries that made up the Allies, governments that the radical Catholic Sinarquistas saw as atheistic. Bueno was not given so much to the fiery speeches of the likes of Abascal, or even Hitler, Mussolini, or Franco in Europe. He was more prone to doing grand scale stunts like taking over Guadalajara, Jalisco and Morelia, Michoacan. These showy demonstrations accomplished little, but garnered support from the peasantry as it sought to incorporate allies to its cause in opposition to the Mexican government. In the absence of his mentor Abascal, Ignacio Contreras stepped in to fill a void, one that Bueno had failed to do as Contreras surmised. Contreras intended to be the flame that would ignite souls with his fiery speech. He would be speaking shortly from the kiosk in a plaza, before a local Catholic Church where robed clerics anticipated the evening. This is where Felipe Gurza was destined to witness whatever transpired.

Felipe had worn a heavy jacket, even a scarf about his neck and had a beret pulled low over his brow, so as not to reveal too closely who he was. The plaza was well lit upon his arrival. Even some of the Christmas lighting was still in place, yet to be removed for some reason. The Party flag of the Sinarquistas, a red field with a white circle in the center containing a map of Mexico, and the letters UNS on the left, top, and right sides of said circle, was draped over the iron railing lining the platform of the circular kiosk. The way people were milling about in front of the flag seemed indicative as to where Contreras would be speaking. The cold of night revealed their breaths of steam rising from their faces that January evening.

Felipe had positioned himself with a good view of the kiosk and speaker, but too with a quick access for an escape if things got out of hand. He thought he was inconspicuous enough, just one of dozens of those mingling in the cold waiting to hear Contreras. He suddenly turned his head when he felt a hand upon his shoulder.

"You here?" commented the hushed voice of a young lady.

Felipe beheld bundled within a jacket a fellow student, Magaly Bedoya, from his study group. She was one that certainly had fetched his eye within the group. But, she was also a distraction for he had found himself studying her more than he thought he should. He knew the purpose of a study meeting was just that, to share and discuss the subject at hand in class. Magaly Bedoya intruded his thoughts, prevented him from truly taking part, being involved. Little did he know he was having the same effect upon her. Now, in this plaza, they who had rarely spoken to each other at all before, and if so indirectly within the group stood side by side moments before Contreras took his place.

"Magaly!" exclaimed Felipe. "You too? I never knew you had any interest in such things." He looked around the plaza, looking for some signs of police activity. "You know this could be a bit risky to be here. I bet many are radical extremists that came out of the Cristeros War, or at least believe it had merit. The Camacho government is not blind. He knows about them. Things could get nasty if police come!"

"Yes, I know that much at least," she replied. "I see you have chosen a good place just in case. It should be easy enough to jump into those bushes and run away from here undetected. Besides, there is that bridge over the street back there." She nodded her head to the side. "We can stand and watch whatever happens from there. I hope you do not mind company!"

"Mind?" he wondered. "Of course not. Glad for the company." He was more than pleased to share the space and time with her. "Any more here?" he referenced to other students from their group.

"I do not think so. I haven't noticed anyone. No one mentioned anything at school. That is why I am so surprised to see you here! Like you, like me, I suppose."

Suddenly a voice called out from the Kiosk's podium. "I am glad to see a good number of you have turned out to see and hear Señor Contreras speak. You will find him unlike others we presently know. Contreras speaks with force and commitment and once you hear his message you too may pick up this banner before you as your own to wave before the government's face. I want to tell you something first. Sr. Contreras was a Catholic priest before and during the Cristeros War. He took up arms to fight against the secular government for our Mother Church and our rights. When all of that ended in failure they never gave up the fight. They formed our National Synarchist Union in 1937 and our numbers have continued to grow. And why? Now, I have the privilege to introduce you to Ignacio Lopez Contreras! He will explain why and much more!"

There were no cheers, just silent breaths of vapor rising above the heads standing below on the plaza floor. There was no one knowing what the spewing rhetoric of this one time priest would be. They noticed an average looking man, nothing specifically appealing. He too was dressed warmly, wearing a fedora to keep his head warm. He removed it and set it upon one of the iron, fleur de lis ornamentals atop the kiosk wrought iron railing. Then he stepped away, looked upon the several dozen gathered below him. It was not a time for children and childish games in the plaza. He was there for straightforward talk to adults. He clasped his gloved hands, rocked a little on his heels, then raised a hand and pointed at various ones below.

"Tell me, sir, and you ma'am, you young lady, and you young

man! Why is it you are here at this late hour? You could be inside where it is warm, enjoying some hot chocolate, maybe something stronger, maybe a tray of treats or something else. I'll tell you why you are here! You know what is happening in our country today, and the world at large. You know that there has to be a better answer to what our President Camacho is doing, and we in the Sinarquista Union believe we have one, and it is time we act!" He clasped his hands again, sometimes behind his back, suddenly bringing them forward to drive a point home by punching his right fist into his left palm, as if imitating someone else, possibly his hero, the Fuhrer of Nazi Germany. His mannerisms were strangely familiar, an intoxicating act he had rehearsed numerous times for effect; a one-time priest within Christendom imitating an anti-Christian. Was he his own man or under the influence and direction of others?

"The Cristeros War, *La Cristiada,* did not end in complete failure. We who had fought the good fight and survived are now in this union. We have a conservative approach to how Mexico should be. We need to return to the days when our Mother Church was stronger, had her place in our lives. Before the devil in the form of Benito Juarez came and robbed her of what God had bestowed upon her, and dare I say robbing you too. The Holy Church of God was, is the light beacon of us all. The priests all over Mexico were good to the people. Then there were those of no faith who did not love the Church. They rallied behind that Indian idol worshipper Juarez and overthrew Maximilian. I tell you we would have been better off if they had failed. But, no they murdered Maximilian and that Juarez devil did nothing but evil since. But, lets look at life more recently. Since the days of the Revolution the federal government has continued to carry out the edicts of Juarez, the 1917 despicable Constitution, mandates to still persecute we Catholics. Why do we Catholics accept what infidels, atheists, liberals, these secular governments do to us? Is it time for another Cristeros War? Is it time for we Catholics to stand up against these secular liberals, even those who see merits in Godless communism?" He clutched his hands behind his back and walked back and forth, getting ready for his next outburst.

"You know of how the United States is now at war with Japan and Germany. The open society of the United States has opened up the floodgates to every sort of liberal quack there is, and their Constitution allows it. Spain, Germany and Japan, Italy too, have fought to rid themselves of these subversives. And, I point out they have been succeeding. We need to look at how they have been doing this. The liberal governments they are fighting against, and we in Mexico, have had one for too many generations. President Madero wanted us to emulate the United States and in the end he too was murdered. So, I ask you this. How do you see we Sinarquistas in all of this? We are opposed to the same elements of humanity as the Axis Powers are. We are conservatives as they are. We want to be rid of liberalism and have a restoration of conservative Catholic values and respect. We want a government that wants the same. But Camacho is someone who knows not what to do and when he does he is wrong. I mean wrong in a big way!" He saw over the heads before him a number of cars parking along the perimeters of the plaza. He had a good idea who they were, but continued with his animated rant.

"For example, Mexico has no part in this world war now raging. We never took a stand in that first one. We have remained neutral. That is a good thing, yes? It is good that the blood of our sons and daughters have not been spilled on some meaningless foreign soil. We have Mexico and she takes all we have! But, Camacho has seemed fit to do unspeakable things to Mexican citizens who just happen to have Japanese ancestry. I ask you why? You all know of how he has sent his soldiers into the border-states and now even into the Pacific Coast states to round them up like cattle and imprison them. What have they done? Is Mexico at war with Japan? No we are not! Even in the United States, who has been at war with Japan since December 8th, has not done such a terrible thing! Why then has our President decided it is best for Mexico to do this? Do we have a paranoid president that cowers at shadows? He is beyond reason and perhaps something is needed to shake him out of his stupor!"

Just before he spoke another word there were whistles blown from various angles around the plaza. Felipe and Magaly could see policemen approaching down the several walkways of the plaza to the kiosk.

"We better go!" he said to her. "Quick!"

They hurriedly backed out of sight into shrubs and bushes, nearly tripping over some protruding, gnarled roots above ground. They then hastened away into the night, leaving behind the illuminated scene of chaos. As they disappeared into the shadows they heard from behind the blow-horn commands of the federal police as they came down the various walkways terminating at the kiosk. The audience of Contreras was milling about bewildered, fearful yet angry, were shouting. Still ringing in their ears were the vitriolic words of the fiery Sinarquista, one of those who had fought in the Cristero War, one who spoke from experience and force, promoting the ideals of another war, one favoring the Sinarquistas and the Holy Catholic Church.

They had scampered up a pathway leading to the bridge, and once there merged with passersby who were crossing over to the other side. The bridge was part of the city street grid, crossing diagonally to offer views of the plaza below. Cars passed by, slowing down as a throng of people huddled at mid span. Felipe and Magaly mingled in, witnessing too the police action in front of the kiosk. They had projected themselves through the crowds. There were shouts of derision rising from the police intrusion, intimidating those present in the plaza below. But, the federals' main purpose was not to disband the meeting, but apprehend the instigating speaker Contreras. They soon stormed the kiosk and had him in custody, ushering him off the kiosk and out of the plaza. Inaudible grumblings could be heard as the audience filtered away by twos and threes. Soon, it was all over. The only semblance of anything or anyone having been there was the deserted Sinarquista Union flag still draped over the iron railing, and too the fedora of Contreras still atop that fleur de lis ornament.

"The Cristeros War still has its players," commented a middle-aged man to another like himself, both alongside Felipe. "Just another time, another place! Same old thing, radical extremists, disgruntled Catholics against the liberal government. Just this time they weren't killing each other as they were back in the 20's."

"That fellow they took away, what do you suppose is going to happen to him?" asked his companion.

The man offered no answer, just shrugged his shoulders. They and others of the crowd began moving away, crossing the bridge to wherever they were destined. Only Felipe and Magaly remained behind, staring as if into oblivion though their faces were turned to the plaza below. Beneath the plaza lights, even from that distance, could be seen the numerous moths and insects hovering in mid-air, drawn to the lights as a moth is to the open flame of a candlewick.

"Well, that man had a good question," summarized Magaly. "What is going to happen to that guy? Not that I really care one way or another. He sort of brought it all upon himself as I see it. I'm too much of a free thinker to get involved with political groups. I suppose I am one of those liberals that he was denigrating." She shivered. "Come! It's getting cold. There's a place on the other side that serves wonderful chocolate Oaxaqueño. A hot cup of that and some churros would be a delight!" She tugged at his elbow and he followed without comment.

It was just a hole in the wall, really. How Magaly had discovered the little place momentarily queried him. There were only two stools inside and two on the sidewalk at a small counter. They sat outside and placed their orders. Two steaming cups of hot chocolate and some churros were soon placed before them. Magaly wasted no time taking a churro and dunking it into the chocolate repeatedly like a donut and then devouring the moistened end with delight, until the churro was gone.

"You are more quiet than usual, Felipe. That back there, does it trouble you that much?"

He stared into the frothy foam of his chocolate, like some crystal ball that had clouded over with an undiscernible future. "I want to know more about those people, just how extreme are they? What are they capable of doing? Just how many of them are like that Contreras? I am going to see if I can get a copy of their published manifesto. It could tell me all I want to know. I surely do not swallow everything he said! But, he caught my ear when he

called the arrests and incarcerations of Mexicans for simply having Japanese heritage an illegal, immoral act. He spat that out as if President Camacho himself was in the audience before him. I fault him not for taking that stand. You don't have to be a Sinarquista to know that is wrong!"

"So, you are going to play the investigative journalist!" she exclaimed as she pushed away her empty mug and wiped some crumbs from her mouth.

Felipe drained his own mug and then set it by hers. "Thinking about it. I could poke around to see what I can find out about this Contreras. I can see what happens."

Political activists from the Cristeros War, like the frustrated ultra radical Catholics as Ignacio Lopez Contreras, looked for other means to express their governmental contempt. The extremist, Jose Antonio Urquiza, had caught his ear. He was in the thick of things as the *Union Nacional Sinarquista* (UNC) was officially formed May 23, 1937 in Leon, Guanajuato. They were comprised of ultra conservative Catholics, aligned with clerical fascism, falangists, fascists from Franco's Spain , and advocates of ultra-nationalism.

In the 1920's and 30's Pope Leo Xlll's *Rerum Novarum* encouraged those in Austria, Portugal, Spain, and Mexico to rise up and oppose anti-Catholic Church governments. Those in Mexico who had done so in the Cristeros War (1926-1929) had left a legacy for future like-radicals to follow; which the newly formed Sinarquistas fully embraced. They countered the socialist policies of the federal government. The government soundly denounced them, had them under scrutiny. After all, the Cristeros War was not ancient history! Whatever course the Sinarquistas embarked upon to oppose their perceived oppressive government, they found support in like radicals in the United States, religious persons as themselves rallied in word and deed.

The Sinarquistas would modify, even mutate. They eventually took on an evident pro Axis Powers stance as World War ll blazed. This was a concern for both Mexico City and Washington D.C. So, having a kinship with Japan did not set well with them when

President Camacho initiated his programs of internment of Japanese Mexicans from the border states and the Pacific Coast. To Felipe and the others who had heard their anti-government stance lingered a question of just how bent they were on terrorist acts. How far would they go? This troubled thought rode roughshod the conscience of Felipe.

They had left the little sidewalk café and were now nearing an intersection where they would part and go their separate ways. 'Have you decided anything yet for your thesis?" she asked.

"Yes and no," he replied. "There has been a new twist in some things. I need to pause a bit. I still have time."

They bid good evening and walked away in opposite directions. While still within earshot Magaly turned and yelled, "If you care to have some company, some help even, in your research, let me know. I am available." She offered him her pretty smile, waved, turned, and was gone.

Help, wondered Felipe? Sure, he would like her with him. Then again, he had this thing to prove to his mother. In the morning he would return to the soccer stadium and Commandant Valenzuela. Perhaps the old man would agree, even if reluctantly, to let his mother accompany him someday, let her too meet Haru Yamashita, his children and behold the sorrows of the compound. One thing the university had done for him, besides allowing him to earn a splendid education, was to foster and nurture his inquisitive mind. But, it seemed more and more that school would have to take a secondary role for a while.

As he walked home Felipe entertained in his mind how the evening had been, political extremists, police intrusions, hot chocolate and churros, and of course fetching Magaly. He was now nearing the doors when they opened unto him.

"Evening, Felipe," greeted Horacio. ""Your mother has been waiting for you, wants to see you before you retire. She has something to say to you. She is in the library."

"Yes. Thank you," commented Felipe, sort of puzzled why she was still up that late hour. What does she have to say that is so important, he wondered? He went her way to find out.

Chapter 6

"Mother and the Commandant"

"Yes, finally you are here!" exclaimed Elisabeth Gurza to her son. "I've been ready to retire the last hour. But, before I do I have something to say to you. In regards to the challenge you presented me with I did some snooping around this afternoon. I wondered about that soccer stadium you had talked about and sought it out. I came across it and went to see things for myself. Well, I did not get past the security guards but I was shown to the commandant's office, a certain Valenzuela. I must say, upon first meeting him I thought the old boy should be doing something else other than that. He has a few years on himself, sort of long in the tooth. Still, he graciously had me sit down to hear what I had to say. Well, he comes across as being quite the gruff old buzzard. But, when I introduced myself he took on another demeanor. His face suddenly developed more wrinkles when I mentioned 'Gurza'. I thought his eyebrows would reach the top of his head. He asked me in a hesitated voice if I was related to you somehow and when I said you are my son he sort of sunk back into his chair, even as if he had stopped breathing for a moment." She held silent, musing in her mind the scene.

"Now why did you go see him?" asked an incredulous Felipe.

"Well now, you were quite emphatic in your assertions in how mistaken I was; even implying I was blind to truth. I was compelled to find things out myself! I am no fool to be blindsided! I wanted to know if these are innocent Mexicans or dangerous foreigners our government is locking up. But, that commandant would not hear of my wants. He regained his stoic composure and told me, no; at least for then. He did say that you were supposed to be there tomorrow." A clock just chimed twelve midnight. "Excuse me, today rather! His advice was to come today with you and accompany you into the compound. So my dear son, I'll be going with you 'today'!" She cast another look the way of the clock. "I suggest we both get some sleep. We have an interesting day before us." She yawned and patted a moistened eye, then rose up for bed. "Oh, before you retire I placed some fresh cookies on a covered dish in the kitchen, just in case. Good night, good morning, whatever. I'll be ready when you are." Then she turned and was gone, leaving behind a bewildered Felipe. He watched her disappear down a passageway, concluding, that's Mother!

It was a crisp morning in Mexico City that January day that greeted them. Elisabeth had been nigh the first up, but Horacio was by a few minutes before. By the time Felipe arrived in the kitchen he found only Horacio tending to some menial tasks at a kitchen counter.

"Your mother is in the dining room, having some coffee," he greeted Felipe.

"Good morning, thank you," replied Felipe and turning to leave he called back. "How is the leg this morning?"

"Oh, about the same most of the time. It never robbed me of sleep though like it has before. Thank you for asking." Then Felipe parted to see his mother.

He found her sitting at the dining table fully illuminated by the crystal chandelier. "Up already?" he asked her, which Elisabeth never promptly responded to. Staring into her coffee she reminisced aloud,

"Your father and I used to get up earlier than this, watch the sun come up, set the sky on fire with all sorts of colors." She paused in her memory, like some wheel suspended, spinning in mid-air. She sipped at her coffee. "Here's a fresh pot," she nodding her head at the pot on a ceramic tile atop the table. "Horacio had this brewed, ready to pour when I arrived. "Of course we had better views of the horizon from the upper terrace." She then fell silent once again, a longer interlude as she delighted in her recall.

"I could use some." Felipe reached to pour himself a cup to the brim.

"I should have warned you to leave some space for some cream. Horacio made a stout pot, knowing we needed a good kick start this morning."

Felipe sat down opposite his mother enjoying again some of the same cookies he had enjoyed before retiring mere hours before. They indulged in the treats and brew and some conversation over the next hour. The sun had already commenced to put to flight the veil of night. The streaking colors of reds, oranges, yellows, purples dazzled them through the dining room windowpane.

"Looking at that, back in the days of Tenotchitlan, before the Conquest, I can see how the Aztecs and others worshiped a sun god," observed Felipe. "I wonder of our day, how ignorant we shall appear to those who look back at us in some four hundred years. Mankind has grown in knowledge. But, what has that done for us really? Morally we all are still the same, like cavemen. Instead of wearing skins and carrying clubs we are only dressed better and do things by push button and levers instead. History proves that! No matter how advanced our minds become we cannot change our base natures."

"Oh my, my son the philosopher!" emitted Elisabeth. "You must continue to stay up late, get too little sleep. That seems to make you wiser. Then again caffeine will sharpen your wit too, and some more cookies will energize." She smiled to herself, thinking of the day at hand. "I look forward to this day. It will be one of an education in one way or another, for you or me, maybe both. Meanwhile I think I'll go upstairs for a better view of the sunrise. What do you suppose, about nine o'clock good enough to leave?"

"Yes, I think that should be fine. We'll find Commandant Valenzuela even at that time probably smoking a cigar and sipping brandy. When I first met him I had thought his eyepiece would fall into his glass. But, I guess those squinting wrinkles kept it secured well enough."

She had excused herself when Horacio entered. They greeted one another in their passing and Horacio angled for a chair across the table from Felipe.

"I hope you did not mind that much about how strong the coffee is," prompted Horacio. "I knew it would probably be needed today. Besides, it is a stronger roast than we have had before."

"It's fine. No need to be concerned, "reassured Felipe, holding up part way a hand to ease any further concern.

"She does that every week, you know. She goes upstairs to the terrace where she and Rodolfo used to spend many mornings before the workdays began, under the stars at night. I suppose in her own way she is up there conversing with him, talking over how things are. Maybe she finds solace in that. It's not for me to question her. But, you shall see. When it is time to go you'll see her energized. Whether it's the coffee or time spent communing with your father up there, who knows? What is, is just that, what is." He poured himself some coffee. "I see you like those cookies. It's a new recipe she tried. It has some ginger and orange peel." While she was mixing everything together she uttered,

"Felipe will like these." He took a bite of one, followed by another, agreeing that they were delicious.

They took the transit to the stadium, arriving at a little past ten o'clock. They were admitted into Valenzuela's office, finding him squinting through some expelled cigar smoke, scrutinizing his pour of some brandy, considering a little more morning delight.

"Good morning to you both," he greeted them. "I know this is not the best breakfast to have. But, at my age caring about nutrition seems ridiculous. I feel it is my due to enjoy some pleasures, before I bid adios to this world. I know others would say a glass of orange juice would be better to start the day," he mused, rubbing his thumb along the crystal glass in hand, holding the amber brandy. "Well, maybe my wrinkled brow and aged frame may just find some spark in this." He took a hefty gulp, felt the burning glow in his chest, followed by a long drag on his cigar. He exhaled a cloud of smoke above his head, then settled back into his desk chair.

"Well, Señora Gurza,"I see you came along with your son as I suggested. Frankly, I doubted you. A woman of your persuasion does not usually commit to such things. They stay home and enjoy their own realm, leave the ordeals to others. I apologize if that seems harsh. But, I saw how those like you, during the Revolution, at least enough to convince me, that they were content enough to hide away from truth, from life, and submerge themselves in a world that was changing all around them, like ostriches sticking their heads in the sand. Stupid? Foolish? Naïve? If I had been a wealthy man as they perhaps I would have done the same." He motioned with cigar in hand for them to sit down, leaving a wisp of smoke eddying above, about his head.

"Now, the same rules apply. The same two soldiers will accompany you into the compound. You will have thirty minutes to do your interviews. As I said before, if anything of a security nature is revealed you must tell me immediately afterwards! Señora Gurza, are you sure you want to do this, go down among all of those undesirables?"

"My dear Commandant, I have been up well before dawn in anticipation. I was never one of those you speak of so disdainfully. I am no ostrich! I assure you! Never underestimate me!" She eyed him with the stare of an eagle. After a few moments she smiled. "I am sure what my son learns that he will clue you into, if it has any such merit. As for me? I am just a mother accompanying her son."

"Very well, señora," responded Valenzuela, aware of her quick wit. "Your son has a favorite down there. Perhaps you'll discover why. I sure do not. They are all the same to me. The government says they must be here and so it is. I never question where my commands come from. Why should I? They know more than I do! They have their reasons for all of this. Now, you best be on your way for the clock is ticking!"

Felipe and Elisabeth stood up to leave. Before reaching the door, the Commandant called out to her.

"You know, I have checked upon you, your family. The name Gurza has ties to the Revolution. Seems your husband was with the Zapatistas. Nevertheless, I am sorry for your loss. When your Rodolfo had died it must have been a hard blow to withstand. But, I must say you appear to have withstood it all in good form."

Elisabeth stood by the door, absorbing the Commandant's

analysis. Valenzuela and Felipe both waited for her response.

"My dear Commandant, thank you for that. I never knew you had such an interest in our family. If I had only known! Yes, Rodolfo's death was a shock, a painful one at that! But, my Felipe is like an exact copy of him; sharp mind, and intellect never satisfied. This is not time wasted being here, not for either one of us. There is something to prove, and it will be. The Gurzas are all about truth, wherever it lies. Enjoy your 'orange juice." She did a slight nod of acknowledgement, smiled, and turned for the door, exiting with Felipe. Valenzuela remained at his desk slowly sipping his brandy, staring at the closed door, imagining the lady departing on the other side. Yes, he surmised, an attractive lady with wit and fire!

"Sergeant!" called out the Commandant. His aide entered. "Place another soldier with their escort!"

There was something in her demeanor that unsettled him, just like her son had. Why had he given into their requests? He certainly was in his power to refuse them. But, he had and now sought some show of his authority with an additional guard.

Felipe lead the way to Haru Yamashita's tent. At first glance the children were playing with some others nearby. Haru was sitting on a makeshift chair, halfheartedly watching over them. He had doubts that Señor Gurza would ever return. He was stirred out of a mild stupor at their approach. Seeing a woman in Felipe's company intrigued him. She appeared to be a woman of substance at first sight. Why would she be with Señor Gurza?

"Good morning," greeted Felipe. "I hope you have been well, despite the circumstances." Haru nodded an Okay at him while looking at her. "I would like you to meet my mother, Elisabeth Gurza. She was insistent to come and the Commandant gave permission." Haru bowed his head in a respectful meeting.

"Good morning señora," acknowledged Haru. "I beg your pardon. I am not in any position to extend a true welcome."

"That is no problem, señor," responded Elisabeth. "I understand and hope to understand more shortly."

"Are you still open to an interview, answer my questions as if you want the world to know of the grave injustice heaped upon you? My mother is here to hear and see things for herself. Do not be intimidated by her." Felipe turned to give his mother a look.

"Yes, I am fine with that," answered Haru. "What sort of things do you want to know this time?"

"Last time we talked about what happened. This time I would like to know something about your home life as it was, how you were part of the fabric of Mexican society up there in Chihuahua. Tell us about your family and business, the community you called home." He watched for some sign from Haru, sitting on the wobbly crate he utilized for a chair.

Haru sat motionless even though the corners of the crate were uneven, caused a slight rocking motion. "My father began a little shop where he sold whatever he could get and resale at a modest profit. The neighbors, all Mexicans, accepted my father and mother openly, and when they realized that they had become naturalized citizens it was fiesta time! Of course I was not around then. But I was told of the celebrations later. My father expanded the business and was able to buy the house too that had an upstairs over the store and extended behind it. It was a general store. Father named it simply "Abarrotes de Yam". That was short for Yamashita as you likely surmised. We were a happy family even though money was tight and the political unrest was terrible. Those Revoultion years were horrible! Despite all of that I thought we had a pretty good life." Then he cast a disdainful look about the tented compound of internees as himself.

"Did you say you had family in El Paso?" asked Felipe.

"Cousins," replied Haru. "When I was just a boy we would take turns visiting one another when the Mexican Army, bandits, whatever were no threat to everyday people. Of course, that is all changed now since Pear Harbor. They cannot cross over the border or can we. Remember! We are the *enemy.*"

"I know it will be painful, but would you care to say something about the cholera and your folks?" asked Felipe.

Haru looked off into the heavens above, the wheels of his memory spinning only five years past.

"They were not the only ones of course. Bad water brings bad things to everyone. They both died within two days of each other. We had several others on our street that got sick, some died.

After mass the neighbors paid their respects. We were not seen as foreigners, but Mexicans as they were. There is no disputing the fact that I have Japanese heritage. You can see this. But, look how my folks and I identify with Mexico. I have a Mexican wife. Her name is Rocio. My son's name is Kenji Carlos and my daughter is Kasue Maria." He waved his index finger at them playing around the tents.

"Kenji was a year old when my folks passed. They were quite happy we gave him a Spanish middle name! Kasue came a year after they died. But, I know they too would have been happy we gave her the name Maria, even though we are not Catholics."

"They are lovely children," commented Elisabeth. "I recall when my son was their age. I sometimes had my hands full of his mischief."

"It seems to me, señora, that your son has grown into anything but a mischievous person. I do not fully understand why he comes to see me. But, he has motives that are intriguing!"

"I assure you, Señor Yamashita, that what Felipe sets his mind to has purpose. I do not always understand him myself. In some ways that is why I am here. I came to see what he sees and if opinions need changing."

"Well, I am not thick headed. I perceived you came for a reason, not to see caged animals in a political zoo. I couldn't conceive the thought that your son would have brought with him someone to see this freak show just for curiosity's sake."

"Believe me! My mother has never been one for that!" assured Felipe. "Time is getting short. The Commandant decided on that extra guard. "But, before we leave I must ask. When you first heard of Pearl Harbor and how Japan had attacked the Americans, what did you feel?"

"Feel?" asked an ashamed Haru. "We were not that informed about Imperial Japan's expansionist dreams, to conquer and take from those people in Asia. Who knows how far across the Pacific Ocean they have intended to go? I understand now that the Americans in the Hawaiian Islands were perceived a threat to them, whether real or imagined. When we heard of their sneak attack and all of the death and destruction I felt shame. Rocio tried to console me. But, I looked in a mirror at my Japanese face and I broke it with my fist. I was angry, ashamed! I did not know what to do or say. I felt sorry for the Americans. But, when President Roosevelt gave that stirring speech to the US Congress, asking for a declaration of war upon Japan, there was something in his voice and manner that suggested America would respond with might. I think Japan smiled broadly after Pearl Harbor. But, the United States I feel will make sure that is wiped away for good!"

"Can you see the reasoning why you have been incarcerated?" asked Felipe, his mother looking on.

"The Americans declared war on Japan last December 8th. They have not rounded up Japanese Americans, placed them in their own concentration camps. We in Mexico are neutral. We are not at war with Japan or anyone else. And yet, President Camacho sees fit to arrest and incarcerate us like this? No, I do not see the reasoning behind it. Are we racially feared for some reason? What about the Germans in Mexico? Has our president dared incarcerate them?" He called his children over to meet Felipe and his mother.

"These are folks that came to see us. But, they must leave. They would like to meet you before they do," he said to them.

The Gurzas smiled and greeted them. Kenji and Kasue did like wise and when their father excused them they ran off to play with some other children.

"There is something innocent at that age," commented Haru. "They have no idea what has befallen us. They think we are on an outing. When they grow tired and want to go home it will be my duty to calm them down, somehow. What can I say or do?"

"In two days I'll return," was all the time Felipe had to say anything for the guards motioned with their rifles that it was time to leave. They could sense Commandant Valenzuela's presence staring down upon them from his office. Haru's question went unanswered, whether an answer was forthcoming or not. As Felipe and his mother were escorted outside they were silent, not a word was spoken. They left behind the tented compound and were ushered into Commandant Valenzuela's office.

"Learn anything of value, Señor Gurza?" inquired the camp's commandant.

"Just personal family history, how they had a general store and everyone respected them," answered Felipe. There was nothing of value to report to the government."

"And what about you, Señora Gurza? Was your female curiosity satisfied? See the foreign critters in the zoo?"

"For some odd reason I recall of a man once running for office who was accused publicly for being a bartender in a cantina. His accuser was his political rival who never disclosed the fact that he was a customer on the other side of the bar. I sometimes see in such a similar oddity, that those behind bars should not be, and those on the outside should be," replied Elisabeth.

"Careful, señora! That is brazen talk and can land you in trouble," warned Valenzuela. "I think it best you not come again!"

"I agree sir. I have seen enough," she replied. "My son's on his own for now on."

"Very well! Stay home do what you do in women's matters. Let this nasty business be done by we men." Then Valenzuela showed them his door and they parted.

Felipe was troubled over his mother's silence on the way home. It was evident that she was mulling over something in mind not yet shared. The miles passed by and soon they were let off in front of their residence and Horacio was there to open the door.

"Good morning," greeted Horacio. "Excuse me, afternoon it is. My, the day is getting by too quickly. Was it an interesting experience for you Elisabeth?"

"Yes, and illuminating too, she replied. "How about some hot chocolate, with a little tequila? There is a chill this day and not just in the air. I have no taste for brandy."

"Yes, there are some conchas left over too. I'll go prepare the chocolate," said Horacio, closing the front portal behind them. He passed them by in the hallway.

"Felipe," she said. "Lets talk in the library." Then she hailed Horacio to serve them there.

The library still contained much of Rodolfo's medical reference books, besides those numerous volumes on world history. He often had several opened books out at once on the mahogany table mid-floor. Now they were silent, not speaking to any academic anymore, neatly showcased on the shelves. Several chairs were grouped about a throw rug with small side tables for drinks, and ashtrays no longer used. Felipe wondered what his mother had had to say all the way home and now perhaps she would reveal what troubled her mind. Elisabeth sat down and Felipe followed. She looked at him long before saying a thing. It was indeed a mouthful in just a few words, something he was totally unprepared for.

Chapter 7

"The Just Victims and Defiant Advocates"

"You were right and I was totally wrong!" admitted Elisabeth to her son. "I just couldn't believe our President would issue orders to do that! As you asked your questions I looked around and could see these people had practically nothing. Of course I could not see inside the tents. But, it seemed evident that not one that I saw had the means to really care for themselves, like they were rounded up out of bed and brought straight here. Even at my age I need some growing up to do!"

Felipe sat stilled, not used to his mother admitting to any shortcomings. "You know, you are reacting the same way I did when I first went there. I had to dance around rhetorically with Valenzuela some, not reveal too much. All he knows is that I am a Sociology major at the university and this is a research project of mine for possible considerations for my thesis. But, it is much more than just that. I want to know just how innocent these people are and why our government has done so horribly wrong in all of this. Why has our neutral country so feared them that it has acted with fear and not with sound reason? It seems like our leaders are scared at shadows. Is there one iota of guilt in those people? Have any sworn allegiance to Emperor Hirohito and Imperial Japan? I doubt it very much!"

"He talked some about his wife up in Ciudad Juarez. Do you know any more?" asked his mother.

"Not really, just that she is Mexican, not Japanese at all, and was left alone. He said she's expecting their child."

"Ripped away from his wife and home like that has got to be

eating at him like some cancer!" mused Elisabeth. "How can he lie in that cold tent at night on whatever kind of bed that was provided and not worry about his expectant wife, and at the same time be concerned for his children with him? Too, you must wonder about the dreadful worries she must have not knowing anything about their whereabouts, how they are, if they are Okay?" She paused in deep thought, then added, "Those children, such darlings! How can Camacho believe they pose a threat? What do you see in them, any sort of national threat?"

"Not at all! But, then again there have always been questions about Mexico City, wonder if they know what they are doing. We expect, even pray they know more about what is happening than we all and and are making sound decisions. It's not a way to govern though, keep the people in the blind! Mexico is not a major political player on the world's stage. The only importance others see in us, those powerful countries with huge militaries, is that they want our natural resources, pure and simple! Our geographical location on the world map, next to the United States, is so key to the motives and ambitions of Japan, Germany, maybe even Spain. I remember in our studies at school how we dissected the speeches of the Americans' President Roosevelt. He said some years ago that the *only thing they had to fear was fear itself!* It seems our own government is guilty of that, of fearing the unknown and acting scared of shadows, whatever; nothing quite definite. Perhaps I might be convinced about Camacho's misguided fears for the adults in that tent compound; but those children? Insane! Absolutely absurd!"

Felipe thought how the previous evening he and Magaly Bedoya had witnessed the police breaking up the anti-government rally in the plaza, and how people risked speaking out against the government. What was he risking by his interviews and any public publication of facts and truth he revealed? What about that Sinarquista Contreras? What did they do to him?

"I can't get out of my mind his wife!" admitted Elisabeth. "I don't know the woman but I feel for her, the pain she's going through." Like some smoker taking in a deep drag on a cigarette, she sighed in reverse deeply, exhaling her breath. She expelled all, resembled the sails of some boat suddenly going limp, motionless. Then, she uttered a pensive inquirey, "You said Ciudad Juarez? You've never been to Chihuahua. Care to go? Would you like to go and find her? See about helping her somehow? Could at least inform her about her husband and children. Can skip school a few days, just say it's all for academic 'research'."

Chihuahua? Felipe had never regarded going up there. After all, a journey to the border was not a walk next door. Still, his mother posed him an interesting challenge, as he had her. Yes, it had merit, possibilities to shed more light on the innocent victims of a fearful government. He took a long time mulling over in his mind what she had said. Elisabeth could hear the wheels of his thoughts grinding on the rails to who knew where. Yes, he's thinking of Ciudad Juarez for sure she surmised.

"When? When do you think I should go?" he asked her.

Hmm, thought Felipe. "I suppose in several days, take care of some things first."

"You find out more information from Señor Yamashita your next visit, where their neighborhood is exactly up there, where to find their abarrotes. You tell him that you want to go see his wife and allay her fears in any way you can. The thing is this poor man is going to have to trust you, basically a stranger. He has reason to mistrust everyone now. So, don't be at all disappointed if he puts you off. If that's the case then a decision will have to be made, just go, or not, snoop around on your own and hope for the best." Elisabeth looked him directly in the eye, choosing her next words emphatically. She looked at him without flinching, with a matter-of-fact emphasis in her eye, blurted out,

"But, I am going with you!"

A shocked Felipe stared at her in disbelief. "With me?"

"Indeed! I stepped my toes into these waters to test how things are. Now I feel compelled to jump in. That old buzzard Valenzuela has denied me any further visits to the compound. But, he cannot prevent me from doing this. Besides, your father would be all for it! In another couple of days you'll see señor Yamashita again. Then perhaps the next day we could take a train up there?"

"Mother, that is not a luxury ride. It will take time and have some rough edges to it. We would need to......

She held up her hand to quiet him. "Listen, before you came along your father and I had some adventures together. He wanted to practice medicine among the Tarahumaras in the Copper Canyon. So, we spent some time up there among those poor people. I am not so contrary to challenges, necessary ones at least. I can check on tickets tomorrow and if a go we can leave in several days. What do you say?"

Felipe stammered briefly, considering them traveling together those long distances. Then he thought of Haru Yamashita's wife, expecting a child, managing the store on her own, all the while trying to function while her family had been ripped apart, fearful of her own unknown.

"That would be fine, maybe in three days? That will give me time to notify the school, others, that I," he corrected himself, "that we will be away for a week or so. I hope so at least, no more than that. I suppose as long as I say it is connected to my thesis research they will be in agreement. First, though, as you say, Señor Yamashita has to be trustful of me to volunteer any information of his wife. I cannot come across too pushy or eager. That could arouse suspicions. One thing for sure, after we return, if we saw his wife, and he and I get together again he will be greatly relieved to hear of his expectant wife and how she and the store are!"

Horacio limped into the library with a pot of hot chocolate and cups on a tray in one hand and in the other a tray of concha sweet breads.

"Here is a treat. I am partial to these myself, especially the chocolate conchas." He set the trays down upon a table between their two chairs. "Hot chocolate Oaxaqueño is so good too!" He poured them some cups and sat down himself with them. "Anything else?" he asked.

"We are likely to be leaving in the next several days and may be away for several more, maybe a week," advised Elisabeth. "You'll have charge of the premises."

Horacio looked puzzled. "Really? Where might you be going?"

"To the border," she answered. "Up there where the

government believes is a nest of spies and saboteurs. We are going up there to dispel lies and fears. It's sort of like having Rodolfo back again," she added. Then she fell silent as she sipped her steaming hot chocolate, reminiscing the past, intrigued with the present.

"Up to see the Tarahumaras again, like you and Rodolfo had done?" inquired Horacio.

"Not this time, no déjà vu. We have a more pressing investigation to make in regards to these forced internments. Felipe has some important work to do and I'll be accompanying him with my own purposes."

"Elisabeth, you are getting more involved with this challenge than I ever expected of you. Something must have happened at that futbol stadium today, something more than I ever anticipated. Care to inform me?" asked Horacio.

"Just that I was illuminated to some things that I never bothered to think of much before. Yes, what I saw and experienced today was troubling, enough so that I need to do something. And, if by going up to the border helps to further educate me as to my errors, so be it! To willingly remain blind is to be a fool! I never want to be regarded as one by others, and certainly not by myself! We'll be gone and back before you know it."

"Very well! I know when you have made up your mind there is no detouring you. What about you Felipe? You ready for the trip?"

"Ready as ever," replied Felipe. "I am certainly adding more perspective to my thesis. But, somehow this seems more than mere academia. As important as that composition is in my life, a sudden turn of events has put that on hold. I have no peace of mind to devote to it until I get some other things taken care of." He held up a vanilla concha. "You like the chocolate. I prefer these. Vanilla and chocolate compliment one another. This combination is what our Mexico has given the world. Now the world wants more, like our petroleum, and with this new world war going on lots of money is to be made by profiteers. It is too bad that Mexicans in general never see the gains of anything that big business does. We seem to have a vault of wealth that other countries enjoy. But, getting back to Chihuahua, it will be my first time up there. I guess it will be an adventure of sorts. In some ways I am looking forward to it, others not. I expect to see pain and misery and that is never a good thing, except for how it educates. One thing about higher education, Horacio, the more one learns the more knowledge can trouble the soul. It's like, the more I know, the more I know just how little I know. But, I must say, the more one knows the less likely is one to be naïve, blind, foolish, and really not easily suaded by others! That is me! Trying to avoid that trap. It is so easy to be complacent and never question things. That's not me!"

"You sound just like your father," commented Horacio. "I remember one night during the Revolution when.........."

"No, not that again," implored Elisabeth. "I know what you are going to say, as you have said so many times before. We know all about how your and Rodolfo's curiosity got you in trouble in Morelos. Rodolfo told me about that convent! Enough is enough." There were some snickers in the library.

"Listen, I have the study group to get to in a couple of hours," informed Felipe. "I best get up and think about that!" Really, however, whenever he thought of the group he really was thinking of Magaly. He wondered how she would take it when he told her of their going to Chihuahua. He drained the last drops from his cup and wiped the concha crumbs from his mouth. "Thank you, Horacio. Mother. Later. When I return after the study group maybe we can talk more." Then he stood up and parted the library.

Elisabeth and Horacio watched in silence the door being closed; imagined Rodolfo's son walking the hallwall to his room. The study group was not on their minds, but that of an impending train to the north, of their being aboard to an unknown reception.

"Spitting image of Rodolfo," interrupted Horacio. "In character that is! Gets a thought rolling around in his head and he's like a hungry dog with a bone, won't let it go! His compass is fixed. He's as good as gone! Well, both of you actually!" Elisabeth offered no comment, just smiled in agreement.

The study group consisted of a dozen students who shared a class or two with one another. They met a couple times each week, usually, to discuss any given subject matter that was common study among them all. However, one thing led to another and often conversation would veer off target, discuss current affairs rather, correlating the past with the present. Each one would often have a different perspective on pre-Hispanic cultures, of the indigenous groups of today, the descendants of those from yesteryear, pre-Conquest of that of the Spaniard and Roman Catholic Church. They usually met at Josefina's. The waiters would always have ready a table with twelve chairs in a side room where they could visit and share their academic studies. Several large bowls of totopos (tortilla chips) were always placed at several locations up and down the long table and by each bowl was placed a carousel of different salsas for dipping, and a couple of large platters of guacamole to enhance it all. Some students had shot glasses of tequila that they nursed for however long the group met. Others were satisfied with just a bottle of beer. Nibbles and sips were hyphenated by lively discussions.

Josefina's was a modest place, beige-colored stucco, arched windows with wrought iron scroll work. A clay tiled roof hung overhead as an eave. A red neon light in a window proclaimed 'cerveza', beers of appeal. Prices were comfortable for students and teachers alike. Their modest incomes were not sorely tried. The aroma of corn masa and tortillas fresh off the grill enticed the hungry and even the not inside. One did not necessarily need to be hungry to venture through the door, but once entered, the inviting ambience and aromas prompted orders for at least some appetizers and drinks. They usually had wafting from some audio speakers music like boleros and romantic songs, even corridos from the Revolution days. Then an occasional guitarist would be heard, usually sitting upon the edge of a fountain that had floral pedals floating in the waters. The fountain's centerpiece had a stone likeness of Saint Francis with a peaceful dove in an uplifted palm, the other at the side as if comforting stone figures of a dog and cat at the feet.

"Ah, nice you made it today," said a greeting Magaly. "You're a senior, doing your thesis. You are needed for your input on Malinche. Was she really a traitor to the native peoples by having a relationship with Cortes, his mistress? We know our history. But, you'd been in the program longer than most and surely have some viewpoints. One comment was that she was similar to the Americans' Pocahantas or Sacajawea. I don't think so. I think she was terrible! She deserves little credit for anything!"

"History can be a thin line separating hero and villain," responded Felipe. "Look at Francisco Villa. There are people today who still curse Pancho and others yet idolize him. He had his own way of meting out justice and that often was the sign of a calloused brute. But, Pancho was Pancho. La Cucaracha was a savvy general. But there are those who say he was just a cheap gangster. Villa would probably spark more heated debate than Malinche. But, our studies are not of this century." He paused briefly. Then, "What did you think of the plaza meeting?"

"I had hoped the police were later. I wanted the man to speak more. He was sort of comical in a way with his energetic prancing about, rocking back and forth on his feet while punching a fist in his hand. I wasn't so much interested in what he had to say as much as I was intrigued by his clownish dramatics. He spouted like some volcano, red in the face and all. I'm glad we got out of there and had the hot chocolate and churros instead. Things didn't look that appealing from the bridge. Why you ask?"

"Just curious. I am wondering what happened to him after the police took him away. Warn him, threaten him, beat him, throw him in jail? The only thing he had said that I paid attention to is the Sinarquista view of PRI (Institutional Revolution Party) and President Camacho arresting all the Japanese-Mexicans without just cause. I'd just like to know more what else they have to say about that."

"How are you going to find out?" asked Magaly. "You have any plans I don't know of?"

"Not exactly! Nothing definite!" replied Felipe. "But, I do have something to tell you. But, after the study group." Then for the next hour and a half the dozen students bounced viewpoints and insights around like some rubber ball until it was time to head home for supper. It had been a lively time of sharing, a stimulating ninety minutes that the dozen students looked forward to each week. They now were pushing their chairs away from the table and standing up to leave, except for Felipe and Magaly. The two of them remained seated engaged in conversation.

"What is it you have to tell me?" she asked as the last of the students exited their academic retreat.

"I'm going to be away for several days. My mother and I are taking the train up to Ciudad Juarez. There is a lady we need to find. We don't know her. But, she's the wife of one of those internees at the futbol stadium. We want to go see her and try to give her some peace, and actually by doing so will give her husband a measure of peace also."

"How do you know about her?" she asked.

"I've been interviewing her imprisoned husband at the futbol stadium. A pathetic scene really! A gross injustice on the part of our government! I'll be going there again tomorrow and hopefully he will give me the needed information to find her up there."

"Why isn't she with him in that camp?" asked Magaly. "Why take some Japanese and leave others?"

"She isn't Japanese. She is a Mexican mestizo. The federals left her alone. All I know about her is that she is with child, lives above a store they own. So, I am assuming she is trying to run the store while worried to no end over what has happened to her husband and children. We are going to seek her out and answer her questions, help her if we can."

"One thing about you, Felipe, is that you are a doer, not just a book person," commented Magaly. "That is a long trip up there. Could be some troubled areas to get through. Sometimes bandits hold up the trains and of course there are still small armies of disgruntled peons that always seem in revolt. You sure you want to do this?"

"Yes. I've had no peace to concentrate on school. Actually, it was mother's idea. She wants to go with me! Until I get this done I am just wasting my time on trying to do my thesis. But, I also have another motive in going. The train goes up through Guanajuato and that is where I understand the Sinarquistas are mainly. My mother doesn't know it yet. But, I intend to do some inquiring up there, see what I can learn, if anything. I know they formed their union in Leon in 1937. We are nigh five years later and I want to know if their 'manifesto' has changed any. They hate the liberal government; call them atheists. I just don't know if they are terrorists wanting another civil war to topple the government and get their religious zealots in to rule with a harsh conservative hand. Or, are they all bluster? What are they capable of doing? The rumors they have ties to the Nazis and Hitler is beyond belief! We Mexicans certainly are not Aryans! What could we possibly have in common with Germany and Hitler's racial fanaticism? So, I have a two-fold purpose in going, to seek out Señora Yamashita and satisfy my curiosity in Guanajuato."

"I somehow wish I was going with you. But, that would not be appropriate. And besides, I have an examination to take in three days. And too you say your mother is going also? Why? What for?"

"Mother has never lost her spirit of adventure! She sees a challenge and she gets energized! Now, we best go. But, when I return I really want to see you and share what we did and found out! If all goes well we should be home in about a week or less. I'll be looking for you."

They parted Josefina's and for the first time they embraced on a sidewalk outside as they readied to go their separate ways. They had not been this close before, even sensing the beating of one another's hearts. In their separate minds they wondered what each heartbeat was for, for worldly pursuits or for one another. Felipe patted her back and they separated with smiles. She stared at him intently.

"Listen! Don't get yourself into any trouble. I know that curiosity of yours. You can be just like a dog following his nose to trouble. Be careful!" She smiled, planted a kiss on his cheek and then went for home.

Felipe beheld her departure, admiring her charm, form, and beauty. Her intellect was sharp as a tack. She was one he could relate to in all ways. He turned to leave himself when he heard a commotion behind him. Spilling out from a bar were several men, apparently having had too much liquor. They had a poor individual on the ground, kicking him profusely in his face and ribs.

"You dirty Japanese scum lover!" they cried out, taking turns at kicking the man. He groaned with each heavy thud. Felipe hastened to help.

Felipe grabbed one of the men by the collar of his jacket and threw him backwards into the street. In quick succession he struck another with a fist alongside his ear and the assailant fell to the ground. The third was so inebriated he fell on his butt not knowing what end was up. Then Felipe focused upon the prone victim.

The man was bloodied. He certainly was not Japanese. But, the drunkards called him a lover of the Japanese. Felipe helped the man to his knees, and when he seemed steady enough he helped the man stand. But, any further help the man refused; begged to be left alone. Felipe watched him stagger away, wondering what prompted the attack. He cast a disdainful look at the three men on the ground.

"You are a dead man!" cried out the one sitting on the pavement. "Dead! We're going to kill you dead!" he said and then hiccupped. Then he babbled incoherently whatever else.

A police car approached with its spot light on illuminating the scene. He was told to halt.

They listened to what he had to say and knowing the history of that bar the policemen were not that surprised.

"Japanese lover was he?" said one officer. "Maybe another kick or two was called for."

"You serious?" asked a shocked Felipe. "They could have killed the man! Doesn't that matter?"

"Listen! You best be about your business and let us do ours. Or else we might have to do something!"

He was angered by their attitude and threats. Who would speak up for the victims, whomever they were? It was the first time Felipe had ever behaved that way. He had no idea what the assault was all about. But, when he heard 'Japanese' he had thought in an instant of Haru Yamashita, and he rallied to the victim's defence. Was there more of this waiting for him and his mother up north? He pulled his collar up around his ears and walked for a bus, leaving behind questions and the wary eyes of the police.

Chapter 8

"Riding the Rails to Who Knows What?"

They were leaving behind the rolling lush hills of central Mexico, continuing north through the state of Guanajuato. Felipe continued to entertain solo thoughts of a stopover there on the return, perhaps in Leon itself, the birthplace of the Sinarquista Union. He mulled over in his mind different what ifs and scenarios he might encounter there. Perhaps Magaly was correct in saying to beware whomever he met and spoke with. He was long in such thought, almost as though he had forgotten his mother was occupying the seat next to his aboard the train. He had been mum for seemingly hours.

"Felipe," Elisabeth said, startled him, nudging his side. "Where are you? You are someplace far away. What are you thinking about? Ciudad Juarez is not that far away now from what I heard the conductor say. Tell me, son, what is on your mind?"

"Oh, I'm just considering what is up ahead," he said, skirting the real issue. "I can see how the landscape has changed. It can look desolate to most I suppose. There is a certain beauty in it though. *La Cucaracha* Villa was comfortable here. I think he should have been named *El Alacran* instead. He was more like a scorpion with a deadly sting."

"They say 'live by the sword, die by the sword.' Well, Villa lived by the gun and he was assassinated in a hail of bullets, even after the Revolution. There is no escaping one's destiny!" commented Elisabeth.

Destiny, wondered Felipe? What was at the end of these rails as they ended at the border? What lay in store for them? What was their inescapable destiny? Thoughts of Guanajuato now faded with each passing kilometer north and thoughts of 'Abarrotes de Yam' and Señora Yamashita began to play once again upon his queries. What would they find at that border town? Meanwhile he stared through the car's window, out unto a wintry scene of strong winds whipping around brief snow flurries as the train railed on.

They had left Mexico City far behind and as they now rolled into the train station of Ciudad Juarez the sun of a new day was fully up. It was the first time that either one of them had been to this small city. The closest Elisabeth had been was years before with her husband when she and Rodolfo had been to the west in the Copper Canyon, working with the Tarahumara indigenous peoples. Now, she and Felipe stepped onto the landing and were greeted by bright sunshine and a biting wind with gritty sands stinging their faces. A tri-colored Mexican flag on a pole snapped and popped smartly its red, white and green atop the depot. Soldiers were evident about the depot, ready to quell any disruptions. They had no intentions of staying long so they had packed lightly, having little luggage. The only personal items they had were what they had carried aboard the train and placed underneath their seats. For Elisabeth any refinements she had taken for granted in Mexico City were for the time being tolerated without. *Just a day there and then they would return* she had planned for.

They took rooms at a hotel named Las Florecitas, named for the numerous little flowers that graced the entry when spring blooms burst forth. Now it was winter and the bushes looked like dried twigs, not a single hint of any flowers in the making. The desk clerk was a small man, stood on a stepping stool to peer over the desk at customers. He wore thick glasses, squinted at them across the desk.

"First time here?" he asked, pushing the registry forward for them to sign.

"Yes," replied they both simultaneously, Felipe signing-in for them. The clerk turned the registry around read their names.

"Gurza!" Knew some a while ago down in Torreon. But, you, I see are from Mexico City. No relatives I suppose."

"Not at all, "replied Elisabeth.

"Well, Juarez is not a place for much fun. You must be here on business of some sorts," he said, 'fishing' for information. "Expect to be here long?"

"Just tonight. We are doing research. My mother, years ago, was helping the Tarahumaras. She decided she wanted to come up this way again and here we are. Maybe we might try making our way out to see them, help if we can. They really suffer during winter." Felipe tried pacifying the man's subtle curiosity. Newcomers to the hotel were not that common, especially in the winter and the clerk was obviously intrigued.

"There is an American here who has a popular cafe. 'Barnaby's' is down that way several streets," he said pointing in the direction of the eatery. "No one really knows his history. Some say he was a farmer, fell on hard times in the United States during the Great Depression; came here to start over. Well, he's still in business after maybe ten years I hear, longer than I've been here. So I guess that speaks something for the food he serves. For me, I am still a beans-and-tortilla man, some enchiladas too. If you want that we have a little dining room off to the side over there. But, I guess many of the Chihuahuenses like his American hamburgers and hotdogs and other gringo foods for a change. Here, let me get your keys." He stepped off his stepping stool and nearly disappeared from behind the desk. Then was heard the sounds of the stool scraping the floor as he moved it to the key rack. He climbed it, selected their keys, and then did everything in reverse, reappearing before them.

"Here you are," he said, handing them their respective keys. "I hope your stay is a good one. Don't mind the army being here. They have kept things in order. Sometimes we get troublemakers who come in. But, don't worry. Nothing like that has happened for a while."

"What about those trains we've heard about taking Japanese-Mexicans to prison camps? "ventured Felipe. "That must have been something!"

The small man peered over the rims of his thick glasses, his face going blank, then a hint of a frown darkened his brow. "A lot of mixed feelings about that," he replied as if deflecting the question. "We're next to the US border and they are now at war with Japan. There are people of Japanese ancestry on both sides of the border. There are those in El Paso who have relatives here in Juarez. It seems both governments are afraid of the Japanese. It doesn't matter if they are Mexican or U.S. citizens. For us, President Camacho just decided to round them all up, put them in camps so they can be watched. I saw no threat from Japan towards us. Maybe Mexico City is just kissing up to Roosevelt in Washington D.C.? Who really knows? Not you! Not me! That's for sure!" Then the clerk changed subjects.

"Sorry about the weather. But, it is January! You should have come in the spring when Las Floracitas lives up to its name! This is really not representative of what we have to offer. Make sure you bundle up if you walk around outside. Those gritty winds can make you raw and you won't even know it for being cold. But, once warmed up inside, especially in the morning you will know it for sure! You can feel like you've crawled around in the desert like a gila."

"Thank you," responded Felipe, holding up his key. "Think we'll walk around a bit just the same and stretch our legs some. A lot of hours sitting on the train you know. We'd appreciate it if you could take our bags to our rooms." The desk clerk agreed when Felipe dropped some coins, a propina, on the desktop. He motioned for his mother to follow and they crossed the lobby floor to the door. Felipe held the knob fast for as he opened a strong gust of wind threatened to blow it wide open.

"Even controversial up here," commented a surprised Elisabeth, stepping outside with Felipe. "We heard of how the Japanese up here are such a threat and to listen to that clerk it seems there are those with doubts. Come, let's try that Barnaby's place, see what it looks like, if it warrants going inside. It might be a good place just to step inside, get out of this cursed wind. We might inquire there where the Yamashita's community is."

Barnaby's Café seemed like a place right out of Oklahoma or Nebraska before the Dust Bowl blew the terrain and businesses away, destroyed the livelihoods of thousands. Like a tumbled-weed Barnaby Patterson had tumbled across the international border with enough Yankee coins in his pockets to meagerly start afresh a new venture, hoping for the best. He had reinvented himself and in relative ease mastered enough conversational Spanish to make his way through this new culture. Offering free lunches to an occasional local policeman or official was a bribe of sorts for their assistance in whatever needs that arose. It paid fine dividends for they indeed smoothed out rough spots that cropped up every so often. *Mordidas,* bribes, were just the way it was here. 'Scratch my back I'll scratch yours' was the modus operandi. But, to Barnaby Patterson it was a small price to pay to be resurrected from the dust blown hell of the American mid-west. His family farm of many years had blown away helter-skelter to all points of the compass as the worn-out topsoil of those states, Oklahoma his, had disappeared in suffocating clouds elsewhere, parts unknown. Hell, he thought, perhaps the dusts blowing about them there in Ciudad Juarez were part of his Oklahoma, still looking for a place to settle even after all of these years. It was far easier now to slap onto the grill a hamburger paddie than be out tilling useless ground.

From the outside stood Felipe and his mother, by the door, looking at a menu posted in the window. Felipe's trousers were snapping about his knees as the crisp wind assaulted them and Elisabeth pulled the collar of her topcoat tightly about her throat. Typical American food they concluded; hamburgers, French-fries, hotdogs, ice cream, Coca Cola. Ice cream, they wondered? Who would eat ice cream on a day like that? What made his burgers special was he placed Chihuahua cheese, dill pickles, yellow mustard and something called catsup on them. People love his cheeseburgers so the hotel clerk had said!

"Let's give that a try," encouraged Elisabeth. "If we like it then perhaps Horacio would like to give it a try making some, someday."

They were quite filled after finishing their orders. Being neither liked sugary drinks like Coca Cola they found a beer more than adequate to wash the salty foods down. Barnaby had shown his Mexican adaptations; for on the table were not only mustard and catsup, but also a molcajete, a stone bowl, filled with salsa picante. They called for the bill and it was Barnaby himself that brought it to them.

"I hope my kind of food satisfied," he said in handing the tab to Felipe.

"I can see why your cheeseburgers are so popular," commented Elisabeth. "The desk clerk at Las Floracitas said your hamburgers are very popular. I can say so too, now. Quite filling though. I feel I won't eat another bite in another day or two."

"Where I come from we talk about foods that will 'stick to your ribs'," responded Barnaby. "In other words, you will not feel hungry for a while. You probably won't believe this. But I nearly starved in the United States some years ago. Every one across the border is not rich like you in Mexico might think. I had lost everything and when I got back on my feet I swore I would never go hungry again and if it was in my power I would make sure others wouldn't either. So, it pleases me much that you enjoyed my food and are satisfied."

"I met a man from Spain once in Mexico City," spoke Elisabeth. "He sat alongside a table of ours in a small café. After finishing his meal he rubbed his hand across his belly, referring to it as his 'Arc of Happiness'. I guess we can say the same here." Barnaby chuckled.

"Maybe that's a more fitting name on the front of this café, 'The Arc of Happiness'." He laughed with gusto. "Sounds kind of Chinese though, and I serve anything but. Anything else I can get you? Imelda, brings in some mighty fine flan, if you'd like that instead of some ice cream."

"Oh no, señor. We are quite full. Thank you though. But, there is one thing you can do," suggested Felipe. "We are looking for this address. Can you direct us there?" Felipe handed him a piece of paper with the address of 'Abarrotes de Yam'.

"Let's see now," pondered Barnaby." Oh my, I believe that is the area where the army came in the other day to round up all of those Japanese folks. There's still talk about that. Bad times to be one of them! They are caught between a rock and a hard place, a no win situation for those poor souls. My gut feeling is that they are victims of fear. But, look, this is your country and I don't get involved in politics. It is prohibited any way. I can't risk being kicked out of here. I have no other place to go. But, listen, the Japanese Americans are in a tight spot too. I wouldn't be at all surprised if Roosevelt does similar as Camacho has done. Just my gut instinct! Say, may I ask why you want to know this?"

Felipe and Elisabeth looked at each other, wondering what they might say. "Just up here for a friend. Doing some inquiries for him. Say! What about how some of the people here being arrested for national security? I tracked down this community where some came from. I would like to see it for myself, maybe do some interviews. Maybe the locals can tell me what they think about it all."

"Social interests is it?" asked a surprised Barnaby. "I have a niece studying sociology in Tulsa, at least she was. I haven't heard from family for some years now. Maybe she's married now with a whole bunch of kids. She was concentrating on the migrations of Oklahomans out to California. They out there call them *Okies*. That is sort of demeaning if you know what I mean. Many of those from Oklahoma who lost their farms and jobs moved out there with hopes of finding work. Those Californians saw them as threats taking away their jobs. It was more like, 'go back to where you came from!'" Then he took a sheet of paper and drew a map on it, showing where to find the Yamahita's community. "Might be some challenges there. People might be tight-lipped, not willing to talk. Best of luck! Listen, we make a good breakfast in the morning. If that burger has worn off, want some coffee and hotcakes come on back."

Felipe and Elisabeth paid their bill and thanked Barnaby. Then they wasted no time in making their way to their destination. In reality it was not that far distant. They began an earnest walk, following Barnaby's map, grateful the wind had abated.

They now stood in front of a store front that had stenciled in white letters upon the windowpanes, ABARROTES de YAM. It was a general store of moderate size, larger than others in the vicinity. Somewhere inside, imagined Felipe from his conversations with Haru, was his expectant wife Rocio.

They had come all of this way and now for some odd reason their feet hesitated from entering the store. They mutually wondered what sort of individual they would encounter, how to introduce themselves. Would she believe them? They stood before the door in contemplation when the door opened and a customer exited, excusing herself as she sidestepped them. Then it was their turn to open that same door, and they did, entering the world that Haru Yamashita and his family had called a joyful home for many years.

Greeting them was a lone lady, sitting behind a counter, her eyes puffy like she had allergies or had been crying, appearing in a weakened state. She dabbed a handkerchief to her eyes and nose.

"Hello. May I help you?" she asked the strangers in a faint voice.

"We hope to be of help to you," answered Felipe, "especially if you are Rocio."

Rocio had an inquisitive expression come over her face. "Help?" she asked. "What kind of help? The kind I need no one can give me. Who are you and what do you want?"

"My name is Felipe Gurza, and this is my mother Elisabeth. We are from Mexico City. We have come all this way just to see you! We come to give you greetings from your husband and children. We want you to know that they are fine, despite what all has happened. We know a terrible wrong has been done to you and many others. We hope by coming here to tell you this that we may give you some sort of comfort."

The slender lady stood up uneasily, sudden tears rushed to her eyes, hungering for more information. Felipe had expected to see a pregnant woman as Haru had said. Was this truly Rocio?

"You have seen Haru, Kenji, Kasue?" she pled. "Where, when? What is happening to them?"

"They are in a compound camp on a futbol field, in a large stadium at Mexico City. I have visited with your husband several times and he trusted me well enough to tell me where you are. That is how we located you up here." Felipe studied the woman's fraught face.

Just then another woman came from behind a curtain behind the counter. She was a neighbor assisting Rocio in the difficult days since her hospitalization. Both Felipe and Elisabeth wondered about her pregnancy and Rocio perceived their dilemma in asking.

"Haru doesn't know," cried Rocio. "I had an accident, a

miscarriage. I lost our baby!" She openly cried. Her assistant gingerly wrapped an arm around her shoulders and settled her back down on the chair.

"It has been hard for her as you can see," said the woman. "I think it best you leave if you have said what you came to say. She still needs rest!"

"No, no! I am fine Aurora," admitted Rocio. "I must talk with these people! They have come so far and after only a few words they cannot just leave. I must know more! Please show them to our quarters in the back. I'll visit with them and you can mind the store for a while."

They were now seated in a room that had served as a family gathering in better days. Just beyond the rear door is where Haru had liked to read his paper and greet the dawn each morning, prior to opening their store.

"Some tea or coffee?" asked Rocio.

"No thank you. We are still full from lunch," admitted Elisabeth. "Listen, we had no idea you were in this way. We do not need to be here! We can talk later maybe."

Rocio held up both her palms, silencing any such suggestion. "No, you are here and I must need to know more now! So, please tell me how you met Haru."

"I attend the Universidad Autonoma in Mexico City, majoring in Sociology. When I got word of how that futbol stadium was being converted into an internment camp I went to see for myself. I was given permission by the Commandant to tour the compound. There are more tents than I could count. Somehow when I saw your husband I was drawn to him. He was reluctant at first to engage in conversation. But, I think we befriended one another regardless of the doubtful circumstances. Your two children seem to think they are on some sort of camping trip, are playing with other children around their tents. Haru and I are only given thirty minutes at a time to visit and we have met only a few times. But, we have grown to trust one another. Believe me! If he had grave doubts about me he would never have told me where to find you. He told me all about his folks, how they began this business and how cholera killed them five years ago. So, in our brief visits I have learned something of his Mexican history and it is a travesty what has happened to them, to all of you! It is shameful, a wrong that needs to be righted!"

"My dear," said Elisabeth. "About your miscarriage, should you not be resting instead of being in the store doing business? Is there anything we can do to help?"

"I must keep busy or my mind will go mad! Aurora and others come to help me and that makes all things possible. Well, maybe not all, but most!" How are Haru and my babies?"

"Well, he certainly is distraught over what has happened. Any sane person would be. He and the other adults know how they must safeguard the children as much as possible. The government is providing them with clothing, blankets and other things to make living in a tent city habitable enough. Even the soldiers will offer them chocolates, whatever they have and can afford on their measly pay. I get the feeling that most of the soldiers do not agree with what has been done. They only assume a soldierly posture when officers are around. If it was up to the average soldier Haru and all the others would be freed. That is my gut instinct! I am not saying this just to pacify you. I really sense this! Your children seem undisturbed, like this is some great adventure. But, the longer it goes on that will likely change. Even Haru knows this and realizes he must be ready to reason with them, calm them when that happens." Felipe observed how what he had said was received.

"Damn Japan!" cried Rocio. "None of this would have happened if it wasn't for that damned Hirohito bum, their god-like emperor. He and his war machine just want to conquer and take resources from other countries. On the other side of the world the Nazis are doing the same thing. This is a greater world war than the first! Will not people ever learn? Haru was so ashamed after Pearl Harbor! Felt like hiding his face some days! Why can't the government see he and others are more Mexican than Japanese?"

"What about your community," asked Elisabeth? "How has the response been since the internments?"

"If you went up and down this street all of the Mexicans cursed the soldiers, during and after. Some were even taking eggs from the abarrotes and throwing at their trucks and buses. Only the officers seemed committed to carry out their orders. I do not recall seeing or hearing of any others taking delight in doing such a thing! I am sure wherever this horrible order was carried out in the country there were similar responses. Camacho is not a popular president now." There fell a momentary silence. "Tell me, what is next? Is that stadium a permanent home or will they be moved? Haru and others have to have something to do! They just cannot sit around day after day doing nothing, just waiting for whatever else may happen!"

"I have heard that this is temporary, that they'll be moved sometime. Where I just do not know. I imagine some sort of labor camp; like farming or industrial, something like that. Commandant Valenzuela is not the most cordial fellow. But, if he knew something I think he would say so. Whatever we learn we will keep you informed. You could write Haru. But, I have no idea if he would ever receive your letter. Here's the address of the stadium." He handed her a piece of paper with the information.

They had talked an hour, the time flying by. Aurora had not reappeared for there had been a number of customers to occupy her. It seemed all the neighbors made the most trivial excuse to come and buy at least something to show their support for Rocio.

"You say you are leaving tomorrow. May I send something with you for Haru and my babies?"

"Of course," answered Elisabeth. "I cannot go to the stadium anymore. But, Felipe will see to it that what you send Haru will get."

She took out from a dresser drawer a locket. She opened it up and inside was a photo of her and Haru. For Kenji she presented them with a whittled wooden toy car and for Kasue a Tarahumara doll. "I'd like to send more but I fear the command will confiscate if deemed too much."

They had not known each other before. But, the past hour bound them in ways never anticipated. They embraced each other before the Gurzas prepared to leave.

"You know, our baby we already had a name for. If a boy he was to be Roberto Jesus. If a girl, we hadn't settled on that yet.

But, I always liked the name Yuriko. Maybe something like Yuriko Citlalli?" She cried openly again, "I'll write Haru a letter explaining all and have it delivered to your hotel tonight. I don't want you to feel the responsibility of telling him of our loss, of our Yuriko. ! It is too personal of a thing."

They parted, pulling the curtain aside and passed the counter where Aurora was serving a customer. Elisabeth was dabbing some tears with a handkerchief. They bid adios to Aurora as they passed her by. Aurora took note how Elisabeth was so moved! They were soon through the store and back out on the blustery street. They stood still and silent, thinking what they had just experienced.

"It seems like there is something we should have done in there," commented Elisabeth. "Something else we could have said or done! I don't feel we accomplished much. I don't feel good about this at all!"

"I know what you mean," confessed Felipe. "I feel the same. There's no more we can do right now. Lets just go back to the hotel. Think things over. That lunch is like Sr. Barnaby says, *still sticking to my ribs.* But, maybe they have something hot to drink at the hotel." How great some chocolate Oaxaqueño would be, he mused! But, that was a fanciful dream of his, way up north as they were.

Unlike when they had left the hotel, greeted by a blast of cold wind upon opening the doors, the winds had abated on their return and they arrived back in a relative calm. The smallish desk clerk was in mid-lobby rearranging a dried floral arrangement in a vase on an oval desk against a wall. Above the desk and vase was a large wall mirror reflecting the lobby environs, at an elevation that Clerk Eusebio Gregorio Ernesto Alvarez Morales could not peer into that well. If his height had kept pace with his name he would have had no problem. There would have been no need for step stools.

"Well, after several hours in our fair town have you decided your trip was worth it?" asked the clerk, rising up from a large floral pot.

"You gave us a good suggestion in eating at Barnaby's. I have had little hamburgers on plaza carts in Mexico City. But, that

American makes huge ones. His cheeseburgers with onions, tomatoes, lettuce are the best, I guess. I have never had one like that. But, I am still stuffed," lamented Felipe. "Any chance you have hot chocolate in the dining room, something hot to take the nip out of the air?"

"I'm sure Arturo can do something like that," answered the clerk. "I'm sure, too, he can add some tequila or whisky to whatever."

They thanked Señor Morales and walked to the dining room.

"No sir, we are still full from lunch," answered Felipe the inquiring waiter. "If you please, some hot chocolate for us if you have any." The man bobbed his head up and down in the affirmative. Soon he returned with two steaming cups of hot chocolate on a platter with a few biscochitos, cookies.

"Well, I know you like your cookies," commented Elisabeth. "You'll make room for those I'm sure."

They had whiled away an hour in conversation, sips, and nibbles. It was now dusk. Lights were turned on and they both were feeling a bit cozy, hot chocolate laced with tequila and free from the winter outside. The dining room had a little wood-burning stove to comfort customers and the lobby had a fireplace with nearly spent wood needing to be refueled.

"I think I'll go up to my room," said Elisabeth. "It has been a long day. See you in the morning. Our train leaves at 9:00 am. Maybe have some coffee here before we leave?"

"Sounds good. Have a good night," responded Felipe. "I saw on a table in the lobby a newspaper. I think I'll sit out there for a while and read some. I'll retire myself in an hour or so. Let's meet here around 7:00?"

"Sounds good to me too. See you in the morning."

They pushed themselves away from the table, Felipe paid their tab, and they made their way for the lobby. At the stairway they parted as Elisabeth surmounted the stairway for her room upstairs and Felipe went to settle on a lobby sofa to read the paper. That evening would pass quietly. But come morning Felipe would awake unto a puzzling mystery.

Chapter 9

"Captain Arestegui, Where is Mother?"

He had sat for the better part of an hour reading with effort the fine newsprint of a newspaper of questionable paper stock. It had no form, just wilted no matter how he tried holding it still, further troubled whenever the main entry door was opened and a gust of wind rushed inside the lobby. His eye had glimpsed the elusive headline reading, 'Mexicans in Question', but the article was undulating, like trying to see a fishing bobber between waves of troubled waters. The wimpy paper took repeated efforts to steady. He finally steadied the paper by placing it on his lap; then he refocused for the evasive article. Once found he was slowly drawn further into the world of Haru Yamashita and the other captives, now wards of the government. It absorbed his mind like quicksand does the body. But, there was no sound reasoning he read why those of Japanese ancestry had been singled out. The free world was at war with the Axis Powers of Hitler's Nazi Germany, Mussolini's Italy, and Hirohito's Imperial Japan. Franco's Falangist Spain was meddling abroad in Hispanic America with aims to reignite its lost Spanish Empire. Germany was active in Mexico, clandestine operations, seeking to corrupt the impressionable minds of university students and peons alike while trying to latch onto as much Mexican petroleum as they possibly could. Wherever the Union of Sinarquistas was strong, as in Guanajuato, German professors were rumored to be promoting Nazi interests, even by manipulating the union subtly through the present Spanish Falangists. All of this was not literally spelled out in the article. But, there were plenty of innuendos, fingers of suspicion pointing here and there, even if at shadows and phantoms. Felipe folded the paper, rested it on his lap briefly, thinking of what he had read. He set it back down upon the table where it had been. A troubled brow spoke of being troubled.

"Señor," spoke a voice. "You seem troubled with what you were reading. I make it a point to read peoples' faces and yours clearly did not like something. Care to share what it was?"

Felipe looked aside, seeing a man in a soldier's uniform scrutinizing him. He wore the rank of captain in the army. He appeared to be an average-sized man while sitting. The striking thing about him though, as Felipe soon discerned, was his brazen-like complexion, odd for that society. His face was void of any expression, almost wax-like, an anemic, translucent appearance. The veins in his temples protruded as one under great stress, intent focus. The only sign of life were his snake-like piercing black eyes. His black hair was neatly trimmed, glistened like obsidian under the lobby lights. Felipe felt a moment of unease, the man being intrusive, wanting to know his thoughts and more. Amazing how a stranger's few words could make one feel like being under a microscope! Perhaps his uniform qualified his person and queries. Still, Felipe was uncomfortable with the man's black-coal eyes boring through him.

"I am Capitan Arestegui. The only article I could see you were apparently reading was the one about the Japanese internments. Am I correct?"

Felipe thought of his answer, careful. "One of several I found interesting. Why do you ask?"

"I was responsible for helping to arrest many here in Ciudad Juarez, made sure we put them on trains south, got them away from the border. We did that and now I suppose the Americans will rest easier. Now they must do their share. There are two sides to the border and Japanese are on both of them. We have done our part, even though we are not at war with Japan as they are. It really is beyond reason we have done this. We are a neutral country. But, orders are orders. That is what soldiers do." He continued to stare at Felipe, not a blink in his frigid stare.

"Why do you think the government was so wrong?" ventured an inquisitive Felipe.

The Captain's hard stare wavered, looked around to see if there were any eavesdroppers. Then he lowered his voice. "Listen, on this side of the world I think Nazi Germany is more of a menace. Before this new war they were buying maybe half our oil. There are German colonies in the country, one even in Mexico City. I bet you that in those enclaves are Nazis up to no good. Germany is at war with the United States and they see an opportunity to do their worst to the Americans through us. Mexico is geographically ideal, located for their easy mischief. Japan? Forget them! They are not here like the Germans are. They are here but never mix in, keep to themselves. The Japanese immigrants, however, freely embraced us and we them. The Italians? Hell, they are not involved in stuff like this. Mussolini and Hitler have different goals. But, I guess President Camacho fears the Japanese more than Germans, even though I see no need to. I think it should be the other way around! But, there seems to be a fear here in the Americas anything Asian. Those cultures are so different and that causes fears in government, and fear causes bad things to happen. Of course, there are the crazies ruling Japan with their imperial designs to conquer others. That surely hasn't eased tensions. That is why Camacho's internment orders. I, though, just don't see Japanese Mexicans doing the devil's work for Japan in any way. If anything, I bet they feel betrayed by Japan."

Interesting, thought Felipe, of the captain's take on the whole controversial issue. "I can not imagine the government having the means to round up everyone suspect, Japanese, German, Italian. The logistics would be beyond logic."

"From your manner I would say you are a Capitalino, a Chilango from some part of Mexico City," ventured the captain. "You are far from home. What brings you to the border?"

"Some research, maybe some humanitarian work too," replied Felipe in partial truth. "I am a Social Studies major and we thought about doing some work among the Tarahumaras to the west. My mother is with me. She had been there some years before. But, I think she is feeling the cold more than when she was younger. I'll see what she has to say in the morning." Felipe paused, considering a question.

"Tell me, Capitan! What do you know of the Sinarquistas? I keep coming across pamphlets of theirs. I've known about some of their public protests and demonstrations. But, who are they really?"

"Young man, I would consider them as rabble. The hotheads could be violent. They have an agenda that is all Church, a far right ideology that sees ultra-conservatism ruling the country with the Church in control, not the liberal secular government as Benito Juarez had put in power last century. They are so anti-government! But as strange as it is, they see a kinship with the Axis Powers. With them it is all about authority, control and power and they like those totalitarian ideals. That is why Camacho has his eyes on them. I have no proof of course. But maybe our president does, that the Sinarquistas can be like Nazi puppets, even without knowing it. We Mexicans have a history of being the pawns of other countries. No real surprise here. They are puppets of bigger fish. The question now is what happens to them after this Pearl Harbor thing? I would think they might be having some internal problems, trying to know what their true purpose is, who to side-up to. With them the key is the Catholic Church, and the Church is always mindful of its public image, and from what I have observed, not so much with their own moral substance!"

Felipe thought of the firebrand Contreras spouting in the plaza, his mannerisms, very much like the newsreels he had seen of Adolf Hitler. Why would any Hispanic idolize the Aryan racist? It was beyond comprehension for Felipe, grappling for reasons why his country was playing the fool.

"What happens to those the government arrests?" asked Felipe. "I saw this happen in Mexico City. The speaker they took away. I wondered where they might have taken him, what happened to him?"

"I think it safe to say his future was not so bright," responded the captain, offering no more with a wry smile.

"Well, it has been a long day and the morning comes too soon," yawned Felipe. "I best go to my room and get some needed sleep." He pushed the newspaper towards the captain. "Here read for yourself."

"Not necessary. I know more than what those reporter fools do. In fact, you might question whatever they write. Have a good night of sleep." He watched in careful study Felipe rise up and stride the lobby floor to the stairway.

Strange, thought an uncomfortable Felipe, that he had felt the soldier's piercing eyes fastened upon his back, until the stairway turned a corner and led him out of sight, and yet he could still sense the scrutiny. He was near the top of his flight of steps when he encountered short Eusebio, the desk clerk, about to descend the stairs in a hurry. They briefly greeted one another. In his walk to his room Felipe neared his mother's, the light still shone underneath the door, saw a shadow of movement suggesting she was still up. He paused, thinking to knock, but decided to pass on. It was time to retire.

Las Florecitas had some attractions but the comfort of the bed was not one of them. He tossed and turned, was not at ease, convinced he could have done no worse by sleeping on the bare tile floor. It's a hard world, thought Felipe, and the more he experienced and learned the harder it was. The winds outside had risen again, rattling a loose windowpane in his room, just another feature of 'welcome' to this remote hotel. Even the cold persona of the Captain lingered in his thoughts. He heard a heavy thud on the hallway floor beyond his door, as if some late arrival had dropped some luggage. Foot- steps then faded away. He gave it no more thought as the windowpane rattled some more. A draft around the frame troubled the curtains. The blankets he pulled overhead and sought the warmth of his breath to warm him underneath.

How he had slept any surprised him as he stirred out of his labored slumber near 6:00 in the morning. The window frame draft still troubled the curtains some, even had a slight whistling effect. Perhaps the hotel had some gaps in the sides, something that allowed the winds to pass through or over and making that monotonous sound of intrusion.

Felipe rose up from his bed of misery. He had agreed with his mother to meet in the hotel café at 7:00 am, have something to eat and coffee before heading to the train station, be aboard no later than at 9:00 am. Yes, he felt his stomach rumble, thinking Barnaby's hamburger had finally worked its way out of his stomach and noted some hunger growls. Yes, he would get ready and go down, be the first to see what was available.

A few others were already at some tables, perhaps those destined for the train too. He selected a table thinking it would suffice he and his mother for the time being. A wall clock chimed 7:00. A middle-aged waitress, her hair in a bun with some loose strands dangling about her face approached his table with a menu.

"Just some coffee for now. My mother shall be here soon. Then we will order." He accepted the menu to consider.

Chickens were a big item on the menu for there was every conceivable means of cooking eggs. An old standby of his was huevos rancheros, sunny-side up eggs over a fried tortilla and bathed in salsa picante. That, with some fresh tortillas and coffee should set him for the day ahead.

He had nearly finished his cup of coffee when the clock read a quarter past the hour. "Where is she?" he muttered to himself. The waitress came again, offering a refill. "I guess my mother is taking longer than I thought. Please, I'll have the huevos rancheros meanwhile. She should be here shortly." She topped off his cup of coffee and left with his order.

Hurry up, mother! The train won't wait for us, thought impatient Felipe. His breakfast was brought in short order and although he found it tasty, he did not relish it, too much grease. He noticed the time. She was forty minutes late. She had never slept so late at home. How tired was she? He paid his tab and hurried upstairs. At her door he knocked. There was no answer. He knocked louder.

"Mother! It's Felipe. We must go!" There was still no answer. He tried the door handle. It wouldn't open.

Down at the far end of the hallway was Captain Arrestegui, just exiting his room. He stared at the heightened agitation of Felipe pounding on the door, walked his way.

"Young man, having problems this morning?" he inquired.

"It's my mother. She's not answering her door. She was supposed to join me in the café at 7:00. Our train leaves at 9:00.

"You try the door?" asked the captain.

"It wobbles, seemes locked though." replied Felipe.

"Here, let's just jostle it around a bit. These locks are not that good," admitted the captain. "They sometimes work or don't. Sometimes people get locked out of their rooms." With a few sharp twists and shakes something came loose, prompting something inside the room to fall to the floor. They hurriedly pushed open the door, it scraping upon something below.

Felipe was expecting to see his mother either in bed or up, getting ready. But, he was overwhelmed in perplexity. She was nowhere in the room! The bed appeared to have not been slept in. Where was she? He looked at Arrestegui in disbelief. The captain himself was now taking an interest for it was all very strange. Strange indeed for the door had had the key inside the lock and when he had shaken the doorknob the key inside had fallen, and is what the door dragged across when they had flung the door open.

"Maybe I somehow missed her? Maybe she's down in the café now looking for me." Felipe bolted downstairs while Captain Arestegui remained behind scrutinizing the room.

Felipe nervously looked all about the café, and not seeing her, hastened to the lobby. He found a different desk clerk at that hour, and describing his mother to him asked if he had seen someone like her that morning.

"No, señor," answered the younger, taller of the two clerks, side-stepping the stepping stool behind the desk with a look of disdain.

"Room 2o2. My mother's room! You know if she went out at all, had any visitors? She is missing!

"Missing? What do you mean by missing?" asked the clerk with an aire of indifference.

"Just that! Don't you understand what that means? Missing! Was here and now disappeared! That is about as clear a meaning as there is!" exploded Felipe. "Where is the other clerk, the small fellow who knows us?" He looked around the lobby with an agitated glare.

"Ah, Eusebio!" responded the perturbed clerk. "I'd like to get my hands on him. He is supposed to be here now, not me. I had other plans. But, he suddenly quit or something without warning and that forced me in. He left me a real mess of work to clean up too. He is a small man even in wit and character, a real scoundrel. I don't care for his friends at all and if you are one, well I am sorry about that."

"Listen, I don't care about any of that. That's between you, he, and the owners of this hotel. But, we are guests here and my mother's room has not been slept in and she is nowhere in sight. She has to be somewhere. This seems to me to be of a concern for this hotel. Right now an army captain is upstairs inspecting her room. So, I better get some considerations here! If not, this hotel is going to be in the news in a bad way!

"Now, señor. Calm down. Let me summon for some help."

"Hello, señor, greeted a senior-looking man, well attired. "May I be of assistance? I am Lazaro Gutierrez, the owner."

"Sir," acknowledged Felipe. "I am in a desperate situation here. My mother and I checked into your hotel yesterday. Last evening she retired before I did. I decided to read in the lobby here for a while and then I too went upstairs to my room. When I passed hers I saw the light on under the door and figured she was still up. I never stopped I just went for my room. I needed the sleep. This morning she is gone. Even her bed was never slept in. We had a train at 9:00 am to catch. But, there is no way now we can do that! Are any police here that would investigate this, or is the army in total control? Who can I see to get some action on this?"

"First of all, I share your concern. When a guest of ours has any misfortune we try to help as we can. My clerk says there is a soldier in the room right now investigating?"

"A Capitan Arestegui," replied Felipe.

"Well, he is as good as they get when it comes to investigations. I would let the army deal with this. Meanwhile, as you wait for whatever, please be my guest free of charge," soothed in vain Lazaro Gutierrez the owner. "At this very moment there is not much that can be done by us. All I can say is to be patient, do not panic!"

Felipe stared at Gutierrez with an incredulous look. He just couldn't stand still and do nothing! Patient? It was never a virtue he ever cultivated. What would his father have done, or could have?

"Señor?" prodded Gutierrez, perceiving Felipe's thoughts were racing around elsewhere. "Señor, is that alright with you?"

"Is what all right?" asked Felipe.

"That you stay here as my guest as the Capitan coordinates his investigations?"

"I do not have much choice. Do I?" answered Felipe with a snide question. "I am grateful for your accommodations Señor Gutierrez. I just have to do something. I can't keep still and wait for others to do the work. I need to do something! She's my mother and this whole matter means more to me than you or any one else."

"Understood!" added the owner. "I am sure this will be resolved soon and then you and your mother will have a longer stay than planned. You can always take another train."

"Yes, I hope so. I suppose so. Thank you. At least you know something is wrong. I am going back to the room where the Capitan is." Felipe turned about and raced for the stairs, bounding up the flights to his floor, hoping that his mother had strangely appeared.

"Find anything suspicious?" asked Felipe of the Captain.

"Perhaps, perhaps not. There is this bag with this toy car and doll, a locket. But, this here note makes no sense to me." Arestegui held out a note he had found on the floor at the foot of the bed, partially obscured by the fold of a bed-covering quilt. Felipe took it. It made no sense to him either. Just two words; "HELP, Rocio". What could Señora Yamashita want her help for? Why was he excluded?

"Me neither," exclaimed Felipe. "I have no idea what this means!"

"Any idea who this Rocio is?" inquired the Captain.

Felipe shrugged his shoulders without answering. Arestegui assumed that meant a 'no'. But, Felipe was now determined to return to Abarrotes de Yam for answers.

"You have a picture of your mother?"

"Me? No! But, she carried an old photograph of her and my

father in her purse. But, even her purse is gone. Just like that midget desk clerk that suddenly quit, gone. What is happening here?"

"Quit?" asked a perplexed Captain, one eyebrow arching high above his coal black eye.

"That desk clerk on duty now is about to pop a few buttons off his vest. He is having a fit about that guy."

Captain Arestegui seemed to be entertaining some thoughts not yet shared, as if he knew something best kept secret.

"I am going to walk around town and ask people if they have seen anyone of my mother's description. When I return, if you are still here, you can tell me anything you have learned." Felipe hastened to his room to ready himself for an indirect trek to Rocio Yamashita's.

Chapter 10

"Barnaby's"

"**N**o. She hasn't been here since you both were in yesterday," answered Barnaby Patterson, the owner of Barnaby's Café. "Your mother wandered off did she now? Juarez is not that cordial of a place for a lady of her character. You best retrace your steps of yesterday. Maybe you will find her strolling around for one last look at things before you leave."

Felipe was disappointed. But, he held in quiet anticipation the possibility of yet finding his mother at Abarrotes de Yam, or at least he would find a lead there.

"Can I get you a cup of coffee, we talk a bit?" asked Barnaby. "No customers yet. It's slow and there's time. Maybe this would help calm you down some, settle your mind, help you decide some things."

"Thank you. But, I have had some already. I best be on my way, look about for her. I have a hunch where she may be. If she happens to come in please tell her I am looking for her. Tell her to return to the Hotel Las Floracitas and wait for me, that I should be back in maybe a couple of hours. Tell her not to go anywhere else!"

"Las Floracitas!" exclaimed Barnaby. "That shrimp-of-a-man, that bug-eyed desk clerk, he was here last night. Really agitated he was! Hardly finished his meal, just poked at it. He just kept fidgeting, staring at the door like he was expecting someone at any moment. Real nervous he was, kept checking his watch."

"He's not a desk clerk anymore it seems. I was told that he

suddenly quit last night without any notice at all, or at least he just didn't show up for work. The clerk I spoke with that had to fill in for him was hot as a pistol!"

"Well, something had him on edge like that and then showing up here like some twitching frog legs in a skillet. He surprised the heck out of me when he bolted out of his chair and ran for the door and then outside, like maybe he saw someone pass by the windows. He never even paid his tab."

Another mystery, thought Felipe. He was now having regrets coming all this way to the border. Mysteries seemed to be compounding. *We should have never come* his wrought mind reasoned. *We should have stayed home. I should still be at school and working on my thesis.* But, Haru Yamashita had intrigued him, and even mother. From his few visits with him Felipe was drawn towards the internee. His impulse was to help him somehow, and the best way he had concluded was to seek out his wife bearing Haru's messages for his 'expectant' wife. He came with the intent to be an intermediary between Haru and his wife Rocio in Ciudad Juarez.

What was it about the short statured man with bulging eyes, underscored by an eagle beak-like nose, and that underscored by a pencil-thin mustache? He had a name fit for two or three people. He was short in stature but long on mystery. Why had he been there like that, even catapulting out the door? Why did he suddenly disappear, just like his mother had?

Felipe departed Barnaby's, and en route to Rocio's asked those he had encountered if they had seen anyone with the likeness of his mother Elisabeth. All seemed futile, until he stumbled into a pharmacist who was placing an advertisement in a window facing the street. Felipe went inside.

"Excuse me sir," interrupted Felipe. He repeated his same line as he had uttered numerous times before, giving Elisabeth's description.

"Yes, someone like that was here early this morning. We hadn't even opened yet and she and another lady, and an odd looking fellow, were pounding on my door. They were in a hurry for first aid supplies. You know, bandages, gauze, iodine; things like that. I didn't care that much for being disturbed so early. But, I assumed someone was in bad shape and these things were desperately needed. I sold them whatever and they hurried away."

"You see which way they went?" asked Felipe.

"No. They just hurried out the door. I didn't ask any questions or see what direction they went. Wish I could tell you more. Why you looking for her?"

"She could be my mother," answered Felipe.

"Well, whomever she was she was not from here, a real cultured lady. Why she was in the company of the others I do not know. I wish you well, that you will find your mother soon."

"Thank you. At least now I know something. If you see her again, ask her if her name is Elisabeth Gurza. If it is please tell her I say to return to the Hotel Las Floracitas and wait for me. Do not go anywhere else!" said an imperative Felipe.

"Very well. I'll keep my eyes open for either of them."

Felipe thanked the pharmacist and now hurried in the direction of the Yamashita community. When aware of his surroundings he hastened to Abarrotes de Yam and Rocio Yamashita. Soon enough he was opening the door and entering into their world once more, a return never anticipated again. He saw the same neighbor lady who had assisted Señora Yamashita yesterday, now sitting at the counter. Aurora had a tabby cat on the counter, was stroking its back, brushing the fluffy tail, offering her own version of purring and baby talk to her feline friend.

"Hello. Remember me?" asked Felipe of her. "I and my mother were here yesterday. We went into the backroom to visit with Señora Yamashita."

"Si, señor. I remember you," she said as the cat scampered away. "Your mother was here again early this morning. She and Rocio were in serious conversation. I do not know what they were talking about. But, I could tell it was something that was troubling them both, had a sense of urgency about something. I didn't think Rocio was fit to leave. But, they left in a hurry about two hours ago. They never said where they were going but Rocio swore they would be back early afternoon. You are welcome to wait if you are a patient man. Then too I could use some help moving heavy boxes."

"*Mother*, thought Felipe. Finally! But, why was there all of this mystery? He looked at his watch and it nearly read twelve noon.

"Very well, that could help pass the time away." Felipe looked around the store's confines, spotting some large boxes stacked up against a back wall. "Those boxes back there?" he asked, nodding his head in that direction.

"Those are just some. Ready?" she asked.

"As ever I will be," he replied.

They busied themselves for nearly half an hour, Aurora only parted when a customer came in, but soon was with him again to direct and assist. They now had cleared floor space for people to maneuver around the store unhindered.

"Now, Rocio will be happy about that. She has been meaning to move those for some time. But, there have been too many distractions. Thank you for your help."

"You are welcome," responded Felipe. They sat down upon some chairs. "May I ask where you come from?"

"Originally my family was from Sinaloa, a fishing village not far from Mazatlan. Why do you ask?"

"Just curious. This seems so remote. It makes me wonder how people ever come here, why." replied Felipe.

"Well, I suppose we fleas like being close to the Yankee dog," she chuckled. "There are relatives on either side of the border. For me, however, my husband is from Chihuahua, here, from Juarez. When we married we moved up here. God only knows why!'" She rubbed her arms. "It is cold. Would you like some hot chocolate?"

Thoughts of Magaly arose as he and she had shared time over hot chocolate in Mexico City after the Sinarquista rally.

Felipe accepted her offer, and Aurora rose up to make them the hot beverage. They were soon sipping the frothy foam delight from steaming cups. They visited for a while when another customer came in. She excused herself to greet an elderly man with a cane. He held up the cane to show a missing rubber tip, asking if they had any.

"Sorry, sir," Aurora said apologetically. "But, the ferreteria at the end of the street should have some."

The man thanked her and exited the door. He had been gone for no more than five minutes when the door opened again. Aurora and Felipe looked that way. He was draining the last

remnants of his hot chocolate when he noticed the new arrivals.
He froze!

"MOTHER!"

Chapter 11

"One Mystery Solved, Another Looming "

"Where have you been?" cried out Felipe. "I've been worried stiff looking all over for you!"

Elisabeth and Rocio now stood before them at the counter, little Eusebio just now entering the door behind them.

"A mission of mercy," replied a tired Elisabeth. "I am so sorry to have put you through all of this. But, timing was of essence! I surely thought I'd be back at the hotel in time to meet you for breakfast, as planned, then catch the train for home. But, that never happened. I am sorry. But, we are here now." Then she looked at their cups in hand. "Is that something hot you are drinking?" She and Rocio were shivering.

"Just some hot chocolate," replied a relieved Felipe, then casting a hopeful look to Aurora to make some more. She rose up in a hurry to do so without haste. "There has to be more than that, just wanting something hot to drink! Where have you been? We've missed the train! I've been worried stiff!"

"I am sorry for that! But, remember how Rocio had said she would send us a letter for her husband? Well, maybe an hour after I had gone upstairs and left you in the lobby someone had pushed under my door two envelopes. I went to see if someone was at the door or in the hallway. But, no there was no one. One envelope was addressed to me, the other to her husband. I opened the one for me. Rocio was pleading for my immediate help. I was really perplexed what this was all about, wondering if I should go or not. The note just said some one would meet me in the lobby as I came downstairs. So, I put on my coat and left. I thought about telling you. I really did! But, I assumed you were in bed, asleep, and thinking I would not be long just hastened downstairs. As for the reason for all of this I will let Rocio explain."

A tired and worn Rocio Yamashita eyed Felipe, knowing he deserved an explanation even as fatigued as she was.

"When your mother arrived with Eusebio I told her why I had sent for her. I felt that anyone who would come so far and help the Tarahumaras would offer help to others also. When the soldiers came and arrested my Haru and babies, all the others, there were some of our friends and neighbors that hid, and escaped. They dropped everything, fled out into the countryside, hid wherever they could. Some fell over cliffs and onto the rocks, others had scrapes and cuts of various kinds. None of them were dressed for the freezing temperatures. Their injuries are why we bought the bandages and things. We have them in a safe house now. But, if word gets out they will be apprehended and we who have sheltered them will be in hot water. I reached out to your mother for help for I wagered her humane character would respond. I guessed right! She has been tremendous! You see, young man, without your mother's assistance we would not have been able to help these people at all. Surely some would have died. Medical supplies were needed and she helped us all with only short notice. She did more than we had hoped for! Rather than fault her you should be proud of her! "

Felipe pondered his mother, soaking-in what Rocio had just said. His mind once racked with queries now relaxed. "I never have had a loss of pride or respect for my mother, and given what I now know I have even more. But, I still have some concerns. This Capitan Arestegui is no fool. He is an intense man investigating your disappearance. He will not let up. Mark my words! To resolve this situation we must stop him. Mother and I must return to the hotel, come up with some sort of story to pacify him. If it works it could call off he and his men from further searches, looking for answers. This would help secure your 'refugees'.

"Felipe," interjected Elisabeth. "We can spend another night or two at the hotel, at least until we know the train schedule. I know we have reasons to get back home. But, while we are here I can still offer help to Rocio through Eusebio here." She motioned to him standing behind them, Rocio's messenger. "But, I am suddenly feeling tired and hungry. Perhaps we can stop at that Barnaby's for something to eat?"

Their visit extended another fifteen minutes and then it was time for Felipe and Elisabeth to depart.

Elisabeth handed Rocio some money. "Here is some extra to help out. Don't worry about Haru and your children. We shall help them the best we can." She saw the pained look on Rocio's face, knowing the news of her miscarriage would greatly trouble Haru. "When we hand Haru your letter we shall assure him that 'you' are Okay. Rest easy about this! Your nightmare will be over one of these days. They'll be home again."

"I have my doubts, Elisabeth," pined Rocio. "Since Pearl Harbor we've heard rumors that Japan has agents in Mexico, working with Nazis here too, planning attacks against the United States across the border. We do not know if any of this is true. President Camacho must think it is. He is taking no chances of any collaboration between Japanese-Mexicans and Japan; even Aurora's family in Sinaloa have mentioned the radical Sinarquistas are showing upon Baja, hoping to do something out there on the Pacific Coast. Speculations are some where on Baja California Sur. It is remote and they could be virtually unseen. This certainly makes reason why Camacho and the Americans are nervous, since the Sinarquistas are like the Nazis and Imperial Japanese. You can imagine if some Sinarquista colony is set up that they would lend assistance to the Japanese on the Pacific Coast. I can't justify what Camacho has done. But, think I understand why. As long as this war is going on Japanese-Mexicans will be suspect. Mark my words!" She held up the wad of cash Elisabeth had given her. "Be assured this will be put to good use!" She now felt faint and begged for a chair.

Barnaby's now had lunch customers. "Well now, I see you found her," commented a welcoming Barnaby Patterson. "Have your Juarez adventures stirred up an appetite worthy of my skills?" His blue eyes twinkled with humor.

"Mother surely has one, a bit more than me. But, yes, I can have something." Felipe was not prone to repeat one of his mammoth hamburgers. He looked around the environs for a table.

"This way," said Barnaby leading the way. "Get away from the door. Every time someone opens it cold air rushes in. Don't get me wrong! I like having customers. But, I am sure my customers, do not like the cold air that comes in with each new arrival. He sat them down at a corner table comfortable for two. "There is still some coffee in the pot. But, being the lunch hour maybe you'd like something else?" He looked at them both, waiting for some response.

"Coffee would be fine," admitted Elisabeth. "I hope it is strong because I need a good jolt."

"Rough night? Maybe some insomnia? There came in early this morning some fellows that needed a jolt of caffeine too. A couple appeared to be Mexicans. But, the other looked like some European maybe. Just his manner and way was different. Then I think that fellow had too much coffee 'cause he began fidgeting about, began arguing with the others over something. Just beware of caffeine. It can be good or bad. You, my good man?" he asked Felipe. "The same or something else?" Felipe agreed that coffee was well enough.

A waitress came with their coffees and then took their orders for lunch. They were half way through their victuals when Barnaby approached them, carrying something in hand.

"Those fellows I was telling you about? They dropped this on the floor. I have no idea what it is about. But, it seemed to be something they got worked up over. Maybe you have an idea what this is?" He handed a small pamphlet to Felipe.

The print on the pamphlet read, *El Manifesto De la Union Nacional de a la Sinarquista* with a Leon, Guanajuato address. Felipe's thoughts boomeranged to the Sinarquista rally in the plaza in Mexico City, of he and Magaly, and all the others that cold evening. He thumbed through the pages, speedily reading the radicals' dogma.

"Radical political activists," commented Felipe. "They have a strong following from Queretaro to the border. It seems that wherever they go they cause strife; like what you were observing maybe. Care if I keep this?"

"Not at all! The last thing I want to be considered is a potential recruit for political activists. Yes, take it with you. I never want those types in here again or anything that encourages others like that. The world is crazy enough these days and I don't want it coming here."

Felipe thanked him, dropping the small pamphlet into a side pocket of his coat for further scrutiny later that day. He and Elisabeth had finished their meals and dabbing their mouths with their napkins when Barnaby passed nearby to serve some others at a neighboring table. Felipe hailed him for their bill, saying they could be in again before long. It all depended on when their train south would leave.

"Look forward to it," commented Barnaby. "You still have things on the menu you haven't tried yet. We'll be ready and waiting for you." He smiled as he hurried to another table. They paid their bill and wove good day to him as they departed, stepping outside into a brisk wind again, the cold air briefly invading the café before they closed the door. They hurriedly closed the door and made way for the hotel.

"Hurry mother! The more we move the more we'll warm up. When we get to the hotel we'll see about the train schedules and extend our stay for however long. I hope Horacio back home isn't worried about us not being on our scheduled return."

"Never mind him. Horacio knows me and how things do not always go according to plans." Elisabeth's mind skipped over faded years recalling episodes, chapters in her life that never had any shortages of surprises. She had a wry smile. "Yes, lets hurry!" She hastened alongside Felipe in a determined gait to step into the comforting confines of the hotel lobby.

The Hotel Las Florecitas was as it had been, when Felipe had hurriedly departed in a quest for Elisabeth. There were diners in the restaurant café, and the lobby had some mid-day activity about the front desk. A few people sat upon sofas and chairs engaged in conversation or engrossed in something they were reading. A porter was pushing a cart of luggage away from the desk. Captain Arestegui was at his customary perch, sitting upon a lobby sofa with a perfect view of comers and goers. He analyzed everyone with his frozen rope stare, pigeon-holing and categorizing each and every one who came in line with his vision. He became enlivened when he saw Felipe with his mother walk inside.

"Ah Ha! You found her! Where may I ask did you finally find her? My people have been scouring for her everywhere."

"Capitan," spoke Elisabeth. "I feel honored to have one of your stature so interested in my well being! But, I'll have you know I am quite all right. In fact I just had a wonderful lunch at that American's place, Barnaby's. You should go there sometime, that is if you have never been before." Then to squelch his curiosity, "I'm a night person really. Felipe found me out and about stargazing. It is simply amazing how many more are seen when there are not many city lights. Then too, this landscape offers stargazers splendid views of the heavens. I just got carried away with the experience, forgot the time. I'm so sorry for what I put Felipe through, and even you too apparently. But, here I am again. Please, Felipe, we need to ask the desk about train schedules. If you please, Capitan." She did a slight nod of her head and backed away, pulling at Felipe's arm.

"Not at all señora," replied Arestegui. "I am pleased to see you are fine and well." He watched them cross the open space of the lobby for the front desk. *A very classy lady,* he concluded, but with a hint of mystery. And, he was one of stature that prided him self upon solving mysteries. He continued to stare their way.

"He's still watching us," muttered Felipe.

"Yes, I know," admitted Elisabeth. "He's not one to take lightly. Those eyes!"

"This must be your mother," commented the same perturbed desk clerk, masquerading a warm reception. "I am glad that you have found each other and are here again. May I be of service?"

"Thank you. If you please, a train schedule," replied Felipe. "We'll be your guest for another night at the goodness of the owner," he added, to which the clerk acknowledged. When their business was done they sat down in the lobby briefly to converse. They had noticed that Captain Arestegui was now focused upon three men in fine, conservative apparel, engaged in deep conversation at a small table against a lobby wall. High above their heads was a large portrait of President Benito Juarez, and when they became aware of it rose up and departed elsewhere in apparent disgust. The captain's eyes followed them as they ventured inside the café. There was something about the trio that unsettled him. He stood up and strode to the café himself in their wake.

"Did you see that?" asked Elisabeth. "You see the Capitan looking at those men?"

Felipe nodded a yes, saying nothing, thinking of that pamphlet in his pocket, something to read alone, in his room later. "What should we do for the rest of the day?" he asked her. "Our train doesn't leave until tomorrow morning. This Juarez really has no culture to offer we 'Capitalinos.' "

"Well, my son. You always want to be doing something. You can take a lesson from that Capitan. Simply be still and observe. There is a time and a place to be doing and another for being still. This is a time to be still. Consider what you have learned this morning, where this knowledge will take you, what you shall do with it. This is a time for thinking, not doing."

They had continued to share thoughts and ideas over the space of thirty minutes or so when the same trio emerged from the café to walk across the lobby and then departed outside. Following them in a lingering fashion was Captain Arestgui, peering after them as they exited the hotel. He summoned one of his soldiers, uttered something to him, and he in turn summoned his own, and soon three soldiers hurried out the door to tail the trio. Then the Captain sauntered the way of Elisabeth and Felipe.

"May I join you?" he asked.

"Of course. This is a public hotel lobby. These chairs and sofas are here to use." Felipe motioned to the Captain to sit at a neighboring chair, next to a small table sporting a small bronze sculpture of Francisco "Pancho" Villa of the Revolution Days.

"Young man," said Arestegui as he sat down. "Last night you had asked me what I know of the Sinarquistas. I believe there were some just here. Sometimes one develops a second nature in sensing certain things in certain people. There were three people here that just left. Perhaps you looked their way but really never saw them for who they are. They seemed out of place in some ways, ultra conservative in their urban attire compared to this rustic place. There were those two Mexicans with that man who seemed European. What was he doing in their company? He seemed to be their mentor or leader of something. It was just a gut feeling; that he was a German Nazi grooming a couple of Sinarquistas for whatever purposes the Nazis have in mind. Imagine such a racist country as Germany is, self-deluded in thinking their white race is far superior than all others, and most definitely we in Mexico. There can only be one motive that Hitler has and that is to get at the United States through us! What fools the Mexican Sinarquistas are, anyone actually, believing Nazi lies and being their puppets!" He cleared his throat, as if his tirade had been choking him. He tugged at his stiff collar.

"Actually Capitan, I know who you mean. We both saw them and thought they were an odd sort. But, it astounds me, sir, how you can conclude so much without knowing any facts. Amazing! Simply amazing! They might have been no more than business men, having a meeting over railroad construction, petroleum, mining, whatever."

Arestegui considered Felipe's comments, questioning his intent, meaning one of keen observation or one of criticism, or perhaps seasoned with both. "Señor Gurza. Don't think that just because I am posted this far away from the capital that I am not aware of what is happening in the world around us or at home here in Mexico. Germany has people here, in their own colonies within our country, and I, although I have no proof, am sure the Nazis and Hitler have an agenda to fulfill in our country. What aggravates me is that too many of our fellow Mexicans are naïve, or just stupid to play right into their hands. The Nazis know how to bait people in order to get what they want. Look down in Guanajuato. There are Germans there, some even professors, teaching our youth their subtle lies, doing their best to convince the students and others that they are the way of the future, and if we Mexicans follow them then Mexico will dethrone the United States from being number one in the Americas. You wonder if I assume too much in analyzing who those men are. Well, I have my ways and then some, to see what is what." Then he faced Elisabeth.

"Tell me, señora. Did you learn anything that may lead you out to the Tarahumaras again? That is a difficult journey."

"Well, I did do some inquiries last night and this morning," she lied. "But, perhaps we'll return in the spring when the weather is more convenient. I am not as durable as I once was. This trip has proved that to me."

"People's needs go on regardless of the weather. When the time is right you'll be back. The poverty of those people will always be there, and when down in Mexico City you can make plans accordingly about returning to the North. Next time though you might make a more direct approach to them. Ciudad Juarez is still a ways to the east of them in Copper Canyon."

"Yes, when my husband and I were up here years ago that is what we did. But, this time I thought Juarez might be a good place for provisioning ourselves. I wanted to see things firsthand, see what was available. Maybe next spring, before the summer's heat of course, maybe we'll be back."

"Well, perhaps I will still be here. If I am I will extend a welcome. Meanwhile, you have the rest of this afternoon and evening in this 'lovely' place." He looked about the lobby with a critical eye, even thinking beyond the walls at the small city about them. "Juarez will be here, waiting as usual for something good to happen for a change." There was a moment of silence but then he added, "If the opportunity arises perhaps we can share dinner together, or at least a drink in the lounge?"

"Perhaps," replied Felipe and Elisabeth seconding him. "Like the idea of relaxing, reading maybe for a while, stay out of the cold. Maybe see you this evening."

Captain Arestegui studied Felipe, pondering if there was truer purpose for his being there, wondering if he cloaked himself with claims of being a student of sociology. Why was he really here, even his mother, he wondered? Odd travelers he thought. Felt out of place. It was a long journey to come, just for a day or two and then turn around and leave again.

"Señor Gurza. You'll be passing through Guanajuato, a stronghold for the Sinarquistas. If you have time you might stop over and see what you see. Learning anything about those radicals will surely help you in your studies of mankind, and just how corrupt a species we are. I have heard from good sources that the University of Guanajuato has on staff German professors. Here we are rounding up Japanese Mexicans and placing them in concentration camps when we should be deporting these Germans for corrupting the minds of our youth! The more you learn the more fodder you will have to chew on as you formulate your thesis. Just beware that the more political you become that you will become a lightning rod for others to strike at."

"Tell me, Capitan! You say there are Nazi agents here in Mexico up to no good. What about Japan? Do you think there are Japanese agents also with the same purpose in mind, to harm the United States?"

"I believe that Japan has had greater plans than just Pearl Harbor. We have a long Pacific Coast line that has many remote areas where the Empire of Japan would love to establish secret naval bases. I wouldn't doubt for a moment that along with Pearl Harbor they had planned operations within our country in order to attack the Americans from Mexico. The Americans' Panama Canal would be a prime target too. Imagine secret Japanese naval bases on our coasts, half way between the US border and Panama, and how easy it would be for them to attack the United States from our border and even the Canal from those bases. So, to answer your question, yes I believe that both Germany and Japan have operatives in our country. Like it or not, President Camacho is a hands-on president. His putting the Japanese Mexicans in concentration camps may seem to some hard-handed. But, he knows what is happening more than we do. Both the Nazis and Japan want our natural resources and try manipulating us politically to get all they can. Camacho knows this! Mexico has some tough times ahead, tough decisions to make, and strong winds to face." He paused, looked at Felipe. "Write a truthful thesis and you'll ripple the waters, maybe even trouble them!"

The remainder of the day Felipe and Elisabeth remained in the hotel. The cold winds outside would not abate, blowing about occasional radical snowflakes that appeared and disappeared. It was more comfortable to lounge inside, read, engage in conversation with others, sip some tea or coffee and munch on sweet breads. Early evening they had dined in the café , Captain Arestegui a no-show, and afterwards they both parted for their respective rooms.

"Mother, now no disappearing tonight!" grinned Felipe. "We have the morning train to catch. Again, I'll rap at your door at 7:00 am and we can go together for some breakfast."

"Understood. I am due for a good night of sleep. See you in the morning." They gave each other a slight hug and then went their separate ways.

Felipe felt the pamphlet inside his jacket pocket jostle against his breast as he walked the hallway to his room's door. He had nearly forgotten it. Now, he unlocked his door and entered his room with thoughts to give it a reading. He stood mid-room contemplating the day, now reaching for the pamphlet. He had used a key to unlock the room door. This pamphlet would twist open, unlock another, of mysteries in Guanajuato.

Chapter 12

"Guanajuato, Guanajuato"

It had been a morning of freezing temperatures. Overhead, low-hanging clouds released an occasional snowflake or two as passengers made their way along the platform en route to their assigned railroad cars. Breezes eddied-about between the train and the station house, catching up within the currents the rogue snow flakes, often having a haphazard course of up and down, even sideways. They had boarded their car and were well on their way in a southerly fashion. The border town of Ciudad Juarez had long-faded in their wake. But, accompanying them were thoughts of Rocio Yamashita, Barnaby Patterson, certainly Captain Arestegui, and others they had encountered. For Elisabeth, dancing continuously before her mind's eye were those unfortunates she and Rocio had helped, those Japanese-Mexicans who sought safety and shelter from the soldiers who had come and arrested their family, friends, and neighbors. It was something that would plague her for the duration of the trip home.

Felipe sat in his window seat, peering outside at the passing landscape. His outward looking image reflected in the windowpane revealed an expressionless face. His thoughts remained in Ciudad Juarez, mulled over that which he had read in the Sinarquista pamphlet overnight in his hotel room, and that which Captain Arestegui had spoken of. The tract troubled him. He found it interesting but absurd; a far right wing dogma that should have set others on edge. Were they truly that radicalized? Were they so opposed to the national government that they even advocated overthrowing it? They flirted with treason! He shook his head in disgust, believing them to be religious zealots with warped, politically - charged agendas that promoted changes even by armed action. In their view President Camacho and his secular administration had to go, and if siding with the Axis Powers would meet that end, so be it! Arestegui viewed that this group of terrorists was being duped and manipulated by Nazi Germany. Cultural differences were being bridged via enlisting the help of Franco's Falangist Spain. Mexico and Spain were predominately Catholic and shared a common language. Germany's goal was to inspire their Spanish friends to woo the Mexicans through their common Spanish language and Catholicism to accomplish the Nazi agenda in the Americas. Felipe strongly considered all as he stared blank-faced out the window. His reflected image in the windowpane was like an apparition, entertaining troubled thoughts. He was forming an opinion, that Germany was pulling all the strings, was the master puppeteer of them all.. And yet ironically, Japan was the focus of national control and irrational fears.

"What would you say to making a stop in Guanajuato, maybe a couple of days?" asked Felipe of his mother.

"Guanajuato?" asked an astonished Elisabeth. "Why? What do you want there?"

"Something that the Capitan had said about the Sinarquistas. They are centered at Leon. But, I am intrigued about how some German professors at the university there are said to be involved with them. I would hope to find out if these Germans are Nazis and if so what affect are they having on students, and actually even beyond the classroom. Sinarquistas, Nazis, and the polluted minds of our young people should be a wake up call to the nation. Maybe I can learn more in Guanajuato itself."

"And just how would this enhance your studies, your thesis?" inquired Elisabeth. "It was one thing to make this long journey up here, be of a help to the Yamashitas and the others. But now you are flirting with who knows what, maybe even danger? I have this uneasy feeling that nothing good awaits us there. Are you sure you want to do this?"

He did not readily answer, thought of how to respond. "It is something I have pondered over night, even more here on the train. I'll think some more on it. There's still some time before a decision is to be made."

Both fell silent. Considering what was said and what was on either's mind. "Very well," interrupted Elisabeth. "Two nights only. The only time I was there was with your father and we stayed at the Posada San Felipe on the main plaza." She smiled to herself; thinking of how that experience had inspired them both to name their son Felipe. "It is a nice place. At least it was, ideally located. We could see about rooms there. It may be a little chilly to sit outdoors in the plaza cafes. But, it could be an excellent place to people watch and eavesdrop conversations. Your call! Just give it more serious thought. If you are bound to go I will go with you. But, lets not stay too long. I have a bad feeling about it."

Posada San Felipe was indeed in a good location. It had been in operation since the 1860's and the hallways and lobby, even the inside dining room, had large oil paintings of historical significance of Mexico's past. The taxi had to drop them off at the rear entrance for the front was on the plaza, an outdoor café gracing that entry. They registered at the desk and were issued their rooms on the third floor. Their neighboring rooms had individual balconies and soon they were standing on them overlooking the heavily treed plaza below. Hidden birds within the confines of the thick foliage chirped and sang their varying songs in non-stop chatter. The thick, green canopy obscured from them the numerous strollers and passersby below. But, there was the constant sound of musicians delighting those sipping coffee and munching on whatever at the outdoor tables alongside the plaza's promenade. It was cool, and the meandering breezes that coursed down the narrow, winding streets and entered the plaza truly convinced all it was winter. Even so, those below were undaunted, bundled warmly, enjoying their hot brew and some galletas, some feasting on meals, listening to the crooners and their harmonious accompaniments at that mid afternoon hour.

"Certainly is a romantic setting," commented Felipe. "You and father were here, at this very hotel?"

Elisabeth reminisced. "Yes, a long time ago it was. That corner café below, across the promenade," she said pointing below to their left. "That is where we had spent a splendid evening. The meal was not our intent. All we had I think was a bottle of wine, some cheese and bolillos. We just spent a couple hours I suppose, maybe more, loving the moment and each other." She fell silent in her further recall. Felipe gave her space and time, thinking he saw her eyes moisten with a hint of tears.

"How about we go below, have some wine and cheese, watch and listen, do the same again?" asked Felipe.

Elisabeth, drawn back to the present, blinked a few times, and trying to be inconspicuous wiped the corner of her eye with a palm. "Oh, but of course. I am ready. You?"

"Let's go! I'll see you in the hallway." They turned about and left their respective balconies, closing the doors behind them to shut out the intruding cold air. They met in the hallway and soon had descended the tiled staircase to the lobby and then strolled outdoors, soaking in the ambience of the hotel as they exited outside. They passed an outdoor buffet cart and a covered platter of various sweet breads which caught Felipe's eye. A cordial waiter approached them, asked them if they desired a table; to which they said in the morning they would. They continued across the plaza to the corner café that they had observed from the balconies, where Elisabeth and Rodolfo had years ago basked in the glow of their mutual love.

"Lovely setting is it not?" asked Elisabeth, noticing the strollers passing by them on the promenade. The canopy of green, the heavily leafed trees that sheltered the plaza, obscuring their views from their balconies, was now overhead. They were now a part of the throng underneath. Elisabeth focused upon an aged artist, a man of barely any means apparently, dressed simply despite the coolness. He sat upon one of the wrought iron plaza benches opposite them. He had his legs crossed and upon his lap he had a large sketchpad. He worked wonders with his worn charcoal pencil, portraits or simply en mass that of the passersby. He seemed oblivious to all about him accept for the subjects he sketched. He was engrossed in his own world, completely oblivious to his intrigued on-lookers.

"I'd like to see what that man over there is doing," commented Elisabeth. "He has an interesting face and demeanor. I wonder whatever he is sketching has such merit also?"

Felipe looked in the direction she was referring, noticing the same man who apparently had a similar affect upon him. He was about to say something when the waiter arrived with their bottle of wine and a tray of cheeses and bread. It was such a pleasant way to unwind from the clickety clacks of the long train ride. The pop of the cork signaled a time to relax. They did not say much, just sat, marveled, and observed in silence. Their thoughts were as pools of water, sometimes clear, sometimes cloudy. The café was not that busy for an hour. Then more began to filter in.

A trio of young people, apparently those of the college, had sauntered in and had taken a table next to them. They were heavily engaged in some topic of conversation that irritated one of them. Felipe identified with fellow students, sensed it was a conversation about some classroom subject, something that generated passion and discussion, something that intrigued him.

"Listen, the very word itself comes from the Greeks. Look at it! Sinarquismo! It means that *without authority and order that liberal anarchy results.* Professor Schreiter brings to us a political agenda. They are wolves in sheep's clothing. He's a German and you know what that means! Nazis! He 's one for sure in disguise, here to pollute our thinking, here for Germany's interests, not ours."

"Ah Carlos! You have him all wrong!" said another, called Ernesto, contradicting him. "Look at the liberals in Mexico City. Look at the mess they have made of our country. It all goes back to Juarez and how he stripped the Church of her rights. The Church meant order. It is us! *Hispanidad!* It prevented chaos and anarchy. We tried to right the wrongs that the federals have done during the Cristero War. But, we failed. Now the Union Nacional de Sinarquistas inherit our struggle, and all the power to them! I am tired of Camacho and his land reforms, like he is giving it all away to the undeserving peons, like some damned Communist. Maybe he should be living in Russia since he is being like one of those Bolsheviks. Mexico is for we Catholics and Professor Schreiter could come from the moon for all I care. At least he sees reality; that the Sinarquista ideology and Catholicism go hand in hand. You should really hear what he says and not judge him out of ignorance."

"Enough, Ernesto!" interrupted Juan, the other of the trio. "Leave, Carlos alone! He has his rights too, to believe what he does. Schreiter I know has been around the Sinarquistas a lot, and I hear he even gives them money to organize and operate. Where he gets the money is speculated, perhaps from the German legation in Mexico City? Maybe even Berlin is instructing him what to say and do. Look how serious this is! Imagine Hitler himself in our classrooms, and if Schreiter is indeed a Nazi you know he is promoting Hitler's interests, and at our expense! Give Carlos credit for thinking about this in depth! He is not some simple minded follower. Isn't it our business as students, to question things and not blindly follow?"

"Juan, you should be in Professor Bueno's philosophy class. He sees history and philosophy are synonymous. And, he knows Schreiter personally, good friends I gather. I like Bueno and I cannot believe he would cozy up to a Nazi. You and Carlos are mistaken about everything."

Carlos began drum beating his pencil upon the table in an agitated state. "We are supposed to be at this university learning good, solid things, things that will enable us to live better lives. And look at us, arguing about social reforms and politics of the extreme. We have a lot of Germans and Spanish in Mexico and it must be figured that a good percentage of them are favoring their motherland. Hitler and his Nazis have raised Germany out of the ashes of World War 1 and they must have lots of pride for that, and have even greater plans for the future. But, they promote themselves, the whites, as the superior race. Tell me, Ernesto, what purpose could Germany have with we brown peoples of Mexico? Why are Spain's fascists here? They see us as inferior beings. I do not need to tell you about what the Spanish did to us, the Conquest and Colonization, Enslavement, how they raped our country, stole our gold and silver and more, and with the Church's blessings really. They only want to get their hands on our country's natural resources as they continue their war of dominance upon innocent people. Franco wants to resurrect the glories of Spain's past at our expense! And too, you know Germany sees in the Americans a possible threat and if they can unsettle them through us somehow they will do it. I see this Schreiter fellow as a Nazi, bent on causing trouble for us all. All I am saying is that we should not swallow everything we are being told. We could wind up choking to death!" There was an interim, each pondering what each had said, Ernesto having an angered brow, and the other two looking frustrated.

"I know you probably are tired of hearing about Pearl Harbor and the Americans. But, listen to what the American Embassy had said last October; the 31st to be exact. In essence they claimed the Sinarquistas is a dangerous, totalitarian group, controlled by Franco's Spanish Falangists and the Catholic Church, but with the Nazis pulling their strings behind the scenes. Why Spain though? Well look! They are Catholic as we and we have a common language unlike the barbaric language of the Germans. We have one of the Romance languages, not one of guttural barking like theirs. The Germans know the stark differences, but feel their culture is far superior to ours. The Americans claimed that Spain wants Mexico to be a part of a New Spanish Empire, ruled by them and the Catholic Church. But, let me tell you, behind the façade everything would be manipulated by Germany, and Germany cannot overtly accomplish this without the lead of Spain. In Europe the Nazis conquer with their invading armies. Here in Mexico they hope to do so by subversion, causing civil unrest, even espionage and sabotage I suppose. They want a new revolution that would draw in the United States in a way that the Americans would pose no threat to assist their European allies against Germany. There are a lot of things to consider beyond whatever Schreiter says."

They continued to debate and argue, sometimes heatedly, and some diners rose up to take other tables or paid their tab early and departed. They wanted nothing to do with such debates, or be in the proximity of them. It was those cursed, university –students they reasoned, a new generation of thinkers and doers that causes social upheavals, ideologues with bias.

Professor Oscar Helmuth Schreiter was indeed German, from Dresden. He was hired by the school to be their Professor of Modern Languages. He was sent to Mexico at the instructions of the *Ibero-American Institute* in Berlin, the strategic seat of Nazi planning for the Americas, with the express purpose of accomplishing Hitler's goals. He would weasel his way into the social fabric where the ultra conservative Sinarquista movement was and there plant the seeds that would eventually lead the way into Mexico for establishing a base for Nazi espionage, to access Mexico's raw materials for its war effort, to make Mexico the center for organized sabotage against the United States and Mexico, disrupt any shipment of goods to the Allies' war efforts against Germany and her Axis allies, establish a fascist center to hassle enough the United States so it would be distracted from Europe, establish a fascist center to broadcast its propaganda throughout Latin America, and to further stir up trouble within Mexico, resulting in restrictive measures that would discredit the Mexican government in the eyes of the citizens, that the people would no longer support liberal President Camacho.

It was an industrious undertaking, requiring patience and tenacity. But, the German dictator had indeed proclaimed the German Reich was here to stay a thousand years! To help facilitate these ambitious goals in the Americas Berlin saw the Mexican Sinarquistas as those whom they could collaborate with, even manipulate, and through Oscar Helmuth Schreiter they helped in the formal founding of the Union Nacional de Sinarquistas at Leon, Guanjajuato on May 25, 1937. He was empowered by Berlin to fund its founding and operations for the first year, and these funds came from the German legation in Mexico City, rendered unto the German colony in the capital, and they in turn paid the funds directly to Professor Schreiter in Guanajuato. He then funded the Union de Sinarquistas. This was done with the blessing of many Church officials, believing that a central authority and order within the country needed to be reestablished, with the Catholic Church holding the reins. But, in reality the Sinarquistas were being duped by Nazi Germany. They were playing the role of the proverbial ostrich sticking its dim-witted head into the sands of denial, swallowing all of whatever the German agents were telling them.

The early leader of the Sinarquistas was the hotheaded and volatile hardliner, Salvador Abascal, self deluded in thinking he was the reincarnation of Catholic, Saint Ignatius of Loyola, the founder of the Society of Jesuits. He had left the directorship of UNS (Union Nacional de Sinarquistas), which was assumed by Professor Manuel Torres Bueno, Schreiter's good friend, on December 12, 1941, five days after Pearl Harbor. For Abascal, he saw his true calling was to establish a Jesuit – Sinarquista colony in the remoteness of Baja California Sur, with a focus just north of Magadalena Bay on the west coast of the peninsula. The bay was remote indeed. The shoreline was rimmed with countless miles of sandy beaches and sand dunes. Saguaro cacti forests lay just beyond the sands. The most frequent visitors had been gray whales and dolphins. But, that would change. In the area of Santa Domingo and Llanos de Irai, just north of the bay, was where Absacal and his followers intended to found their colony. This mission, as all others of the Jesuits, he believed had been thwarted by freemasonry and how the Revolution of 1910 had resulted in their expulsion and loss of rights. Now he was bent on establishing this religious-based colony associated with the Sinarquistas far removed from the scrutiny and intrusions of the detested secular politicians in Mexico City, and their liberal ideals.

"That was interesting," mused Felipe to his mother. "Same university and such varying opinions! Stimulating but troubling! I think I'll ask them something." He stood up and approached them.

"Excuse me. May I ask you something?" asked Felipe. "We could not help but overhear your conversations. It all sounds so intriguing. Have you any opinions of the Japanese? Do you ever discuss in class what Japan's goals are? Are you in favor of Camacho's interning Mexican citizens who just so happen to have Japanese ancestry? Why do this and the Germans have so much liberty? Why do anything at all since we are not at war?"

The trio of students fell mum, considered Felipe an intruder at first. But, they understood the poignancy of his question. There were no Japanese teachers at the university and it had not been a topic of conversation, at least openly. But, within informal groups a comment would arise here and there.

"I am a sociologist in Mexico City and have wondered about this myself," added Felipe. "It just seems so ironic that Germans and Japanese are allies and yet Germany preaches their fanatic racism, that the whites are superior to all others, and that Japan does similar on their side of the world. How can they spout such garbage and be compatible allies? And here in Mexico, where most of us are mestizos, brown people, Hispanics, it's not a stretch of the imagination to know what Nazis truly think of us! I think it deserves deep thought why the Germans are here. They have a history of getting a lot of oil from us, and we know how important that is during war and conquest. In fact all raw materials are needed to feed that hunger and thirst. They must be here to accomplish those goals in one way or another, not for Mexico's benefit. But, why does Camacho focus on the Japanese, put them in concentration camps and not the Germans? And of course, Spain has been hell for us! We are not even at war. We are a neutral country and none of this should apply to us. I'd appreciate hearing what you have to say about this, if I may? Mexico should be for Mexicans! Not others!"

Carlos scrutinized Felipe. "Good question. At our university we have some Germans on staff, no Japanese. They don't speak about Japan, and not even of Germany really, other than saying they want the best for Mexico. But, I question whose best and so should everyone else. Cortes and his Spanish hordes led the Conquest of our country and since then it has been foreigners who have continued to victimize us while we argue among ourselves. You name them, the Spanish, French, English, Germany, and even the Americans despite Roosevelt's *Good Neighbor policy,* have all plundered us. And now, these days, Germany has designs on us in ways none of us fully comprehend. But, we better wake up and be wise for once. If not we will find ourselves poorer yet and under the heel of another foreign tyrant. What about you? What do you think? What are people thinking down in the capital?"

"I am not one to speak for them," answered Felipe. "I do know that we at the Universidad Autonoma have free thinkers. Our professors and students are not promoting ideologies. I really enjoy what our History Professor Arellano has to say, whether of long ago or contemporary, even of civic matters of today, how he ties it all in for cohesive understanding. When I return I would hope to hear what his comments are about what is happening in Mexico today. We are in precarious times and we Mexicans seem to be a playingfield for the bigger nations to do their mischief. I have more concerns over the Germans than I do the Japanese. I have wondered just how just and wise our president has been by incarcerating our own people, even if they have some Japanese ancestry. So what? Why fear them and not the Nazis?"

Again, a silence fell over them all as they pondered an answer to Felipe's question. Ernesto saw an opportunity to say something.

"How would you like to come meet Professor Schreiter and maybe his companion, Otto Gilbert? Even Professor Bueno may be on hand. There is a Sinarquista meeting tonight. Father Garcia has invited them to speak. He and other priests have compiled lists of potential new members for the Union Nacional Sinarquista. Please come and hear for yourself what is said." He took out a slip of paper from a pants pocket and handed it to Felipe. "There, that tells you when and where. See you there maybe. Right now I have class to get to." Ernesto parted with an aire of contempt for them.

.

"It may seem like we do not like each other by how we carry on," said Juan. "But, we have been the best of friends as long as we can remember. But, even good friends have different opinions about some things. Sometimes our differences can be passionately displayed. Ernesto comes from an ardent Catholic family. Some of them fought in the Cristero War. Father Garcia is his uncle. I think some day that Ernesto himself would like to be a priest. I wonder about that though, if it is because he has faith and wants to do the Lord's will, or if it is because he likes all of the rites and empty rituals of the Church and wants to be in its administration. Just the same, that meeting could be an interesting one just for curiosity's sake. Mind you, I have no intentions of becoming a Sinarquista! But, I might go just to hear what that German has to say."

Juan and Carlos stood up simultaneously ready to depart themselves. They exchanged 'good-days' and maybe 'see you later.' Felipe and Elisabeth watched them fade away among the passersby on the promenade.

"What do you say about that?" asked Elisabeth. "Do you think you'll go to that meeting?"

He did not answer right away, just shrugged his shoulders a 'maybe'. He reasoned that this was the very crux of his being in Guanajuato, why they had made this a side stop en route home. He then spoke, "Yes, I think I'll go. Like that one had said, just for curiosity's sake, no intention of getting involved. Like him, I'd like to see and hear this Schreiter. I'd like to compare what I have read and been told about him and the Sinarquistas, see if he is what I expect." He wondered if there would be any likeness to the firebrand talk of Contreras that he and Magaly has witnessed in Mexico City.

The hour had come when it was time to hail a taxi. Elisabeth had perceived that the meeting was for men only and had opted to remain at the posada. Soon Felipe was on his way to whatever was waiting for him. The cabbie zipped along through a subterranean maze of paved tunnels, once upon a time underground rivers that had been drained away during the silver ore strike many years ago during Spanish colonial rule. It amazed Felipe how anyone found a way through the maze. But, the cabbie knew the tunnels well and soon they emerged topside again, slowing down to a stop before a stone building that pressed hard upon the narrow sidewalk bordering the street. It was a short step from the taxi to a large, age-worn wooden door. He confirmed with the cabbie this was the address written on the slip of paper. He paid his fare and then stepped out for the door when he heard a shout from behind. Across the cobblestoned street were the same students, Juan and Ernesto, without Carlos.

"You came!" they shouted. They looked at the steady stream of taxis and cars winding down the narrow, meandering street. "See you when we can cross."

Felipe waited until they finally saw their opportunity to hurry over. "So, this is the place?" asked Felipe when they approached him.

"Yes. Let's go inside," said an eager Ernesto, who appeared to have been there before, for he displayed familiarity.

They encountered some robed clerics inside as they entered, as if it was a sanctioned edifice of the Holy Catholic Church. There was a mix of people milling about in the elongated room. On the far wall were some glass doors, yet unopened, portals unto a larger room where the meeting was to convene.

The trio of newcomers stood aloof, watching intently those about them, noticing the make-up of personalities present. A voice suddenly resonated over all their heads to enter the now-opened doors and take their seats in the interior hall.

They noticed a grouping of chairs set up for an audience and before the chairs was a podium. Behind the podium on a wall was the same red flag of the Union de Nacional Sinarquista, the banner of ultranationalists and clerical fascism. Every one took their seat in relative silence. Father Garcia took to the podium to address the meeting, welcoming all that had come.

"Why, you may wonder, why the Church is allied with the Sinarquistas, why we encourage membership in the conservative and faithful of the Union Nacional Sinarquista. We follow what Pope Leo XIII decreed in his *Rerum Novaru,* telling us to mobilize and resist any 'atheistic and communist' efforts to take control. The Austrians, Portuguese, and Spanish obeyed. We in Mexico followed, in the failed Cristiada movement. We made every effort to have social co-operation. But the liberals only brought class conflicts of socialism. We stressed a respect for authority, law and order. But liberals brought chaos. Our brothers during the Cristero War fought against the socialist and anti-clerical policies of Mexico City, and we failed. Now, the Sinarquistas, God bless them, have embodied the same ideals we fought for in that past conflict. I hereby encourage you to get onboard and support these same ideals!" He paused, looked them over before him. "I will quote the lyrics of the 'Battle Hymn of the Cristeros'. May you take these words to heart and they become your personal hymn of life!"

The Virgin Mary is our protector and defender when there is to fear. She will vanquish all demons at the cry of "Long Live Christ the King!"

Soldiers of Christ: Let's follow the flag, for the Cross points to the army of God!

Let's follow the flag at the cry of "Long Live Christ the King!"

He bowed his head in a show of silent prayer, and then raised up and promptly introduced Professor Manuel Torres Bueno, the national leader of the UNS. Since he had ascended to that leadership he had brought in a totally different approach to promoting the views of their organization. Unlike the previous director, Salvador Abascal, a hard-liner, a no-nonsense, don't-waste-my-time personality, Bueno was a showman given to public stunts. He had led large scale 'take-overs' not that long ago of Guadalajara, Jalisco and Morelia, Michoacan. His stunts had resulted in a measure of jocular responses, winks of the eye, popular among the peasants of the western states, a humorous slap in the face of the status quo government.

"Good evening," greeted Bueno. "I am glad to see you all here tonight. Some I recognize from the university. Others of you I do not know. I see our Spanish brothers are here and of course those from the Ibero-American Institute. To all of you I say thank you for coming. You are here with a purpose and I hope to give you just that. Let me start by saying what you already know, that the world is in a mess right now, and Mexico surely has its share of trouble. President Camacho is demonstrating his love for socialism. Look what the Bolsheviks have done to Russia, total chaos. They think that in their revolution they brought parity among the peoples, no more Czar, no more class distinctions. Every one is a copy of the same, no differences. What a fallacy to believe in! Why has Camacho shown a particular zeal to give away the Church's lands and possessions, to redistribute to others, repeating the atrocities of Juarez? He wants to terminate any viability we Catholics have in our country. I believe him to be an atheist, even a Communist! His stance against the foreign oil companies is like President Cardenas had had, when he nationalized our petroleum industry. Camacho detests foreign powers monopolizing our natural resources and believe they prevent him from fulfilling our Constitution of 1917, as he sees fit, for Mexico to be a sovereign nation in control of our own natural resources. Many are labeling him an atheist and communist. This I believe is true. We know that Russia favored Camacho's election." He stepped away from the podium to cough, and clear his throat.

"Excuse me. I have a raspy throat. This winter weather is giving me a cold. Our problem is not with the world. It is with the secular liberals that control our government. They have an anti-Church agenda. If we wish to be faithful to God the government is against us. Fortunately we do have friends that see our plight, want to help, and they are not our fellow citizens in the Federal District. As you know we have on staff at the university a certain professor who has proved his worth beyond just academia. Those in his class of Modern Languages know first hand his worth. I have become a good friend of Professor Schreiter. He has been very instrumental in the founding of our Union. He has funded us and now beyond his duties at the university he has been devoting much time to assisting us, in ways that the Cristiada movement never had. I could go on a bit more and talk about how it has been to direct the affairs of the UNS. But, I think it would be more important for you to hear from Professor Schreiter. So, without any more delay, I give you the professor."

'Professor Schreiter'

A tall man in a simple suite strode to the podium as one with purpose. He placed a hand on either side of the lectern, gripping it as if his vitriolic speech would blow it away. He came with no written speech in hand. He was one who spoke spontaneously, off the cuff. He stood for several moments saying nothing, just making eye contact with those before him. Slowly, he began with a determinate face to speak.

"You may wonder why we in Germany have an endeared interest in you and Mexico. We are quite familiar with your history, how foreigners have intruded into your lives, takers who never give back. Your wealth has made other lands wealthy. They have lived well off of you while they have subjugated your country, in many ways, unto poverty and void of dreams. This in turn has led Mexico into a lot of bickering and infighting. My country at the end of that Great War lay in ashes. Our people were homeless and starvation was real. We were under the heel of the English and French and they thrilled at grinding us asunder in our defeat. But, look at us since those days. We have surmounted all obstacles and have had no nation stand in our way as we recovered and much more. We are now once again supreme in Europe, the envy of even those who had conquered us. They fear us unlike before. They see what we German people are capable of." He looked over the several dozen brown faces in attendance.

"We in Berlin know of others who have their own kind of ashes to rise up from, ashes of defeat and despair, just like that phoenix bird had done, just like we have done! Our government has an agency in Berlin that was created to consider how we might help those in the Americas. 'Hispanidad' we call it. Those of your Catholic faith, Spanish and Portuguese ancestries bind you in unique ways that are contrary to the Anglo-Saxon Protestants of the United States. President Roosevelt has his *Good Neighbor Policy*, tabbed *Pan-Americanism*. It collides with your *Latin Americanism*. Unlike those Yankee programs of false friendships our *Ibero-American Institute* in Berlin has created programs, with the blessings of the German government, to come to Mexico, and on down to South America, to lend our people and funds to assist when we are welcomed to come. We are actually doing something substantial while the Americans are all talk. Mexico has an open door of welcome and the *Institute* communicated with the university here for me to come and teach and also to help the factions of disgruntled Catholics unite once again in a common cause, the same cause that the Cristeros had gone to war for. We helped in the founding of your Union Nacional Sinarquista. We have taken great pride in what you Mexicans have accomplished, and are ready to help you achieve even more." He paused, letting soak in what he had said before continuing."Remember! Our Fuhrer is a champion for Catholics!"

"The liberal press of the United States can say anything they want. They spread lies about we in Germany. Even Roosevelt's government is a victim of theirs, believing what they feed him. And your President Camacho is not so much his own man. He is under the shadow of Washington D.C. It is really time for you Mexicans to take control of your own country; not be coerced by others. The Americans declared war on our ally Japan, and we reciprocated in defense of our ally by declaring war on the United States. Mexico needs to control its own destiny, fight against the tendencies of your president to make Mexico a communist state like Russia. If that happens you can kiss good-bye any rights to private property ownership and maybe worst of all is the banning of your church! Mexico used to be a strong Catholic country. Now look at what is happening! The national government is instituting national reforms that are socialist. The only ones we know of that are truly opposed to this and are willing to go to any length to do so, are the Sinarquistas. I implore you to rally behind Professor Bueno and make the numbers swell and cause Mexico City to moderate its ways, until a more favorable candidate is elected president. The time to act and do something begins now. Become a Sinarquista member. Join all the others who wish to save Mexico from secular chaos and restore the Church to its moral leadership and guidance, flee from the catastrophes of liberalism!"

There were some exchanges of questions and answers that extended the brief meeting perhaps twenty minutes. A few individuals rose up and sauntered forward with apparent interests of joining the UNS. Others procrastinated, continued sitting and mumbling to those next to them.

"Well, it was not a long speech," admitted Ernesto, the one who was so ardent with Schreiter. "But, it was long enough for you to get the gist of what he stands for, of his and Germany's commitment to help us."

"Still, I think he has something up his sleeve," suggested Juan. "They are not here as philanthropists, do-gooders, paying out all that money and expect nothing in return. They have an agenda and surely have not disclosed it. Germany is not here without a political purpose. Mark My Words!"

"Doubters! You all are trouble, spoilers. Here we have a grand opportunity to accomplish what we all want. You doubting the hand that feeds you will cause you to starve! What about you?" he asked Felipe. "What are your thoughts?"

"It depends what that hand is holding, food or poison," replied Felipe. "Mexico must think beyond our borders. Pancho Villa, Zapata, the Revolution, the Cristero War, all of that domestic chaos! In this day and age we cannot afford to be so self absorbed as we were then. There is a world war going on now unlike the first. This war is sucking in many more countries than the first, and unless we Mexicans begin to have an international mindset we will be played by those who do, will seek to rob us of our natural resources for their war efforts and we shall be the ignorant fool again. This liberal vs. conservative nonsense is detracting us from what really matters. This consumes us as a country while others see us as ripe pickings. We need to think about now and tomorrow, and not be enamored with singing *corridos* of a bygone era."

'Well said," gleamed Juan. "I couldn't have said it any better!"

"You too?" expressed a surprised, disgusted Ernesto. "Well, maybe you should hasten back to Mexico City where there are more of you with that archaic opinion. If you learned anything at all from tonight it is that the Nazis are not our enemy. Reluctance, procrastination, doubting are. Fear of change! That is one thing about Roosevelt had said that I agree with; "*the only thing to fear is fear itself*". Professor Schreiter and the Sinarquistas represent change, a return to law and order, and our conservative Church overseeing all things. Hitler is a friend of we Catholics. You can bank on that!"

All Felipe could do was swallow hard. There was no use arguing with a deluded soul. To those who have ears to hear, they will hear indeed. But, Ernesto was one that had had his ears severed, was void of understabnding. He swallowed with ease the dogma coming from the Ibero-American Institute in Nazi Germany. The meeting was now breaking up, a good number were sauntering out of the hall and were making their way for the exterior door. Left behind was Ernesto in serious conversation with those he identified with. Juan and Felipe exited onto the narrow sidewalk, pulling their coat collars around their throats.

"Temperature has dropped some. That cold breeze makes it feel even colder," surmised Juan. "It is too bad you will not be around any longer. I think it would be worthwhile getting to know each other better. But, your life is back in the capital. You must get back to that! You have just tomorrow here and then you leave?"

"Yes. Maybe if you have time you can stop in for breakfast at the Posada where we are staying, where we first met. We could discuss more all of this."

"Well, that is something appealing. Maybe I will. Maybe I'll surprise you!"

Chapter 13

"What Mother Has to Say"

Felipe hailed a taxi and oddly enough it was the same cabbie that had brought him to the meeting who now was picking him up for a return to the posada. En route Felipe ventured a question.

"You have any Germans staying here in Guanajuato?"

It was an odd question thought the cabbie; but, then again maybe not. He had noticed some, those who had a strange demeanor about them, ultra serious, never a smile. They were an abrasive sort thought the cabbie; a people that never were to be warmed up to, always argued about the cab fare.

"Yes. Not my favorite people really," admitted the driver. "They seem harsh and not given to friendliness. Those who I know seem involved with education in one way or another. It seems like controversy is always hovering around them. If that is what it is like to be educated I am glad to be just what I am. Why do you ask?"

"That meeting I was at? Well there was a German speaker there and many seem to think he is the best thing since bread and butter. I just have a hard time with what he was saying. I came away from that wondering if all the Germans in Mexico hold the same beliefs. If so, then I think we all should be concerned."

The cabbie did not reply, just clammed up as if mulling over Felipe's comments. They once again meandered under the city through the maze of tunnels and emerged topside. The Posada San Felipe was located close by; but was hidden from view due to all the trees in the plaza. Felipe called out, "This is fine. Let me out. I can walk from here". He paid his tab and prepared to walk across the plaza, like a fish swimming upstream as he looked for a way through the teeming strollers, about to buck the tide. Before his first step the cabbie called out to him before he closed the rear door.

"Be careful who you talk with about this German thing," cautioned the cabbie. "You never know just who will hear and there is an element of people in Guanajuato, Mexicans mainly, that think of the Germans highly. Speak anything contrary and you may have some trouble. There are some students at the university that I worry about, and they are prodded along, encouraged by a German professor I hear about. I am not sure what his name is or what he teaches. But, some of these students get fanatical in their political and religious views. Like I say, just keep an open eye. You never know just who is who, who you can trust. That can get you into trouble here."

Felipe thanked the man, watched him drive on in search of other fares. The red taillights disappeared as the car meandered down the narrow street obscured in traffic and rounded a bend. He had been let off on the far side of the plaza. He made his way laboriously through the crowds and approached the posada's outside café. He saw his mother sitting by herself next to one of the prized gas heaters on elevated stands, engaged in conversation with a middle aged lady at a neighboring table.

"Are you not cold?" asked Felipe approaching, feeling the heat radiating outward from a bright flame.

"Not really," answered an inquisitive Elisabeth. "How was the meeting?"

"About what I had expected and then some," replied Felipe. "More people there than I had expected, which should be a real concern!"

Elisabeth looked at him with an odd expression, at least he had noticed that; hoping the person she had been talking with he would detect something also.

"This is Frau Schmidt of the small German colony here in Guanajuato. We were just talking about how interesting this city is. She has had some interesting experiences being here." Elisabeth had purposely spoken up as a forewarning to Felipe as to whom the woman was that she was talking with, knowing of Felipe's forebodings of Germans and the purpose of the meeting he had attended. "May I introduce you to my son, Felipe?"

"Pleasure to meet you Frau Schmidt," said a cautious Felipe with a side-look at his mother. "So you like Guanajuato! How come?"

"Ah, it is so picturesque and has an interesting history, going back to 1548 when it was founded. Amazing engineers here; how they diverted that river through a subterranean tunnel they made to prevent further flooding in the city above! Those street musicians and singers are delightful! Just everything about the city is appealing accept those cursed mummies they keep showing up in the hills. Really though that is such a minor thing when considering everything else. What about you? What do you find appealing here, and maybe what is not?"

"As you say, I agree. Some of the political leanings are a bit strange I do say. But, this far out of Mexico City there are always contrary things to hear and see, even at times a challenge to understand. Tell, me, how did you decide to come to our country and live? What is it about our Hispanic culture that has drawn you from Europe?" asked Felipe with a hint of interrogation, knowing enough about Nazi bigotry and hatred. Was she a Nazi, he wondered?

"My nephew is the German Consulate in Leon. But truthfully I like it here better. But, one goes where one is ordered. We had lived in the colony in Mexico City for a few months. It is such a beautiful city. Devils like Cortes tried destroying it. But, he could not kill the spirit of the people. You have an amazing country, sir. I like being here very much!"

"Well, the way it is back home for you now in Germany and others it probably is best to be here in a neutral country. Mexico is pretty safe in comparison."

Frau Schmidt delayed her response. Then, "Well, our Fuhrer will see that we all will do well, wherever we are, and I am sure he and all the others will take care of business back home. Meanwhile we are here and seek to be good for Mexico. When opportunities arise we shall be of assistance to the Mexican people as well as we can, if we are asked to, of course, only by invite."

"Why come so far to be of help to we 'lowly' Mexicans?" asked Felipe, challenging her, feigning humility. "We in the Americas have our own friends and foes, just like you have in Europe, and historically speaking Europe has not been good for us. Do we hold some special place in the heart of the German people?"

Frau Schmidt felt somewhat uneasy before the youthful, handsome Mexican. Elisabeth suddenly interrupted!

"Did you know they are presenting a Beethoven concert tomorrow night at the Teatro Juarez? Maybe we should go, see something grand like that before we leave in the morning. The Fifth Symphony should be quite stirring!"

Frau Schmidt simply smiled, said nothing, still sensing what had felt like verbal jabs by her son.

"Mother it is a bit chilly out here for me. I think I'll go upstairs, do some reading." Then he faced Schmidt. "Señora, may you have a pleasant evening and further enjoy Guanajuato for however long you shall be here." He did a slight bow of his head with a hint of formality, never saying it had been a pleasure meeting her, which she had taken notice of.

"Well, young man, that has been my intent and so far that has been my experience. Unfortunately, when you board your train to Mexico City we depart for Leon. But, business calls and we must get back. I love a man who reads. Enjoy your book. May I ask what you are reading?"

"Well, I just bought it today. It's about Bolshevism. It is a subject of concern for many and I hope to understand it better, for all of its pros and cons. I know for the Nazis the Bolsheviks are a wary subject to talk about. I beg your pardon if my choice of reading troubles you. But, I say it is best to know who your enemies are, be they far away or close at hand."

"It depends who wrote it I suppose, one for or against them. Stalin is a beast and those people lack purpose and quality. Brutes they are! If the author of that book favors that sort then I do not applaud it and caution you about such rubbish. Our German culture has more merit. You will see that tomorrow night at that concert. Beethoven is far better than any Tchaikovsky!"

"Hold on, Felipe! Walk me up to my room. I agree the evening temperatures are too cold now even with those heaters. I must bid you a good evening Frau Schmidt. I found our conversation stimulating. It is always better to have someone to talk to than sit alone in the cold. Maybe we shall see you tomorrow evening at the theatre. But, for now I am going to retire, get a good night of sleep in that warm bed, be ready in the morning for our final day here." She offered her a smile and then turned and left in Felipe's company. Frau Schmidt called out in the parting.

"Yes, it is always best to have someone to share with. Perhaps we shall see one another in the morning over breakfast. Good night."

Elisabeth smiled and resumed her walk inside with Felipe, he casting a brief look of good night at the German lady. Frau Schmidt stared long at their departure, wondering about the persona of Felipe Gurza, perhaps a name she should remember.

"How did you engage in conversation with her?" asked Felipe. "Was she legitimate? Or, was she there to test you?"

"Good question! It seems this hotel is a hotbed of questionable people. There were plenty of empty tables about me. Why she selected the one right next to me is puzzling. I thought it odd at the time. She sat down directly facing me. I got the feeling she was there for something other than friendly dialog. She said something about how cold it was and was grateful for the heaters. Well, that opened up a conversation about innocent things. Maybe she was subtle about what she wanted. Then you came in, and probably just in time. I ran out of empty conversation to continue with. Tell me, how was that meeting?"

"Well, a priest blessed it and quoted some lyrics from a Cristiada song. He made the occasion seem to have some sort of holy unction. He introduced the Director of the Union Nacional Sinarquista; a certain *Manuel Torres Bueno*, one of the professors at the university here. He did not speak long, appeared to have a cold. But, he introduced Professor Schreiter from the university. He spun lies around in circles, weaving together a cloak of mystery and something to be feared. I could not believe what he was saying that those in attendance could not recognize it for what it was!

Only Juan did, and I too. That Carlos knew better than waste his time in going. But, that Ernesto fellow, a naïve follower of anything that the church blesses and whatever Schreiter says. It's Mexican youth like him that scare me, intelligent but stupid. I could see right through the guise of Schreiter that he is a Nazi through and through, one of twisted lies and deceit." They passed several people waiting at the reservation desk, stopped shy of the staircase. Felipe leaned her way.

"I wonder if that Ernesto had had anything to do with that Frau Schmidt being here, to spy us out. He knew quite well I did not follow his lead. What do you think, Mother? You think she was a plant to get information from you?"

"I began to think of that and played along, acted naïve. It was sort of fun in a way, sort of like acting in a play. Set it to music and perhaps it could be the basis of some new opera."

"What sort of things did she talk about?" asked Felipe. "Did anything seem too overt? Did she reveal anything about herself?"

"Not that much. She talked about the city, how cold it was, the heaters, what was on the restaurant menu, asked if I had family. I mentioned you and she asked a few things, some made me wonder why she asked this and that. But, I deflected most questions, was able to change the subject. Then you walked in and it was so timely! You certainly came in not that friendly! Was the meeting that bad?"

"It sickened me about the religiosity of it all, equating the Nazi agenda with the Church; just a charade, baiting we naïve Mexicans. I could not believe all those gullible imbeciles who went forward and became Sinarquistas, like it was some evangelical calling."

"I wonder if we should believe this woman, that she says she is the aunt of the German Consulate in Leon. Just a minute!" Elisabeth walked back just enough to have a view through the windows of where they had been sitting, and where Frau Schmidt had been. She was still there, but sitting with her now was the student Ernesto, the ardent follower of the Nazis. ""Quick! Come see this!" she implored Felipe. He was soon at her side looking her way.

"What did I tell you! What did I suspect!" Felipe looked on with contempt. Then they stepped away unobserved and began to ascend the stairway.

"Tell me, Felipe, is it true you bought a book about the Bolsheviks?" she asked him with a slight twinkle in her eye.

"No! I just said that to see how she responded," he chuckled. "Clearly she had a typical Nazi reaction to anything pertaining to Stalin, Russia and the Bolsheviks, or Communists as you may. I was just seeing what she would reveal of herself if anything at all. One thing about it all, I am now questioning why any German national is here in Mexico. It can't be for our good regardless of what their rhetoric is."

"Listen, here's my room. I want to talk to you some more. Come in with me." She inserted her key to unlock the door, but was surprised the door ajar. A bit hesitant they entered the room a bit wary, slowly edging the door open.

It looked like a whirlwind had twisted its way around her room. The bed had been stripped and the bedding piled in a heap upon the floor, and across the bare mattress were the contents of her luggage spilled out. The dresser drawers were all pulled out and the closet door was wide open. Who had done this? What were they after? What could Elisabeth possibly have had to attract such attention? Personal items of value were kept in the posada's safe, and the cash she carried never was in an amount conspicuous. This intrusion temporarily ceased all further thoughts of Frau Schmidt and Ernesto below. They would later see there was a link to them. Just as a boomerang returns to its source, so would their doubts and suspicions of the two below.

Frau Schmidt had been alerted. Her Nazi accomplices, thanks to their minion puppet Ernesto Maldonado, were informed of the Gurzas recent arrival, and that they had exhibited contrary opinions of their cause. Being from liberal Mexico City was also a red flag. They instructed Maldonado to notify Schmidt and she in turn sought out subtly Elisabeth at the hotel, delayed her with meaningless conversation so she would not return to her room. They needed time to pore over her things for any incriminating evidence.

"Your room!" suddenly blurted Elisabeth.

They hurried next door to Felipe's. The door was also ajar; some muffled voices were heard inside. He raised his index finger across his lips, a sign to be quiet. He gently edged her aside, away from the door, and then with his toe silently pushed the door open just enough to peer inside. Whoever was inside were none the wiser of his presence. Felipe caught a glimpse of two young men, perhaps students, plundering through his possessions. Just as his mother's room had been his was now being trashed in a like manner. Nearby were two carts, a maid's and another of custodial supplies. From one Felipe instinctively grabbed the handle of a mop and drew it out. He then entered like some avenging phantom. One of the men sensed something, raised-up and turned around. Felipe without hesitation swung the mop head across his face and then ran the blunt end of the handle into his stomach. Down the intruder went upon his knees and Felipe kicked him a hard blow across his jaw. The lights went out for the man. Surprised, the other one now drew a knife and nervously pointed it at Felipe while edging his way around him for the doorway and his escape. When he felt he had been successful he dashed outside into the hallway, promptly clobbered by Elisabeth. On impulse she had grabbed an iron off a linen cart and wielded it as a weapon, striking the fleeing man alongside his head. He was now sprawled out in the hallway.

"Best get security, if they have any!" exclaimed Felipe. He went to the telephone and called the front desk in the lobby. He had barely hung up the phone when two uniformed policemen appeared out of nowhere. My, that was fast he thought!

The two policemen wasted no time, hurried the semi-unconscious perpetrators away. They took the men downstairs via a servant's stairway, not for public use. Felipe and Elisabeth watched them disappear from view.

"I guess going that way helps to avoid bad publicity, keeps the public from seeing a crime had been committed here. The manager needs to protect their image of course."

Just then the manager and another policeman arrived.

"Where are they?" asked the agitated manager.

"The police just took them away, went downstairs over there," pointed Elisabeth.

"Police?" inquired the other policeman.

"Yes! We were so surprised you guys got here so fast!" replied Felipe.

The policeman appeared perplexed, wondered who it was that had beaten him there.

The manager checked both their rooms and winced at the total mess they had made. "Listen, we have never had anything like this happen before, at least on my watch. We are so sorry for this! Just leave things to us. Pack up your personal items and we'll move you to our suites, no charge. Just our way of hoping this you will not hold against the San Felipe." He summoned a bellhop to assist them in their move to the new rooms. As the bellhop led Felipe and Elisabeth down the hallway he commented to them,

"I came up the service staircase, saw those policemen carrying those two fellows," spoke the boyish man as he placed their luggage down at Elisabeth's door. "That was the quickest I had ever seen the police respond to anything, and then vanish just as fast. I usually know most on sight. But, those two officers I have never seen before. I guess maybe they are new."

He handed the key to Elisabeth, asking if he could be of any further help.

"No thank you, young man. You have been most kind," replied Elisabeth. She was about to drop some coins into his hand for a tip when he waved her off.

"Please! Don't think of it! This was a move you should never have been forced to make. Just get over the ordeal. I'll be content with that. We here at the San Felipe do our best to please the customers, and hopefully they, you, will be encouraged to stay with us again. Sir," he said turning to Felipe, ready to usher him to his room next door.

It had been a mere five minutes since Felipe and the bellhop had departed her, and now there was a knock at her door. Felipe stood before her with a grin on his face.

"What is so funny?" she asked.

"You! You tagged that fellow a good one. Remind me never to be in the same room with you if you are ironing! *Wrinkles no more, ironed-out in a jiffy before the lights go out* should be your motto.

I'm sure you gave that young fellow a triangular imprint to remember this occasion by. I wonder how he will explain it all, that he was laid-out cold by an iron lady?

Elisabeth had surprised herself by that impulsive act, something that perhaps her husband Rodolfo and Horacio would have done. But, she had acted so much out of character. She shifted the conversation.

"What do you suppose those guys were after? What on earth could we have that would cause such interest, and for whom?

"Good question! I have no idea," replied a bewildered Felipe. "That's a good question. I find it suspicious though that that German woman and even Ernesto were together." He looked at his mother, voicing a concern on the train that no good would come of their coming to Guanajuato. Maybe that was proving true!

"I like this Juan fellow," admitted Felipe. "I'd like to know more about him and his outspoken friend Carlos. Funny, I never heard their last names. Maybe I'll know tomorrow. Juan told me that he might come here in the morning for breakfast, might see us. I hope he does. But, I will not be surprised if he doesn't. But, if he does he will be shocked when we tell him of all of this, and how Schmidt and Ernesto met."

Elisabeth admitted, "I thought on the train that we should not come here, should have been firm in saying 'no'. But, that insatiable curiosity of yours cannot be pacified. You must do what you must do; like father, like son. I told you two days only. Now, well, I just don't know. I am not feeling like I want to leave here until I know what is happening, why we have been targeted! I never thought of myself as a coward and if we leave it will seem we are getting out of Guanajuato because we are afraid, are being chased off. I know we need to get home, get this letter to Señor Yamashita. She held it up for him to see. "It has been in my purse all this while. I had forgotten all about it. I can't imagine anyone would want this." She pressed her purse to her side.

"No," offered Felipe. "They were looking for something more than that, but what? I hope the police get answers out of those thugs. I want to know just how they and that German woman and Ernesto fit together. There's something suspicious here, the timing and all. On our way to the train tomorrow we should stop at the police station and ask if they found out anything from their investigations."

Elisabeth said nothing, as if her thoughts were considering something else other than what Felipe was saying. She was surmising their whole trip to date, troubled, intrigued.

"You know, I bet that Capitan Arestegui would have a way of finding things out here in Guanajuato. He is one that has focus, determination. His ideas on the Germans and the Sinarquistas and what is happening here deserve attention! Even the meeting you just attended, are all so mysterious, even worrisome. I feel like we have stumbled upon something others don't want us to know. We must be making someone really nervous. Maybe someone is thinking we are some one we are not, have us confused with someone else?"

"Maybe this, maybe that, Mother; a lot of maybees. I feel like you. I certainly had no idea how involved the Church is with these people. Then again there were some Spaniards at the meeting, fresh from Franco I suppose. But, no mention of the Japanese, not a sign of any! I wonder if President Camacho is aware of any of this, if he's s concerned about what Japan may be up to? He certainly should be with the Germans and Spanish!"

"I know we have to get back home. You have more pressing needs than I do. But, what do you think? Should we stay here a little longer, a few more days?" asked Elisabeth.

Felipe knew his mother had grit and tenacity. Perhaps if he had been there solo he would have had no compunction in staying longer. He was of a mind, however, not to risk her in any way. There are some things confronted that are just too convoluted and mammoth to comprehend.

"First things first. Let's see if this Juan comes in the morning, and if he does, see what he has to say. Then afterwards we can go see the police and see if they have found out anything. I think we should still leave as planned. Our purpose for this trip was fulfilled in Juarez. This Guanajuato business was just a side stop. Our main concern is to return to that futbol stadium and convey this letter to Señor Yamashita. There are bigger things going on here than you or I can determine, and even if we did, what should or could we do?"

"You suppose the Japanese are here too but no one knows about it, or at least cares?" asked Elisabeth. "It would be obvious, wouldn't it, if they were? I bet that Camacho knows they are in one way or another and that is why he has incarcerated them."

"After we return home I want to confer with Professor Arellano at the university," said Felipe. "If there is anyone that understands history, and what is happening today, he is the one! He can tell me all about these foreigners here in Mexico, and our own Sinarquistas.

"Let's invite him to the house rather than just you two meeting at school. I want to hear what he has to say also!

"Really? You want Professor Arellano to come to our place?" asked a doubting Felipe.

"Indeed! It would be a good thing to have him educate us. Maybe he has an idea what is happening up here in Guanajuato, even Queretaro and Zacatecas I heard. If the Germans have a foothold up here, somewhere, somehow, he may know all about it, might even understand Camacho better than most. He might even have something to say about Japan."

"Very well! You and Horacio will have your work cut out for you. The professor is quite fond of good food. You can tell that by just looking at him." Felipe grinned at the thought of his former professor's girth. "He is a lonely man in some ways I think. You remember? His wife died several years ago and I think socially he just buried himself in work. It has been all school. He may or may not accept the invite."

"We can at least make the effort," commented Elisabeth. "If it is 'no' then perhaps we can at least see him at his residence."

They continued to debate this and that when Felipe noticed his stomach had rumbled. "You know, I have forgotten about eating dinner! I wonder if the hotel's restaurant is still open. Maybe some tortilla soup and bread would suffice me until breakfast. How about you? You think you could eat something, this time inside where it is nice and warm?"

Elisabeth had agreed and they securely locked their doors and ventured down the long tiled stairway to the lobby. They emerged before the front desk where the manager was poring over some books.

"Everything alright now?" he asked them.

"Quite! Thank you very much! We were wondering if the dining room is still open, for just something simple," inquired Elisabeth, looking around and seeing no customers.

"They are closing in ten minutes. But, let me see what they can do." The manager went to inquire in the kitchen. He reappeared signaling for them to come. "Please, sit where you may. They were served promptly. Bowls of Sopa Azteca and a basket of bread more than sufficed them. They made no delays in finishing for the hour was late and they knew staff had to close the kitchen. They left a generous tip and parted for their rooms upstairs.

Standing before her door Elisabeth called out to her son. "You know, you surprised me too how you took care of that guy with just a mop and a kick to his jaw. I never knew you had that streak of fight in you."

Felipe just smiled; bid her a good night as he entered his room. Yes, he sort of surprised himself, but not as surprised as the one he had mopped. Then he thought of the two men being led away by police officers that had appeared out of nowhere so fast. Enough of that, he thought. It had been a long day and sleep was calling. Tomorrow, yes tomorrow, perhaps Juan would show up.

Chapter 14

"Juan Campos and Carlos Olivares, Police"

The sun shone brightly that early February morning, casting shadows of the tall buildings that rimmed the perimeters of the plaza. The outdoor-dining of the various restaurants had areas that were yet- cold within the shadows and those few tables that were bathed in sunlight is where the customers gravitated to. Songbirds chirped and sang their early morning rituals of welcome within the confines of the thick-foliage trees enshrouding the plaza. Across the narrow, cobble-stoned street lining the south side of the plaza stood an antiquated, large church alongside the grand opera house. Both stone structures cast long shadows across the street and merged with the dark foliage of the many trees in the plaza.

Felipe and Elisabeth had been enjoying the setting, limbering up in the sunshine that was putting to flight slowly the earn morn shadows, delving into their breakfasts of chilaquiles. Each plate had a spread of beans in the center chilaquiles in red and green salsas on either side. They savored the brew of Veracruz coffee. Even a platter of pan dulce was brought to them for their choices of sweet breads. Felipe now held up a freshly poured refill of coffee to sip when he noticed over the rim two youths approaching. One was Juan, carrying a small scroll in hand, and in his company was the vocal and opinionated Carlos.

"Good morning," the two young men greeted upon their arrival. "May we join you?"

"Yes, of course! Grab a couple of those chairs behind you." They drew some away from a neighboring table and slid them up to theirs.

"Señora," they greeted Elisabeth before sitting. "We have a little time before classes begin. But, we thought it a good idea to see you before you left."

"I really thought you were just talking last night. I never thought you were really serious. But, I am glad to see you again. Coffee?" Felipe looked for the waiter when they replied in the affirmative, and seeing him raised his suggestive cup.

"You met Carlos Olivares here yesterday," informed Juan, introducing his companion.

"Yes, of course, the rather vocal orator!" smiled Felipe, reaching across the table to shake their hands. The waiter interrupted them with two more cups to fill.

"Tell me Señor Gurza," requested Juan Campos. "It looks like you have had a good breakfast, and that papaya helps with digestion. But, were you able to digest all of that last night? There were plenty of things to chew on, some meat, a lot of fat. All in all, a bad diet!"

"That's an interesting way of putting it," commented Felipe. "I was chewing it all over like some horse when I arrived here last night. I shared it all with my mother. Really, nothing appealed to me. On the contrary, there was plenty to be alarmed with. I mean truly concerned!" Although Felipe was speaking to Juan his eyes had a tendency to keep reverting to Carlos.

"Carlos, we were quite impressed with what you had said yesterday, the manner in which you voiced your views. You had a way of describing this Professor Schreiter and things that set me on edge. I took notice. I saw and heard him last night at that meeting with Juan here. Like you, I fault every word that came out of his mouth. He's a dangerous man!"

"I am glad to hear this from you," responded Carlos. "That dogma is laced with poison and I am in awe why so many fools are swallowing it all. One can shout themselves hoarse to wake up others, the naïve and unsuspecting, even stupid if I may. But I have been labeled as being unpatriotic, even unfaithful to the Mother Church, and dare I say even to our country. I ask you, unfaithful to whom; the corrupt church? I have spoken out for

Mexico. Religion has nothing to do with what I say and do. It is religious people, our Catholics who have been cuddling up with the Nazis and now the Spanish Falangists. Religious people caused the shameful Cristero War. Wasn't it Christ who said, *put up the sword… that His kingdom is not of this world; if it was then His servants would fight,* or something like that? Now those religious zealots, those fanatics, have formed this Union Nacional Sinarquista. What is their purpose other than being anti-government? Now you have German Nazis and Spanish Falangists here grooming those Sinarquista puppets however they want. What deluded souls believing all of that trash! Spain has their motives. But, it should be clear as day that Hitler wants to get at the United States through us somehow!"

The three others sat in silence absorbing the tirade that Carlos had wasted no time spouting. Passersby on the plaza paid little attention to him. The growing procession of passing people went non-stop.

"I apologize Señora Gurza," admitted Carlos. "Sometimes I get so wound up, just like a clock's spring. Sometimes when I get talking I just go on and on. Perhaps it is best to talk about something else, like where you come from in Mexico City."

"Don't concern yourself about it, Carlos," calmed Elisabeth. "It is all very interesting, very stimulating! I think it is a good thing we talk about this. Please, continue."

Carlos curiously looked at her for sincerity. "You are from the capital. What do you suppose Camacho and the government know about what is happening up here? Are they dumb, naïve, stupid or what? Don't you think they should know what Hitler and Franco are up to in Mexico? It seems he is more concerned about Hirohito in Japan, and that is why he has interned all of those Japanese-Mexicans. He should be wary of all three, Germany, Japan, and Spain! Berlin, Madrid, Tokyo should worry him!"

"Perhaps the imprisoning of the Japanese-Mexicans is just a start?" suggested Elisabeth.

"Misguided or over-reacting!" blurted out Carlos. "Camacho needs to have eyes up here too. Mexican citizens are not rallying to support Japan. The Mexican Sinarquistas are supporting Germany and Spain, and trying to convince more to follow their lead. Who knows? Maybe even Japan is figured in somewhere." Carlos sipped some coffee, leaned back into the chair. "Juan told me last night's meeting showed again how Professor Schreiter is wooing more and more Mexicans to join the Sinarquista movement. Fools! Can't they see that everything that Schreiter says is cloaked in religion and shady politics?" I bet no one swallows Nazi lies in Europe anymore, except maybe the German people! Even they may know truth but are afraid to say anything!""

"Well said, young man!" praised Elisabeth. "Well said!"

"How is it, I wonder, you have been spared this poison?" wondered aloud Felipe. "Why do you see what things really are and all the others don't?"

"Maybe because I do my own thinking and don't let the priests think for me," replied Carlos. "Too many follow blindly what ever the clerics say, and they are telling us all that the Nazis and Fascists are here to help us. Someday those imbeciles will wake up and see that they have been listening to the same serpent that beguiled Eve in the Garden of Eden. All lies and deceit!"

Juan had been tapping the end of the scroll in the palm of his left hand. He suddenly held it up.

"This here is for you." He cleared away some things on the table and spread out the scroll, securing the four corners with the coffee cups.

"This illustrates what we know and suspect. It really creates more questions than gives answers. Take it with you and study it. Maybe back in Mexico City you can make more sense out of it if you share with others, those who have influence." He and Carlos began to explain the scroll.

"Here at the top we have Adolph Hitler, like a master puppeteer, manipulating the strings he has to all of his puppets. He conducts his business through here, the Ibero-American Institute in Berlin. He barks and they pull strings for him. The institute manipulates Spain and Franco, conducting the operations of the Spanish Falangists in Mexico, probably all over Latin America. Attached to another string is this here, the German legation in Mexico City, and they in turn are connected to Professor Schreiter and other German nationals operating here in Guanajuato, and most assuredly in Queretaro also; even in San

Luis Potosi and Zacatecas. We Mexicans are being stupid! We should be questioning why Hitler and Franco are really here, not what these puppets are saying to us with the blessings of Mother Church! Look, wherever they have gone the people have suffered. These devious people are pulling the strings of the Mexican Sinarquistas, manipulate those radical fools to dance for them. They control them through the masquerade of the Church's good graces and guidance."

Felipe and Elisabeth had leaned forward to pore over the scroll, noting the diagrams and notations. It reinforced the thoughts Felipe had had. Elisabeth frowned as she studied the legends.

"It is one thing to think about it all, try making sense of something so convoluted. It's another thing all together to see such considerations diagrammed so expertly like this. It brings things into focus. You sure you want to give this to us?" asked Felipe, Elisabeth seconding him.

"Never mind! We know all of this like the back of our hands. You are just passing through. We live here. Share this with others in the capital so they will know what is happening in our country," encouraged Carlos. "We better get going to class."

"One other thing before you go, there was a German woman here last night. She just introduced herself as Frau Schmidt. She talked which seemed forever with my mother, just empty talk. When I arrived I had a few exchanges with her and then mother and I retired for the evening. The odd thing was upstairs we found our rooms had been broken into and ransacked. We caught them in my room and we laid them out on the floor. The police took them away. You care to guess what they were looking for?"

"Frau Schmidt? It seems like I have heard of her before. I just can't place where," said Juan. "What about you?" he asked Carlos.

"No. I haven't heard of her. I bet that Ernesto had said something to someone and you became suspect. Sort of feels like the Gestapo are here now. Maybe they were just looking for something that would incriminate you, find out more about who you are."

"You mentioned Ernesto. When we had left Schmidt last night, actually at that table over there," said Felipe pointing to a table just beginning to catch some sunrays. "Ernesto came and was visiting with her. They must know each other."

"Seems so," responded Juan. "It just goes to show we have a nasty situation here. It's getting to be you just don't know whom you can trust." He looked at his watch. "We must run! Have a good trip home tomorrow."

There were cordial good byes and both students suddenly hurried away, leaving behind the scroll on the table, now stained with coffee rings. They watched the young men fade away from view, swallowed up by the passersby.

"Professor Arellano! That is whom we need to show this to!" blurted out Elisabeth. "We'll have him over for dinner, see what he has to say."

"Yes, that's a possibility," reasoned Felipe.

"This is all so fascinating, intriguing, and threatening!" said Elisabeth. "But, before the day is far spent I want to browse some of those shops on the other side of the plaza. I know of a candy store over there with all sorts of things. Then, just down the street a little ways is a ceramics store of renown. Perhaps I can get a new butter dish, teapot, something for the dining room or kitchen. Maybe even a new cookie jar," she winked at him.

They paid their bill and joined the strollers and others on the plaza's promenade, strolling their way, occasionally drawn into some of the numerous shops. They meandered down narrow, serpentine streets. A ceramics storefront display caught the eye of Elisabeth.

"Wait!" she told Felipe. "I won't be long."

A brief glimpse of a cookie jar had caught her eye. Felipe waited for her outside, tiring of the window-shopping stroll. She soon reappeared with a package in hand.

"What do you have there?" he asked.

"Just something for the kitchen," she replied with a smile.

The evening shadows were now creeping across the environs, suggesting it was time to return to the hotel. They summoned a taxi and before long he deposited them at the rear of the hotel. That evening was uneventful. They retired early for in the morn they were to depart for home. The sidestop at the police station en route to the train station would require extra time. The night passed rather quickly for them. Morning came and they were up and about eager to meet the day. A brief breakfast and the taxi soon had them wisked away from the San Felipe, leaving behind uneasy feelings.

"Please, could you make a brief stop at the police station?" asked Felipe of the taxi driver. They soon came to a stop before the stone edifice. "Please waite. We won't be long," Felipe said to the driver. He and Elisabeth stepped out and went inside the station.

"Yes," greeted the big man behind the desk. "What is your pleasure or complaint?"

"Sergeant, we are here for an inquiry about last night's incident at the Posada San Felipe," said Felipe to the officer at the front desk. "Two of your officers brought in two young men who had broken into and ransacked our hotel rooms. Nothing was taken but we are curious why they did it. Did we have something they wanted? Did you find out anything in your interrogation?"

The desk sergeant looked perplexed. "You said the San Felipe?" He hailed another officer. "Alvarez, did we have a couple of arrests last night from the San Felipe?"

"No. I was on duty and no one came in from there."

The sergeant looked at them again. "Are you sure about this? As you just heard none of our officers brought in anyone from there last night. In fact it has been a long time since we have ever had to go there. It's a very respecatable place!"

"There were two uniformed officers that suddenly appeared out of nowhere," commented Elisabeth. "We saw them haul away those two fellows. Is this where they would have come to, or is there another station?"

"Only here, señora," answered the sergeant. 'You say two uniformed officers?"

"Yes. I guess they were maybe around thirty years of age, both average height and slim," answered Elisabeth.

"Well, the only officer that we had on duty in that plaza last night is Perales, sort of on the hefty side, tall. These two you suggest I have no idea who they are. I must do some inquiring.

Any more information you have would help."

"Well, as my mother explained they were around thirty, average height, but too slim for their uniforms. The fit was terrible!" added Felipe. 'They did not say a thing, just hurried those guys away."

"This is strange," admitted the sergeant. "All I can say is those so-called prisoners are not here and those officers you described I have no idea who they are, none of us do. I tell you what. Here is a pen and some paper. Write down your names and address and if we learn of anything we will send word to you."

"Thank you, sergeant," said Elisabeth. "But, we are leaving now. We do not live here."

"Well, as I said, if I learn of anything I can contact you." He pushed towards Felipe the pad and pen. "If I may have your names and where to reach you at?"

Felipe wrote down some gibberish, not wanting to risk anyone knowing their wherabouts in Mexico City. He and his mother thanked the sergeant and departed the station. They felt his stare upon their backs as they made their way for the door. *Hurry,* they both thought!

"You had had that premonition on the train that nothing good awaited us here. Your intuition was right. It's a good thing we are leaving now, that our train is waiting for us. This city is interesting for sure! But, there is this current of suspicion, some kind if intrigue going on here, maybe even danger? It's time to get home!" emphasized Felipe.

The depot they now saw through the taxi's windshield. The cab came to a stop, the driver hopped out and assisted unloading their bags, and a package with string tied around it for carrying with a fashioned loop to slip some fingers through. A porter was soon there to assist them inside. Felipe paid their fare and they were on their way inside to board their train home.

The depot loomed ahead, visible through the cab's windshield. The driver came to a stop and helped them with their luggage when a porter appeared. The fare was paid and they followd the porter into the station.Thoughts of home now replaced what they were leaving.

Chapter 15

"Homeward Bound, Home at Last"

The new ceramic cookie jar had been packed well inside a cushioned box for the travel home. The large jar was fashioned in the form of a monk, having an apprehensive grin on his face and an eager hand reaching for the lid, with a caption saying, *Thou shall not steal!* It was humorous, something that Felipe had yet –seen. Elisabeth knew it would please him. He now had the box resting securely underneath the seat he occupied on the train they had boarded that morning. Elisabeth had only said that it was something for the kitchen. Little did he know of the grinning, sheepish monk underneath his seat; well packed inside the box. Schreiter! The German Nazis! The Spanish Falangists! Even the corruption within the Church! The Sinarquistas! They all played upon his imagination more than any curiosity for the package. The kitchen was his mother's domain anyway. Then too there were the strange break-ins and the phantom-like police that whisked away the perpetrators! Where were they? Mysteries compounding mysteries! Felipe and Elisabeth sought the temporary solace of being home; temporary for they were bound to be caught up again with all the strangeness. Elisabeth intruded into his world.

"I really wish I knew more about those police officers, what they did to those young men! Where did they vanish?" Each passing kilometer was putting distance between them with what lay behind them. But still, her mind was jostling thoughts of what had occurred.

Just over an hour into the journey home she stared out the window at the passing landscape of rolling green hills spotted by farms and open fields She thought of how she and Rodolfo had been to Guanajuato many years before, how they enjoyed it then. It still had its historic charm, nestled below in a narrow, elongated cut between towering hills on either side. The subterranean tunnels traversing beneath the city imparted a mystique of sorts, making it unique. It was a serene setting but had a turbulent past and nowadays, socially, there was a current of turbulence generated by the outside influences of the Nazis and how they conducted business through Franco's Spanish Fascists. They had weaseled themselves into the social unrest of the country, especially in Guanajuato and Queretaro. With the leading of Professor Schreiter the movement had organized, became the Union Nacional Sinarquista. Its purpose was simple, carry on the Cristero War, *La Cristiada,* and oppose Mexican and Continental Democracies. Members were recruited through efforts of Schreiter. Their organization had been named and was continuously educated by Nazi agents, and these agents in turn directed the Sinarquistas through the Spanish Falangists present. Mexican Sinarquistas, like those in some other countries, were under the directives of Hitler whether or not it was known.

"Hard to say," answered Felipe while he studied a lone man seated mid-car. "I wonder if that sergeant did any inquiries." He continued to stare at the man. "Well, that's behind us. Let's just leave all of that back there. We're going home. Let's concentrate on where we are going, not where we have been." It was a hypocritical exhortation for he had felt the same, a feeling that would not depart and leave him entirely at peace. He had uttered it with hopes of pacifying her. But, he too needed pacification, especially now with an added mystery, real or not, the stranger aboard the train just down the aisle from them.

Felipe continued to stare the way of the distant stranger. It surely seemed to him he had seen the middle-aged man before; but where? He was dressed in a gray suit, one that had needed pressing, and the hat he wore was pulled slightly forward. A vendor strolled the aisle selling peanuts and snacks, stopped by the stranger when he was hailed. Felipe saw the two talking and the stranger accepting a bag of peanuts. As the vendor approached

Felipe he asked the salesman about the stranger.

"Excuse me. That man up there in the gray suit, did he speak with an accent?"

"He's a gachupin, probably from Madrid," answered the vendor.

"Thank you," responded Felipe. A Spaniard? One of Franco's Falangists? Was he trailing him and Elisabeth? The man's face now was buried behind a newspaper. Was he actually reading the newsprint or was he seeking to be undiscovered? Felipe stared intently his way, as if he could bore a hole right through the paper. Spaniard! There had been those, as Juan had observed at the meeting that had been huddled about Schreiter before the professor spoke. Perhaps this man was one of them?

He felt unsettled. Felipe did not wish to alert his mother, said nothing of the stranger. Besides, they should enjoy the ride home; have no lingering concerns to trouble them.

The stranger now set the paper down and rose up, walked Felipe's way. He swayed from side to side down the aisle reflecting the movements of the train. Felipe anticipated something as the man neared him. But, nothing transpired. The man passed him by and exited the car. About 20 minutes later he had returned taking his seat once more, and resumed reading the paper.

"I know that man! Surely I do," muttered Felipe to himself. He was vexed that he could not place the man. He retraced in mind his steps, from Ciudad Juarez to Guanajuato, to their duration at the Posada San Felipe, to the Schreiter meeting, even Frau Schmidt and Ernesto, all the while trying to identify the man. All was in vain. But still, the feeling persisted he had seen the man before. All through the ride home Felipe kept an eye on the stranger, ready for any act from him.

The train rolled to a stop in Mexico City on schedule. The serpentine, iron horse huffed and puffed, fatigued, sighed relief with a jet of steam, as if saying finally glad to be home. Passengers were slow at first to rise up, stretch their sinews and begin to disembark. But, once they had there was a steady stream. Felipe and Elisabeth had stepped upon the depot landing and were now entering the depot, crossing the depot's floor for the exterior doors to the streets and a parked line of waiting taxis, their porter in tow.

"I'll summon one of the cabs," Felipe told Elisabeth. Soon they were commencing their ride home in one, the driver one of non-stop chatter, his way of welcome home. As they drove away Felipe noticed through his side window the same mystery man waiting for his own ride. *Well, adios to you whoever you are,* thought Felipe. He was glad to be leaving the mystery man behind, just as they had the other mysteries in Guanajuato. Strange, he thought. Perhaps he was one of those Spaniards with Professors Schreiter and Bueno at the Sinarquista meeting back in Guanajuato.

Horacio met them in the entry hallway, underneath the chandelier as they entered. "You were away longer than I thought," he said in greeting. "Was it a good journey?"

"Interesting," injected Elisabeth. "Educational, but troubling also. It seems the more one learns of things the more troubles can arise because of what is learned."

Horacio's face said it all, 'what does that mean?'

"We'll explain later," said Felipe. "Let us get settled first. Then we'll be in to see you, have something to eat. Peanuts and tortas go just so far on the train." He began to walk away for his room, completely oblivious of the box he still held in hand. He suddenly halted and turned, held the box out for Horacio.

"I almost forgot. Here. Open this. There's something inside for the kitchen. Set it on the kitchen counter." Horacio took the box and then parted for his way.

Horacio held the package by the loop of henequen string, which wrapped about the four sides.

He now held the box out away from him, as if it was suspect. Inside the kitchen he placed it on the counter. "Now, let's see what this is. He cut the strings, opened the box and drew out the jar. At first glimpse of the comedic, ceramic monk he burst into laughter. "Ah ha, Felipe," he thought aloud. "That is you! I guess we need to have this new cookie jar filled all the time so you can help yourself whenever." He began to fill it from the older, worn and chipped jar, one that they had had since Felipe was a child.

They were now gathered about the dining table, as they had done since they had all lived together under this same roof. Occasions around the dining table served a purpose; not only for eating, but was for sharing and debating life itself. It is where Felipe had challenged his mother, and she had taken him up on it. By doing so Elisabeth had matured in her thinking, had become more aware of how the world at large was now infringing upon Mexico's sovereignty. It unnerved her. The wars raging around the world were being felt at home in her neutral country, and it worried her how her country would further react, besides the internments.

"Did you find that lady up in Ciudad Juarez?" asked Horacio of Felipe.

"Indeed! Quite a remarkable person! She has suffered losses that should never have been, and still she is able to think of others. I think Señor Yamashita will value the letter of hers we brought back. I intend to go to the stadium tomorrow, see Commandant Valenzuela and see Haru and his children again."

"Elisabeth, how did you view your experiences?" asked Horacio. "Was it worth your while?"

She did not readily answer, but did raise her hand in circles above her head, looking around the dining room, envsioning beyond also.

"I must say, I left the comforts of all of this," she replied looking about the room and environs. "I felt well enough, secure in my own world I suppose. Seeing others who are not so blessed was really eye opening.. I went with the understanding our government was doing what is best. But, I must say seeing that man's wife up there, I now have doubts that President Camacho has done right, incarcerating those unfortunate people. What I saw, they are upstanding citizens, well respected by most or all others in their communities. I think it a travesty!"

"Why were you late in coming home? You should have been here two days ago," asked Horacio.

"We stopped in Guanajuato for a couple of days to satisfy my curiosity. Something I learned in Juarez told me I should see for myself if it was true. It is!" replied Felipe.

"What is that?" inquired Horacio of Felipe. Felipe replied,

"That this organization of Sinarquistas is really being spurred on by German Nazis and Spanish fascists. Hitler and Franco are active in Mexico! I never knew that for fact. Now I do. Even mother here is beginning to see that!" Felipe looked her way.

"True!" Elisabeth replied. "Too many questionable people are up there. For some reason they took an interest in us, and I don't mean a friendly one! We left Guanajuato at a good time. But, we are back now, a bit more knowledgeable and hopefully wiser."

"Oh, Felipe, your friend Magaly from the university has been asking about you. She actually seemed worried since you did not return on schedule. You might let her know you are home," suggested Horacio.

He had certainly thought of her while he was away, especially in Ciudad Juarez at Rocio Yamashita's while he and Rocio's friend Aurora enjoyed hot chocolate together. That brought to mind how he and Magaly had enjoyed the same with some churros after witnessing the debacle in the plaza, when the police broke up the Sinarquista meeting. He looked forward to seeing her again, relate to her how the trip had been.

"Magaly again?" said Elisabeth with an arched eyebrow of wonder. "You two spend more time together than ever. You just friends or is there something more we might know?"

Felipe skirted her question. "Our study group at Josefina's is a good venue for studies and sharing. Our trip up north to the border intrigued her. I bet she would have liked going herself. I'll see her later and tell her all about it."

"Academics, or studying one another?" mused Elisabeth in a tease.

"Tell me. How it was meeting that man's wife up in Juarez?" inquired Horacio. "How did you find her, in a bad way?"

"Quite an amazing person really," exclaimed Elisabeth. "She had been dealt a terrible injustice, as they all have. I had believed that our president wouldn't have done what he did without good reason. He must have known something that threatens us in order to justify singling out these Mexican citizens. They haven't even done this in the United States, and they are at war with Japan. We aren't! Were there valid reasons to incarcerate all of those people just because of their race? Or, was it fear overreacting?"

"Rodolfo and I saw what fear can do during the Revolution. But, that was a civil war. We Mexicans sought to kill one another. Some will argue for good reasons, and others will find fault in everything. These days things are different. There is another kind of fear now, a fear of people from the other side of the world using Mexico as a staging ground for their plans of world dominance. Perhaps, indeed, President Camacho was aware of things, saw the need to put these unfortunate people in compounds to keep an eye on them. Everyday people like you and I will never know." Horacio then looked to Felipe, subduing a chuckle.

"For your information, there is a monk ready and waiting for you in the kitchen. Whenever you wish to make his acquaintance he is ready to receive you. Quite the sweet fellow, really." Felipe's look was of surprise. Really? A monk? Elisabeth stifled a laugh but her eyes twinkled. Felipe dismissed it all.

"Mother, after I see Yamashita tomorrow I plan to see Professor Arellano, ask him about dinner, see if he has any interest. Also, tomorrow night the study group meets at Josefina's. I need to get back into the routine of studies. I'll probably see Magaly there and tell her about our experiences. I'll probably be getting in sort of late. It will be a full day."

"Thank you for saying so. You know, I wish that Commandant Valenzuela was not such an ogre. As long as an old man as he is can still put on a uniform and follow orders without question that they'll find something for him to do. I suppose he feels important at that futbol stadium. He has his own fears, that of obsolescence. I have faulted him for banning me from going with you. But, the more I consider him the more tolerant I guess I have become. I won't be with you tomorrow. How I wish I could be there and hand Rocio's letter to him! Well, what is... is what is. When you come in tomorrow night if I am still up I will be eager to hear what you have to say of your day!" She valued her sleep but that could wait if Felipe had much to talk about.

"If Doctor Arellano agrees to come, and if Magaly has a mind to, invite her also. Knowing something of her studies at the university would convince me she would find the discussions of great value. The five of us sitting around a table asking questions, sharing answers and opinions could be most enlightening!" further encouraged Elisabeth.

"Rocio's friend Aurora, your remember her? She and I were having some hot chocolate when you came into the store. She is really an interesting person. Her family history stems from Sinaloa, from a fishing village not far from Mazatlan. She told me that when she was still living there that they had heard rumors of how the Japanese had been for years trying to establish fisheries, even a cannery on the Pacific side of Baja California. Maybe there is more to that than just rumor? Maybe it is more than fish today?"

Japan indeed had had a long-standing interest in Mexico's Baja peninsula. Early in 1908 several Japanese companies began efforts to invest in Baja California. Those many years ago a certain *Aurelio Sandoval* in Los Angeles, California led the *International Fisheries Company*. Mexico had granted him the exclusive rights to establish his fisheries up and down the peninsula. But, Sandoval lacked the capital to fund his grand schemes. It so happened that a Japanese professor from Tokyo's Imperial Fisheries Institute was on a world tour to promote the Japanese fishing industry. This tour took him to Los Angeles where he had met Sandoval. The Californian failed to court the representative from Japan to finance a large-scale operation on the Baja. Still, Sandoval was able to commence operations of a small lobster company on Santa Margarita Island in Magdalena Bay, on the Pacific side of the southern portion of the peninsula. Sandoval hired a Japanese fishing expert, who had been trained at the same *Imperial Fisheries Institute* that the professor represented, to manage the operations.

These initial years of Japan's interests in Mexico were perceived with concern in Washington D.C. There were speculations as to Japan's truer ambitions in Baja and throughout the Pacific. That year, 1908, the U.S. Navy sent its 'Great White Fleet" of sixteen battleships and escorts on a world tour as a show of strength. The fleet rounded South America and steamed north. Coming up the Pacific coast of Baja the fleet entered remote Magdalena Bay, a show to any present that the United States had to be reckoned with. In the following years Japan fashioned other desires. In 1912 they made vain efforts to purchase the Bay, having a desire to establish a naval base and an agricultural colony.

Now, it had become a question that spearheaded more conversation. Just how involved had Japan become in any form whatsoever on Mexico's Pacific coast? They bounced back and forth ideas and different scenarios, what if this, what if that. The monk had some of his own input. But, the hour came when they retired. Felipe knew he had a long day ahead of him. Elisabeth was glad to have her own bed again. She had tired of the clickety-clacks of the train's wheels on the rails. It was far better for her to be home and enjoy the rest. She bid them a good night.

For Horacio he too was happy they were home again. He did not care to be alone in such a large house. It was better to have them home to talk with. How he missed his dear friend Rodolfo! He too would be gone some day. Just now, however, he still felt he had some purpose to hang around a bit longer. But, sleep too was calling him and he retired.

For Felipe, he was yet - intrigued by some silent monk in the kitchen waiting to see him. Why did he not present himself? Before retiring he sauntered into the kitchen alone. He looked about and saw on the tiled countertop the jolly fellow with an impish grin reaching upward to get a cookie. He laughed aloud. "Mother!" "Is that how you see me? Excuse me my friend. But, I am going to get a cookie before you do." He helped himself to several, hurriedly placed the lid back on. "Sorry, amigo. You have to reach down, not up to get the prize!" Then he left.

The last conscious thoughts Felipe had that evening before falling asleep were of the morrow when he saw Haru. How would he take the news of his wife's miscarriage? Would it be more sorrow upon sorrow? Then the final thought was that of Professor Arellano. Would he come to dinner? Would he further enlighten them as to the realities of the day they were living in? Then seemingly moments later he wondered where the evening had gone, for he had awaken to the bright beam of a sun's ray intruding through a curtain, bathing his face in light. He lay there silent, thinking the day was at hand. It was time to rise up and meet it head on, embrace it.

Chapter 16

"Haru Yamashita and Dr. Arellano"

"You surprise me Señor Gurza," exclaimed the old, crusty Commandant Valenzuela. "After what, a week that you haven't been here, and now you've returned? Have you matured any? Where have you been, schoolboy? You here to see that same prisoner again?"

"That is my purpose, sir. I have come a long way to see him. I went to see his Mexican wife and to report to him how we found her." He reached inside his vest pocket and withdrew Rocío's letter to him, held it out for Valenzuela. "She wrote him how it is at home, all in Spanish. Remember, they all are Mexicans. I suppose you need to proof it first before I can hand it to him. And, she sent this wooden toy and doll for the children." Felipe handed him a small bag.

"Exactly!" He took the bag and examined it and the envelope too. He was more interested in the letter and scoured the print. Then he folded the letter once again and inserted it into the envelope, remained silent for a few minutes considering what she had written. "Seems innocent enough. More hardship has befallen them, with the loss of that baby. Here." He handed the letter back to Felipe. "I really have no empathy for those folks down in that compound. But, I must say this will rock that man even more. You best get it over with. Clock is ticking. Tell me, did you really go all the way up to the border just for that? That's a lot of trouble and for what? Nothing changes. You young people!" He shook his head in disbelief. "Idealistic, naïve, even stupid at times. But, you'll learn. Life over time is a stern teacher!"

Felipe dismissed the rude commentary. "I have brought him a pen and some paper, an envelope too, to answer her. May I give it to him? When I come again I can take his letter and let you approve it to be sent on to her."

"I have no problem with that," replied Valenzuela. "As you say, I must approve of whatever he writes her and she him."

Felipe thanked him and was met by two soldiers to escort him within the compound when the Commandant halted him with a question.

"How is that mother of yours?"

"Tired from the long trip. Even so she wanted to be here today," replied Felipe.

"Yes. I remember how that last meeting with her went and I forbade her to come here again. Maybe if she apologized I would let her return."

What, considered a humored Felipe? "I'll mention that when I see her tonight." Then he turned and joined his escort.

He found Haru sitting on one of the crates, whittling on a piece of wood some figurine. He had been working on it for sometime for there were whittlings about his feet. He was totally engrossed in the object as he rotated it in his hand, completely oblivious to Felipe's arrival. He raised his head and looked Felipe's way when he spoke.

"I see that horse figure is taking shape. You have talent, a good eye and hand coordination," commented Felipe. "You know how to rid the excess to reveal the hidden truth you hope to share."

Haru was startled, had a brief smile that faded. "Back again?" he asked. "It has been a while. I thought maybe you had changed your mind about coming to this place again."

"Not at all," replied Felipe. "It takes awhile to go up to Ciudad Juarez, and then come back. We did find your wife Rocio. Despite everything that has happened she is doing well, as well as can be hoped for. How about you and your children?"

"The same," replied Haru. "But tell me! How is my wife? Don't tell me what you think I want to hear! Tell me the truth!"

"She is coping, worried about you. She is an amazing woman!

Even with what has happened she still thinks of others." He leaned forward and inconspicuously told of how she had been helping those refugees that avoided being interned. "I have something for you and the children." He reached into the pocket and retrieved the letter. "She sent this to you. I am sorry it is opened. The Commandant had to approve it before I gave it to you." He handed it to Haru who eagerly accepted it. Rocio! The baby! "This is for your children." He handed the bag of gifts to Haru, and he set it on the ground as he read the letter.

Haru pored over her words and when he came to those that informed him of the loss of their child he winced, and tears welled up in his eyes. His jaws tightened. He gingerly folded the letter along its creases and replaced it inside the torn envelope. He stared at the ground about his feet, feeling wasted like the spent wooden chips about his feet.

"How about her? How is she doing? How is my wife's health?" asked a sorrowed Haru.

"You needn't worry my friend. She is doing well. She has plenty of support from your neighbors. They help around the store, help with the boxes, stocking the shelves, and even serve customers. It seems whatever Rocio needs the neighbors just know beforehand and help her. She doesn't need to ask for anything. I never saw any lack of customers either. People just want to make sure she is Okay through this ordeal. I have some paper and a pen for you. You can answer her if you wish. I'll be back in a couple of days and can take it with me to post. "Haru accepted the stationary. "What about you and your children?"

"The boredom is trying. But, we've heard from some of the guards, who really haven't been that bad at all, that we may be moved soon to some sort of labor camp. It's best to get some productivity out of us, free labor. The government should like a free labor force. The people outside of here wouldn't. We'd put some out of work. The children? That is a real concern of us all!"

Felipe knew that he could not frequent the camp as often as he wanted. He had is studies to resume, his thesis to complete. He had his own life to live. There was Magaly, someone he wanted more time with. The Sinarquista movement and the intrusions of

Nazis, Fascists, and perhaps the Japanese were concerns that dogged him. He looked upon Haru, wondering how to respond to him.

"Perhaps the government may seek to school them while older children and adults are put to work, doing something, whatever," offered Felipe. "Just a guess!"

"I had similar thoughts," replied Haru. "I cannot imagine them being put to forced labor!"

"I was talking to your neighbor Aurora, about her family roots in Sinaloa. She told me of how Japan has had years of interest in the Baja Peninsula, mainly the fishing industry but also agricultural.

Did you know about this?"

"Oh, my folks would say something about that from time to time, make comments about the Imperial Fisheries Institute in Japan. They never seemed to think anything would ever come of it being Japan was so far away. But, whatever might have come of that I understand there are Japanese migrants who have settled in fishing hamlets on the Pacific coast. I have no idea if they are still connected to Japan in any way. I always thought that they were in Mexico to make a life for theirselves not contribute to Japan in any way. Why do you ask?"

"I'm not implying anything," replied Felipe. "I want to make that clear! I am not casting suspicion your way! I have been trying to make sense out of President Camacho's actions against you. I must tell you something! On this trip we were rudely awakened to what is happening in Mexico. The German Nazis and the Spanish Fascists are here, seeking to cause trouble for us, and the Americans. And, since Japan is allied with Germany in this war against the Democracies, if Japan has any foothold on the Pacific Coast then their military may embark upon some adventures against their enemy, the United States. I have wondered if the president knows more about what Japan is up to, what their emissaries and agents in Mexico are doing. By incarcerating you Japanese-Mexicans he may be thinking that there will not be some racial bond that still esists, that this will prevent any assistance for the Japanese Empire on Mexican soil. At least that has been some considerations of mine. It doesn't excuse the injustice heaped upon you. But, it may give rise to understanding why it happened."

Haru said not a word, just thought in depth what Felipe had said, feeling a wave of shame of his heritage. He dropped his small knife and the wooden horse he had been carving, wrung his hands in despair. "That is a logical thing to think. But, why not do something about the Germans and Spanish too in Mexico? Why fear one more than the others?"

"That is THE question!" emphasized Felipe. "I have no answer. I cannot even speculate." He paused in thought and then said, "I will not be coming as frequent as I have. I'll be here in two days of course. I need to know if, when, and where you will be moved. Meanwhile, I have responsibilities at the university and must devote myself to my thesis. But, I shall try to see you each week for sure. I just don't know how often."

"I understand," responded Haru. "You have a life apart from all of this. You have done so much. Rocio and I are forever grateful. It's just too difficult to express gratitude now."

"I fully understand. My mother and I never expected anything from you. We did what needed to be done and we shall do more as we can. I just wanted you to know not to expect me every other day. Please know that just because I do not come as often it is not because I have stopped thinking about you. Not at all! There are just some things I must attend to. I will be here though in two days. Have that letter ready and I'll get it posted. Just be careful what you say in it or the Commandant will not allow it to be posted if you write anthing controversial."

Haru acknowledged that as the soldiers beckoned Felipe it was time to leave. He said in parting, "I never saw your children. I hope they are fine."

Haru called out, "They are several tents down that way playing some games with others. Thank you for bringing these things for them. I'll have them here when you return so you can see them again. Please give my regards to your mother. She's an impressive person!"

Felipe nodded with an affirmation and then was escorted away from the compound. He departed the stadium and made way for the university, and with any luck would find Professor Arellano open for a brief visit.

Professor Enrique Arellano, a man of average heighth and a rotund belly, was cleaning a blackboard of chalk drawings. The white powder had dusted his person and sleeved arms, even dusting his rosey cheeks. The hour was in between classes and Felipe entered the classroom.

"Doctor Arellano, may I have a word with you?" he asked.

The doctor turned and recognized Felipe. "Ah ha! So it is Felipe Gurza, one of my proteges! Yes, by all means come in! I was just cleaning up some, getting ready for the next class. Come in and tell me how life is for you." He set his chalk down, and wiped his hands on a towel before swiping the white dust from his sleeves. "Well, perhaps chalk dust should have been black. Black clouds of dust would be more appropriate these days for how the world is now, full of bolts of lightning and thunder! Tell me, what do you wish to see me about?"

"Does there need to be a reason just to stop and see a respected friend?"

"One thing I have learned in life, especially here at this university, is that people often have multiple motives, whether stranger, acquaintance, or friend. I am not suggesting anything negative pertaining to you my dear friend. It's just that it has been a long time. I do not think you came here just to chat. What is it that you really want?"

"My mother and I were up to the border, Ciudad Juarez to be specific. Then on our way home we stopped at Guanajuato for a while. What we experienced was quite troubling, even had a hint of danger. Mother suggested we invite you to our residence for dinner and talk about it all. We would like to get your impressions, hear what you know. We do hope you will come. We would value your views and would share what knowledge you have."

"Chihuahua, Guanajuato? Those are states most intriguing. Of course up that way there has always been a history of unrest. Tell me, what inspired you to make that journey?"

"A long story, really," answered Felipe. "We could discuss it more in detail after a worthy dinner. I will say this, that it has not that much to do with history, but certainly does with current affairs. This world war raging now certainly is tugging at us too. What we observed up there, what happened to us, all indicates that Mexico in one way or another cannot escape destiny. There are too many outside interests ruffling the feathers of our Mexican eagle."

"Among my colleagues we have exchanges, talk about the present political turmoil, the various factions of rebellion, and labor unrest in the country. We find it a wary time to be living in, wondering what next may befall us." Dinner, he thought! Oh my! How long had it been since he had had such an invite? His considerations now returned to the days with his wife, when they had a social life. But, since her demise he had withdrawn, devoted himself to the university and students. In its own way it compensated him for his loss, helping him to focus on life outwardly and service unto others, rather than being self-absorbed in grief and sorrow. "Most gracious offer. Thank you. Now, I really do not know what is more intriguing, what the meal will be or what you have just told me. But, yes, I would be pleased to come. Thank you."

It was agreed to the day and hour of the dinner. Felipe offered him tidbits of what they hoped to discuss with him, reminisced the days when Felipe was in his classroom. Even in Felipe's young adult life he had a sense of nostalgia for those days. They visited until the next class was minutes away from starting, when the first students would begin sauntering in. They bid good day to each other and Felipe headed to the library to finally do research into his thesis project. He knew it was a laborious task to grapple with. It was difficult to coral his rambunctious mind, to focus on his studies. Intrusive thoughts kept derailing him, those of Juarez, the Yamashitas, Guanajuato, Schreiter, Spanish falangists, and the Sinarquistas. What good was coming out of that university up there? What was fomenting in the classrooms and hallways, in private gatherings, to spew out into the general public, perhaps even the country at large?

He sat at a table with several opened books about his note pad, poring over each book, jotting down notations. A gentle tap on his shoulder drew him out of his inner world, only to see Magaly standing alongside him.

"When did you finally return?" she asked him straightforwardly. "I've been wondering why I haven't seen or heard from you. I thought you were supposed to be home maybe two days ago."

"Magaly!" stammered a surprised Felipe. "I was going to look for you at the group study later at Josefina's. Well, whenever or wherever it is always good to be with you! Here" He pushed a chair her way. "Sit down for a while."

She sat alongside him, noticing something different about him, even if subtle. What was it up there at the border that affected him like that? "Tell me, what happened up there?"

He knew she was thinking of Juarez, not knowing of their time in Guanajuato, where his mind was now affixed. He set his pen down and spoke with her in a hushed tone within the library.

"Ciudad Juarez is not my kind of place. There are some interesting types of people there. But still, it is too far removed from what I would deem a meaningful life. We did find Yamashita's wife. She is a most extraordinary person! To meet her is to respect her, and that respect only magnifies when one considers the travesty just heaped upon her, the losses she has suffered. But, I must say, we stopped off at Guanajuato on the way home and what we encountered there really troubled us! Earlier today I was at Dr. Arellano's. I discussed things with him. He is coming to dinner and we shall discuss openly what we experienced up there and what he knows. It stands to be a most illuminating time. I do hope you will join us!" A library aid signaled to him to be quiet. He whispered the day and time and she heartily agreed.

"I'll come for you," insisted Felipe.

"I will be ready!" responded Magaly.

"Great! I am sorry," he apologized. "But, I need to delve into these books. I really need to get busy on this. But, see you tonight at Josefina's?"

"Of course!" Magaly stood up and just before she turned to leave planted a kiss on his cheek. "There! Something else to distract you!" She gave him one of her bewitching smiles and then strode across the library floor and outdoors. He watched her disappear from view, subconsciously felt his cheek while admiring her beauty. He too smiled, and once again picked up his pen to return to pressing demands.

Horacio and Elisabeth had always worked well together in the kitchen. Others, as they, would likely have hired help. For Elisabeth, she preferred to be a hands-on person, do things herself. Horacio was an extension of herself, and he was completely at ease following her lead. Creating a dinner for a special guest was a delight. First things first, the savory dishes upon the table, followed by some dessert. But, the true icing upon the cake would be their exchange of information post dinner in the parlor. They eagerly anticipated Doctor Arellano's commentaries. She and Horacio had prepared a fine meal and all was now in a ready state to serve when Horacio opened the main entry door to the professor. Elisabeth was present to greet him.

"Señora," greeted Dr. Arellano, removing his hat and slightly bowing his head as he entered the Gurza estate. "I feel quite honored to be invited. It has been a while since I have been out like this. I am very grateful."

"The pleasure is ours in having you here," responded Elisabeth. "1942 is just underway and we promised ourselves to reach out unto those we have valued but have seldom expressed so. You are number one!"

"Really? Such a double honor! Thank you again!" replied Arellano. Horacio took his coat and hat, took the items to the coatroom.

"The evening is cold. I feel winter more each passing year," lamented Arellano. "Whether it is colder or just me is a valid question to consider. I've lost some weight and I think my bones feel the cold more now since there is less flesh insulating them. But, as you can see, I still have ample cushioning." He chuckled, rubbing his rotund belly.

"This way please," motioned Elisabeth. She led him down the hallway to the parlor. In his gait the professor marveled at her residence and furnishings.

"I never knew Rodolfo that well," he recalled of her deceased husband. "But, one thing I do know, out of the ashes of that

Revolution he came with an appreciation of the arts. I see that you and he graced your home with some fine pieces."

Elisabeth did a quick survey of the parlor, recalling the various pieces they had bought together, even some being gifts from appreciative peoples from various walks of life, but most came with inherited estate.

"Yes, we did work well together furnishing this place. We actually owe it all to a certain Englishman we once knew many years ago. He was a very grateful man, thankful that Rodolfo had saved his life those many years ago. As far as the artwork goes, we learned to invest at one piece at a time, even resold after the values appreciated. Then we'd reinvest in other purchases. After a while I said enough is enough. That is especially true after Rodolfo died. My zeal for any continuance died also." She did a fast sweep with her eyes of the room, taking in the views of items that she had grown so used to over the years and seemingly had lost their glitter of appeal.

"My son Felipe should be here shortly. He went to see his friend Magaly Bedoya. I believe you know of her. She will be coming with him"

"Magaly! But of course! Such a bright and inquisitive mind!" replied the professor. "It shall be a pleasure to see her again. We need more bright ladies like her, and they are around, just lack means and opportunity. Too many, though, think it is more important putting a baby in the belly than substance in their pretty heads!"

Elisabeth and Arellano were enjoying a glass of Jerez sherry when Horacio interrupted them in the parlor with Felipe and Magaly.

"Hello. We finally made it!" said Felipe. "There's some sort of labor demonstration affecting traffic. It took some time to get through all of that. But, we are here!"

"Glad you came, Magaly. Of course you know Dr. Arellano here," said Elisabeth, introducing the professor.

"Quite so!" responded a smiling Magaly. "It has been a while. But, nothing could dim the memory of your classes! I'm pleased to be in your company once more."

"It was so special to have you in my class! Your academic zeal made me a better teacher! You kept me on my toes. I looked forward to you in class. It certainly is a pleasure to see you again. You are marvelous as always!" he exclaimed, eying her striking beauty and charm, marveling her wit too.

The five of them visited in the parlor for a while, enjoying the sherry. "Some like a little sherry before a meal, some after," commented Arellano. He turned the crystal glass in his hand marveling at the color and bouquet. "I for one would enjoy this whenever, wherever!" He semi- raised his glass in a salute to them all as he downed the last drop.

Elisabeth then encouraged everyone to the dining hall. There was no pre-determined seating for anyone at the table. There were no formalities. They sat at will around the large hardwood table finely dressed for the occasion. Horacio took delight in ferrying the preparations in the kitchen to the table. But, Magaly believed he could use some assistance and she rose up and helped him. They all openly conversed in between bites of food and sips of drink for the better space of an hour. When they all had their fill Elisabeth said,

"Perhaps we should retire to the parlor. We do have some things to discuss in there."

They began to stand up and push away from the table when the professor spoke. "I must say señora, that was a marvelous meal! It has been a long time since I have enjoyed such fare, and in fine company too."

Elisabeth smiled an acknowledgement and escorted them to the parlor. Inside the parlor they all took a seat, some in chairs and some on a sofa, the guests anticipating something. Felipe took the lead.

"This whole business of how our president rounded up our citizens of Japanese ancestry and interned them in camps, which are basically hastily improvised prisons, really troubled me, my mother also. I was aware of how a trainload of these prisoners had arrived here and they set them up in the middle of a futbol stadium. At first I did not know where they came from. Later I found out they came from Ciudad Juarez and parts of Chihuahua, anywhere near the American border. I went to see the camp commandant and he gave me permission to browse through the compound, and interview anyone I chose if they were willing to talk. I met this one man, well spoken, no hint of a Japanese accent. He spoke Spanish flawlessly. We befriended each other. Granted, he was hesitant at first. But we did connect. This led my mother and I to go up to Juarez and confer with his Mexican wife, tell her that her husband and children are fine. That was not totally true of course. But, we thought they needed to know how each was doing, that no one was in immediate harm. That experience was quite illuminating, just how grievous Camacho's act was! The thing that troubled us more than anything else was our stopover in Guanajuato." He looked directly at Dr. Arellano. "We encountered German Nazis and Spanish Falangists there, stirring up a fervor within the radical group of Sinarquistas. This Mexican terrorist union is being fed a diet of lies and deceit by these Europeans. There can be dire consequences if Mexico plays the part of an ostrich, hides from the truth." He poured himself a little more sherry. "There is a German influence in the University of Guanajuato. To what extent I do not know. But, a certain Professor Schreiter is a dangerous man, spouting how the Nazis want the best for Mexico and then backs away a bit and lets Spain carry out their directives. For some reason the Nazi thought must be that it is easier to achieve their goals through Franco, a Spanish speaking Catholic country as Mexico is." He looked for some facial expressions he could read of the professor. There were none.

"I attended a Sinarquista meeting when I was told Professor Schreiter would be speaking. I went in the company of some others, one ardent supporter of the Nazis 'for' Mexico and another totally opposed to them as I am. It was alarming to see at that meeting the stranglehold the Germans and Spanish have over that Mexican union of conservative malcontents, their would-be recruits. I can see the whole purpose is not for any good." He sipped some sherry to moisten his lips.

"At the hotel we lodged at there was a suspicious German woman and then our rooms were broken into. Misterious policemen showed up to arrest and take away those guys. But, there is no record of such policemen or of any arrests. Even on the train home I felt someone was following us. It could have been my imagination. I just don't know." He stepped backwards a few steps and picked up the scroll that Juan and Carlos had given him. He held it out. "This scroll was given to us by some very concerned students from that university. It depicts what they know and strongly suspect what is happening in that world of Nazi and Spanish collaborators, what their intents are for being in Mexico." He moved some items off a desktop and unrolled the scroll, anchoring each corner with an ashtray here, a paper- weight there. The others rose up and gathered around Felipe and the scroll to see firsthand what he was introducing.

Doctor Arellano stood beside Felipe, his arms folded, in deep thought of what Felipe was saying and explaining, observing how Felipe with his index finger was pointing out how the flow of German funds had supported the Sinarquistas. He leaned forward, placed his elbow on the desktop and cradled his chin in his palms, scrutinizing the scroll as Felipe concluded his presentation.

"We invited Dr. Arellano to come, not just to enjoy his persona, but to hear any commentary he would like to make about all of this. We value his opinions." He looked to his side at the professor, offering the opportunity to him.

"Thank you," responded Arellano, risng up from his survey. He stood silent for a few moments, yet - considering the scroll, in deep thought. "Yes, I have some things I can share with you. But, the first thing I must say is that everthing you have just said is most interesting! It just goes to show, casts further light upon what is happening from Queretaro to the border, but also in places like San Luis Potosi and Zacatecas, and dare I say on the Baja also. It adds to any insight I have had, and now has even educated you! I have a colleague at the University of Guanajuato who writes informative letters to me of what is happening there. He has told me about this German, Oscar Helmuth Schreiter, Professor of Modern Languages, and another named Otto Gilbert, and even some other questionable people. But mainly, he says that Manuel Torres Bueno, Professor of Philosophy, is apparently his closest associate. He's observed them spending a lot of time together and has wondered if it is more than just school life. What has concerned my friend, Doctor Hernandez, is that they and the radical group Sinarquistas are joined at the hip. Outside of the classroom Bueno is the national director of the Union Sinarquista. The first one, Salvador Abascal, had quit last year and disappeared somewhere. Hernandez thinks he possibly went to the Baja to establish a Sinarquista-Jesuit colony in that remote area." He slightly rocked back and forth on his heels, rubbing his chin, staring down at the scroll but not necessarily looking at it. His thoughts were racing.

"Does Hernandez say if there are any more staff at the university that are suspect?" asked Felipe.

"No. But he gets perturbed when he overhears students talking about things that have nothing to do with academic studies. Clearly, Schreiter and Bueno have greater aims outside the classroom, to politically educate the naïve and gullible youth in ways that should never be! All of that nasty business starts in their classrooms; where they subtly inspire and recruit the unsuspecting to follow them beyond. Indeed Schreiter is from Germany. He got his appointment at the school through the influences of that Ibero-American Institute in Berlin, and of course most likely continues to receive his orders from there, and money too I suppose, like that scroll suggests. You and I know that is where the maniac Hitler is. What comes from that institute comes from that lunatic dictator, a demon from hell!"

"Yes, I am seeing how these German agents have weaseled their way into our culture, and very subtly I might add," commented Felipe. "But, what about Franco in Spain? Why are the Spanish fascists, these falangists, here also? I should think they would be more interested in rebuilding their own country after that insane civil war of theirs, rather than trying to fashion something similar here!"

"No surprise there!" commented Arellano. "Spain and Italy are similar. Mussolini wants to resurrect a new Roman Empire, and Franco wants to do the same with Spain's so-called glorious past of conquest. Spain wants Mexico back, part of a resurrected Spanish Empire, with they and the Catholic Church in charge. First things first though! They seek to do so with groups like the Sinarquistas. This is not a case of conquering by military invasion! No! They hope to do this through subversion, divide and conquer by pulling strings they have subtly attached to those they have duped, and the ones who are pulling the strings of all, even those controlling the Spaniards? Nazi Germany of course. It's a *you scratch my back I'll scratch yours* world for them. I don't know if the Spaniards know the Germans are using them or not. Even if they do, if Franco feels that he and Spain are getting what they want then they don't care. Their goals are to topple the secular government of President Camacho, reestablish the controls of the Catholic Church, and Berlin surely hopes this succeeds, to disrupt things in Mexico so much that it draws in the United States and the Americans will not get involved with the war in Europe, will be consumed about their *Monroe Doctrine* being violated. The real tragedy here for us is that these home groups like the Sinarquista fools are playing into the hands of bigger interests beyond Mexico's borders. I think, and mind you this is only my opinion, that currently the Sinarquistas pose only a regional problem, not a national threat, eventhough the Nazis and their duped Spanish Falangists have them slated for bigger things. Dr.Hernandez warned me about how Spanish military officers have set up secretive paramilitary units within the Sinarquista Union, drilling select members with German military overseeing things, training with weapons like they were part of the German army, that these secret groups are always active, go on cross-country hikes supervised by these military veterans. They masquerade themselves as hunting and marching clubs. The ultimate aim is to carry out sabortage missions in Mexico and the United States. We have heard they have been behind the killings of hundreds of people in the states of Queretaro and Guanajuato. Their movement so far is concentrated in the north, and now maybe on the Baja peninsula. The greater concern about them is for their attempts to establish their own colony on the Pacific coast of Baja, and knowing Japan's interest over the years of that area, and how the Sinarquistas favor the Axis Powers, that they may lend assistance to any Japanese adventures on Mexican soil. I am quite sure that Roosevelt and the Americans and our own government are quite aware of this. Even here I have discussed this possibility with some of my colleagues in between classes. We have even heard through sources that the Japanese have secret naval bases for submarines on our coast. We are not aware of any proof. But, you know, *where there is smoke there is often fire!* Just that you know, I mean all of you," he looked at each one, "this is not only about the Nazis, the Spanish fascists, the Sinarquistas! You can be quite sure that the Japanese are here too, somewhere in the country doing their wiles! It could be that American naval interests and fuel depots in Southern California are targets for them. The Panama Canal would be a prize! It could be their legation here in the capital is up to something. But, my intuition is that any Japanese involvement is not with Japanese Mexicans, but of their own doing, in league with the Nazis. It is beyond my comprehension how the racist Aryans and the racist Japanese could ever be allied. But, they are! I believe any overt acts of the Japanese would be up north and on the west coast. What a golden opportunity for them to masquerade any clandestine operation under the cloak of their fishing industries on the Baja peninsula. After Pearl Harbor they must be looking for another grand victory. You can be sure of one thing that they are certainly meddling somewhere! My friends, if you come across any information of an American named, Van Zandt, consider it! Rumors have it that he knows for sure of Japanese submarines off our coast. Rumors say Magdalena Bay, west coast of Baja. I don't know more than that."

There was a pause. Everyone was absorbing his words. The only sounds came from the ticking of a wall clock, and when it chimed it jarred them 'awake'.

"That is quite disturbing, professor," uttered Elisabeth. "Do you suppose President Camacho knows any of this?"

"Indeed I do!" replied Arellano. "The university has made him aware of what we know and of our concerns, and I am sure his own intelligence people have kept him informed. You mentioned the Japanese-Mexican internments. Believe me! Knowing the President as we do I am sure he knows much more than we and this had compelled him to act as he had. Herein lies another tragedy. Many of those people, perhaps even all, are totally innocent, and they have suffered much in vain and continue to do so. They are of the wrong ethnicity, at the wrong place, at the wrong time, scapegoats! It's just one of the unjust things in life, that there are always victims of the masses. I am not excusing what has been done. I am just standing apart from it all as well as I can, analyzing, clarifying in my own mind how the absurd is qualified. "Again a silence ensued, time to measure the content of what he had said.

The professor turned and looked upon the scroll again. "That says a lot but not all! Those university students are no fools! But, they should be aware of Baja also! Look here!" he pointed with his finger. "Directives and funds come from Berlin through the German legation here in Mexico City. Then those funds have been distributed to the German community in the city. They in turn send the funds to Schreiter in Guanajuato. He then uses those funds to support the Sinarquistas. At least that is the way it has been and perhaps continues." He began to have a sense of being a detriment. "I apologize to everyone for all of this. Such things can overshadow a fine meal and company. I beg your pardon."

"Not at all, professor," jumped in Elisabeth. "This was our main purpose to have you here, to have you educate us to reality. We have had gut feelings of what is. What we needed was true input of what truly is, not just suppositions. The question I suppose for all of us is, what should we do? What can we do? Sometimes in life there are things just too big to grapple with. This seems like one of those times."

"I have no definitive answer to that," said Arellano. "We in academia study the past, learn from the present, and share with others, hoping that good comes from it all. When we do, we can only hope that shared knowledge will be used by those in positions of power wisely and that the nation will persevere and even thrive. Mexico seems to be at another crossroads now. These days carry much apprehension. Sometimes I think knowing too much is a curse. Knowledge can be a burden, robs one of peace. 1942 has just begun, really, and I feel that before summer Mexico will be engaged somehow in this world war. Don't ask me how or when! It is just a premonition I have. It unsettles me!"

His premonition unsettled them also. Was his anxiety now

becoming theirs also? Yes, perhaps the billowing chalk dust upon the professor's person should have been black, symbolic of the black clouds looming over their land.

Felipe was further ill at ease since the professor had emphasized the possible dangers on the Baja penisula. Who was this Van Zandt? What did he know? How could he learn more?

"How can I learn more about this American Van Zandt?" asked Felipe.

"If you wish, come see me," replied Dr. Arellano." I hope you do. I have some reads for you. They will make you more aware of things, and in so doing will make you more nervous. Just remember, the more you learn the more you are robbed of peace. I have nights I don't sleep that well. I don't wish that on any one. It seems only the naïve and ignorant can sleep these days. But, come see me if you want to know more. I'm always available, my dear boy! Especially for you." Looking around the room he added, "Any of you are most welcome!"

Felipe nodded, said he would. Submarines? Mexico? That truly troubled him in view of Pearl Harbor. What could they be planning now? It was just another burden to worry about, but something that had to be concerned with. The Germans, Spanish, and Japanese all up to mischief in Mexico, and all the while the Sinarquistas playing their foolish puppet. Idiots!

Chapter 17

"Rufus Van Zandt"

Just prior the bombing of Pearl Harbor on December 7th, 1941 Japanese submarines had lain undetected submerged in Baja California's Magadalena Bay. At night they would surface to recharge their batteries, take on fresh air. One particular night some vagabond Mexicans saw a sub on the surface and promptly reported it in La Paz. As rapidly as it could be done the US navy was alerted.

Rufus Van Zandt had been a Texas Ranger with an impressive record. He had left the service and when the War began was courted to be an undercover agent for the Special Intelligence Service.

"Mr. Van Zandt," greeted the Bureau's Chief. "We'd like for you to work for us, do your country a great service to boot! We know of your stellar record as a former Texas Ranger and believe you have what it takes to do what we are asking of you. All those years of conducting hunting and sports fishing tours on your free time to Mexico we feel you can put to good use for us now. You would not have to be concerned about money. The government would cover you. You know this war is a desperate thing! The Axis Powers are seeking world dominance. The Nazis have broader plans than just Europe and that part of the world. The Japanese, of course, demonstrated at Pearl Harbor how they want to kick us entirely out of the Pacific and have that side of the world all unto themselves. Both, we feel are up to no good in Mexico. They surely have set their sites on getting to us from there. This is why we hope you will be willing to conduct more of these adventurous tours of yours, even if by disguise, and while there keep your eyes open, snoop around to see if there are any indications they are there and what they are up to. Information that we have suggests your main focus should be on the Baja Peninsula, especially the Pacific coast side. We have heard reports of strange submarine activities down there. If true they are assuredly Japanese. Coming this far to our doorstep means only one thing, that they have intents to do us harm again, maybe as big as Pearl. What do you say? Would you be interested? This surely could be more adventuresome than your Ranger days!"

Rufus Van Zandt listened to the offer, was intrigued for sure. In a flash the former Ranger invisioned what life could be, a bolstered income and the thrill of being in the field again was appealing. His escorted tours were certainly on shakey ground since the war began for fear and economics were keeping many at home. Still, he figured he could make it work, could establish a network of informants who could pose as hunters and sportsfishermen. It had been suggested to him to focus on Baja's Pacific coast, enlist the help of fishing charters, people he had known.

"I believe I am your man," admitted Van Zandt. "How soon do you want me to go?"

"As soon as you can," replied the Chief. "We'll assist you from here on. We'll set things in order to get you going, tell you who and how to pass information on to, funds and such. Now, are you sure about this? We don't want you to have any regrets and bail on us! You must know this could be a dangerous assignment! It is not the same as chasing down outlaws. There are real bogeymen there. You'll be up against Germany and Japan, and maybe some others and they play for keeps. They kill without a flinch! This will be your baby, your project to gather as much information as you can and get it to us as soon as possible."

"I'm alright with all of this," he answered. "I'll leave within the week. I will make first contact with friends in Sonora, and then go on down to Mazatlan. I have friends there that run charters for marlins. I know some people too at Cabo San Lucas that will be of great help. I've got the people. I can get it done!" They shook hands to seal the verbal deal, formal documents and oaths followed. Van Zandt then bid them good day as he had preparations to make.

Rufus Van Zandt had crossed the border at El Paso and en route to Mazatlan stopped to see friends in a Yaqui village. They had assisted him on past hunts, and fishing trips off of Mazatlan. They were glad to see their old friend for it had been a while since they had been together. He explained that this time he was hunting and fishing for something else, information. He advised them that he was there this time to gather proof of clandestine activities of any Germans or Japanese, asked if they would assist him.

"Claro que si," assured the Yaqui spokeman. He voiced what past and present rumors had been, coming from across the Gulf of California and the Baja Peninsula. Rumors flourished from the Pacific side; was a wonder why because it was so desolate and remote. The latest one had to do with some people seeking to set up some sort of strange colony just north of Magdalena Bay.

"We've heard fishermen coming up into the Gulf make comments about seeing submarines on the Pacific side of Baja," continued the Yaqui. "Then again you know how those guys can talk; catch a minnow and say it's a whale! Be best to go for Cabo, ask the Ramirez brothers for some help." The Yaqui spokesperson then held his peace.

At the extreme south end of the Baja Peninsula lies Cabo San Lucas. Van Zandt and his small group of Yaquis appeared there, approached the Ramirez Charter Service. They found their friends inside a shack-of-an-office.

"Ignacio, Chema," greeted Rufus and his friends. Chema sat on a stool alongside a grimey window so thick with film the bright sunlight had difficulty shining through. Fishing tackle was strewn about the floor and up against the walls. At Chema's feet was a tabby cat feasting on bits of fish from the day's catch. Ignacio was intently focused on repairing the rings on one of the fishing poles.

"How can we be of help, amigo?" asked Chema, dropping another morsel for his feline friend.

"I must say, my friends, that all is not fishing and hunting in life, at least not the kind you know me for. Of course, I'd like to give that pole there a workout. But, I have bigger things on my mind this time. I am after information! I need to know if rumors are true, if Japanese or Germans are around here, up to no good. Rumors are rumors unless proven for real. You know, where there is smoke there is often fire. Think you can run us out, up the coast to look around? See if there are any signs of submarines we've heard about up at Magadalena bay?"

Ignacio looked up and down the fishing rod in hand, then out to them. "This pole has had some hard use." Ignacio Ramirez eyed the rod up and down. Satisfied, he set it down in the sand and rested it up against a wall.

"The marlins take a toll after a while." He faced Van Zandt. "Submarines? Yes, we've heard things like that. We haven't given it much thought though. It doesn't seem to matter that much anyway. If they come they also go. Doesn't matter that much to we fishermen. But, sure, if you want to go out we can early tomorrow before sunrise.

"Up the coast?" asked Rufus to confirm.

"Well, for us that is where the best catches are right now. For you, you can look for those subs. Tonight, though, you can stay in that cabin behind us," offered Ignacio. "It will be a bit crowded. But, it's just for the night. Japanese you say! Interesting! Pedro came back yesterday and said he thought he saw a submarine on the surface just as night fell. No telling whose it was of course, or if it was a sub even. It might have been a Jap sub. It would be no coincidence, I suppose. There are groups of Japanese that live around here, doing fishing like us, some canneries too, and any of these subs might pop up. I bet the Americans want to know this! Are you working for them now? Is that why you want information?"

"Ignacio, I can't say one way or another," replied a smiling Van Zandt. "The less you know the better."

"OK. There are different kinds of fishing, some with a pole, some with a net. So, you want to fish another way this time. No problem! Will have the poles out but we'll really be fishing for submarines. Meanwhile, come up to the house. We have some sopa de pescado. Have some fish soup and bread, some beer. We can talk more about tomorrow."

As the western sky's flames of red and orange faded into dusk and nightfall was about to claim them they lounged about with bowls of soup and bread, sitting outside on the ground about the house, cans of beer at their sides. The stars were out in force.

"What do you intend to do if we see a Japanese sub tomorrow?" asked Chema of Rufus.

"Act like we never saw them, and if I can I'll identify what class it is, what the apparent course is. Then, I'll just pass the information along and then let those higher-ups do what they do."

They got an early start as Ignacio had advised. That morning the sunrise was like last night's sunset. The swells of the seas reflected the bright colors of the fiery red sun as it rose over the eastern horizon. The poles had been put out, their lines cutting through the foaming wake behind the Ramirez's boat. They were nearing the mouth of Magdalena Bay when Ignacio shouted out that it was time to head back for fuel's sake. The trailing lines crossed as he swung the bow around for a southerly course.

"Look!" shouted one of the Yaquis. His sharp eye had detected something of interest, pointing its way. Chema followed his lead and raised his binoculars for a sweeping view. He suddenly halted. "Dios Mio!" he exclaimed, handing the glasses to Rufus. He looked in the same direction and froze just as Chema had. On an apparent course ahead of them was a periscope cutting through the gentle swells, leaving a frothy white wake. Rufus lowered the binoculars, stared that way. Rumors now seemed justified!

"Looks like she's headed for the Bay," commented Chema. "I can't figure why! There's not much there. Hardly anyone is there! It's a terrible place from what I've seen. I know after storms or before some trawlers will put in there for safety and repairs. It's such a desolate area. Maybe that sub goes in there so as not to be seen?"

"You know of any backroads that go along the bay?" asked Van Zandt. "Is it possible to get up there and have a look at the bay and not be observed if anyone is there?"

"I don't know. I've never been ashore. When we get back home we can ask Pedro. He knows more about that area than we do," replied Ignacio at the wheel. They continued south for Cabo leaving the sub in their wake.

"Fish on!" cried Chema as he grabbed a pole. He pulled and reeled, pulled and reeled, and far distant a marlin leaped, breaking the surface in hopes of throwing the hook. He fought the great fish only to lose it somehow. It had broken free and avoided its doom. He cursed his bad fortune.

"Just like life my friend," commented Rufus. "Win some, lose some."

Back home at Cabo they sought Pedro Gomez, found him in a cantina with some others, loud and noisy with beer suds on their whiskered faces. They called him outside. "Pedro," said Ignacio. "You know if there is a backroad to get around Magdalena Bay unseen?"

"Maybe," he said, rubbing a grubby hand across his whiskered face. "Used to be an old trail through all of the cactus. It is really rough and ugly ground. Why would anyone ever want to go there?" asked Pedro.

"There might be some things happening up there that the government may want to know, because of the war," injected Rufus. "Japanese Submarines for one!"

"Japanese!" exclaimed Pedro. He paused in thought. "Makes sense I suppose! There are those crazy people looking to start a colony or something up there. The word is that some religious-political types are teamed up to build some sort of mission or something up there, in the northbay area somewhere. Why, only heaven knows! We have heard they favor Japan and Germany in this war. Maybe those subs being up there have purpose? Maybe they are getting help from that community of crazies? Then again the Japenese fishermen around here might know something, maybe they are involved somehow?"

"If that is so," said Ignacio. "I suggest we look for a way to get up there and look the bay over without being seen. We should be able to find a place to set a launch ashore south of the bay. Then you can make your way to the bay and check it out," he said to Rufus. "But, you better go prepared. You'll need guns, weapons. Where you going to get that at?"

They were not commandos. Van Zandt had no call or means to

engage in a firefight. In his Texas Ranger days he had had gunfights with outlaws, but nothing of this scope. Besides, what could small arms fire do to a submarine? His job was to snoop around, observe, and whatever facts he learned to pass that information onto Washington D.C. What they did was their business!

Biscochito, one of the Yaquis, spoke. "Leave that to us! We'll take care of that!" he spoke in his native dialect to the others then said they had to leave once back in Cabo. But, he swore they would return with what was needed. Indeed, they had left as soon as they had docked. They did not tell Van Zandt where they were going; just assured him they would be back in a couple of days with what was needed.

Meanwhile the others with Van Zandt waited, tread the water of time, worried they had been deserted. But, true to their word they returned, and with boxes of rifles and ammunition, even explosives. Where had this come from questioned Van Zandt? As much as he had regarded the Yaquis as friends they yet had a mysterious streak through them. Perhaps their long battles with the federal government they had learned to stockpile arms. Whatever the case they were now prepared, but still not in ways to take on the Japanese Navy!

The following morning they set out, Pedro guiding Ignacio at the helm. He directed Ignacio to where he could set them ashore, a shallow cove where the surf was gentle. Once ashore Pedro would lead them through and over the rough terrain where the old trail was, as best as he could remember.

"It is really rough ground in there," cautioned Pedro. "That forest of cactus can be wicked! Be careful! They can do more harm than any Japanese you might see! A little dingy ferried men and supplies ashore and then waited in secret for their return. Van Zandt, Pedro, and his band of Yaquis stumbled over rocks of all shapes and sizes, wondering if what they had selected was indeed a trail. Sprained ankles and worse were always a possibility. They spent more time watching their footing than where Pedro was leading them. They carried rifles in hand with boxes of ordinance strapped to their backs. It was a hot sun to labor under and sweat poured from their persons. Thick growths of cacti threatened to stab them with their spines. Frustration and weariness made them wonder if they were headed the wrong direction. But, when a breeze coursed through the cacti it hinted the bay was nearby and they sighed a hope that was true. Dusk was approaching when they neared the crest of a small hill, seeing the southern waters of the bay stretching before them, sparkling the last remnants of sunlight. Nothing was visibly apparent in the approaching darkness. But, Van Zandt raised the binoculars for a sweeping view. Far distant there appeared some craft, some lights on decks, already reflected in the darkening waters. Nothing much could be determined.

"We must move further up the shore, get a better view," said Van Zandt.

They slipped back down the crest and began meandering through thick groves of cacti, then actual forests of it, some flinching, wincing from the invisible spikes and thorns they inadvertently brushed up against. They came upon a small break, just room for a couple of men, which led to another rise. Van Zandt hoped it would offer a better view, and now he and Pedro worked single file through the cactus forest, crawling upon their bellies like snakes to observe unseen. Muffled voices could be heard below their perch, on the shoreline by a launch. Voices shouted commands and men scampered up and down the sandy beach, some armed. Just off shore were the two anchored trawlers they had seen, tethered together. Van Zandt raised his binoculars for a closer look. Sure enough there were two ships, with lights illuminating the decks, reflecting shimmering lights upon the waters. Shadows of silhouetted men scurryied about as if in a hurry, carrying crates and boxes from below decks. He took note of a low-lying, dark shape in between the two vessels. He tried focusing further the binoculars. Yes! His jaw dropped as a submarine's image came into view, even in the shadows of the increasing night he could make out the conning tower. The submarine was being refitted with provisions. Hatches appeared open and crewmen were scurrying across their small deck and disappearing below with crates and boxes from the phony trawlers. The two vessels alongside posed as trawlers. But, in reality they were tender ships to provision this sub, maybe some others yet due. Shouted commands on the beach VanZandt swore were in Japanese. Dam the darkness, he thought! He needed better proof! But, then what should he do if he got it? Should they just leave and return to the coast where the men waited with the dingy for them? What would happen if they were discovered; or even caught? They US Navy needed to know this. But, they were so far away! Mexico? What did they have that could stop this? Before them was a threat from the other side of the world; a threat that needed to be dealt with now!

Outside the actual participants what truly happened then has remained a mystery. In the days that followed reports reached Washington that a battle had occurred on the bay in which Van Zandt and his Yaquis had sunk the sub and damaged the tender ships, that even a good number of Japanese had been killed. But, where was the proof? There was no wreckage found and no tender ships remained in the bay, not even were any bodies found. Pleanty of doubters arose disbelieving small arms fire, even the explosives they may have had, could have done what Van Zandt and others claimed happened. There was lots of circumstantial evidence and verbal testimonies but no literal proof.

Rufus Van Zandt and his troupe insisted that Magdalena Bay was a refueling point for Japanese submarines, and that the trawlers were in actuality tenders to reprovision them. If his assertions were true, and they had engaged in battle at great cost for the Japanese, this made Mexico City very nervous, threatening her neutrality status. In Washington D.C. there was great alarm. What was next? However, the bay was more of a transient site for resupply. Everything hinged on whether the tender ships were there or not. It would seem more likely that a supply base would have been somewhere else, somewhere that was land based. Unknown to the government was Japan's secret supply base on the Chiapas Pacific coast where they had a more permanent base, named *La Palma*. Plans for Magdalena Bay may have had more sinister purposes, like picking up special ordinance and weaponry to attack the Panama Canal. The *Galapagos Islands,* because of their close proximity to the Canal, was also of strategic interest for establishing a base. It had been reported that an unidentified fleet of submarines, said not to have been American, was spotted off Cristobal Island / Galapagos. Japanese submarines had ventured across the Pacific to reconnoiter currents and winds in preparations for an attack on the Canal. A growing U.S presence, however, in the Galapagos denied them that and they returned to their home base at *Kwajalein*.

Throughout early 1942 Felipe and others continued to wait for something to happen. Japanese submarines had been and would continue to be active on the Pacific coast of the United States and Mexico. On February 23rd, at 7:15 pm their submarine I-17 shelled the Ellwood Oil Fields near Goleta, California, some twelve miles north of Santa Barbara. More attacks would be planned from there up to Washington State. Mexico was still in the cross-hairs of warring factions. Mexico City was perplexed what to do, but had to do something, and reluctantly would eventually.

Chapter 18

"World Events Dictate to Indecisive Mexico"

When news had arrived of the Russians defeating German forces at Stalingrad, February 2, 1942, leadership within the Union Nacional Sinarquista began to rethink their course, how the Union, as a whole, had to rethink their relationship with the Axis countries anymore. The dastardly and cowardly attack on the Americans' Pearl Harbor in December and now Stalingrad convinced them to cozey-up to an anti-Roosevelt faction within the United States, Anglo-American clerics led by Cardinal Francis J. Spellman of New York, and Bishop Fulton Sheen. These two Catholic clerics worked with the Sinarquistas in Mexico, to begin efforts to 'reschool' the members towards a universal form of having more appeal with a 'cleaner' slate, distancing themselves from the Nazis, Imperial Japan, and Fascists, now tabbing themselves as the *New Christian Social Order*. The Union had taken on more of a religious front rather than adopting one of armed conflict and subversion.

In Japan, the preceding month, preliminary plans were being made for their Imperial Army to invade the United States' Aleutian Islands of Alaska, and for the Imperial Navy to totally eliminate any remaining strategic power of the Americans in the Pacfic at Midway Island, at the extreme west end of the Hawaiian Island chain. Infighting within both departments of the Japanese military had been making it difficult to plan cohesive, coordinated, and decisive battle plans involving their army and navy.

For the Gurzas in Mexico City, they still had held onto the tenuous hope of security for being a neutral country while the world burned in war around the globe. And yet, Professor Arellano's forboding words still resonated in their ears, as winter's months of 1942 fell from their calendar akin to leaves from trees in the fall. Felipe had immersed himself at school. Haru and his children had been moved elsewhere to an undisclosed farm, the adolescents and adults were put to work harvesting crops. Their young children were relegated to makeshift nearby schools, just to keep them occupied. The world at large raged on in madness. The world's antagonists of Berlin-Rome-Madrid-Tokyo drafted their wiles and orchestrated their respective plans to control events upon the stages they favored. Nazis had arranged for the Spanish Falange to assist the Japanese to take over the Philippines, and their lofty goals to operate against the United States *from* Mexico. There had been talks in Madrid with the Japanese about forming an alliance, or collaboration, for the conquest and occupation of the Philippines. The two countries concluded negotiations and entered into a secret pact. Spain's partner in wanton crime had bombed Pearl Harbor on December 7th, 1941 and the Japanese Air Force raided Manila on December 29th. To begin 1942, the Japanese army marched into Manila on January 2nd. This rapid success inspired Nazi encouragements to have the Spanish Falange and Imperial Japan focus upon fashioning similar plans for Mexico, and enlisting the Mexican Sinarquistas to unravel the social fabric of the country

Japan's aim was similar to Germany's, latch onto Mexico's oil and raw materials by any means. Unlike Germany, however, Japan had desires to literally attack the United States from across the Mexican border. Japan maintained a skeleton army, tabbed the *Mexican Military Service Men's Association,* under the direct command of Japan's Minister of War, *General Hideki Tojo.* The states of Sonora and Sinaloa had many Japanese farmers and fishermen, and one of their fishing fleets was known to frequent Magdalena Bay on the Pacific Coast of lower Baja California. To accomplish their ambitious goals in Mexico the Japanese-Spanish Falange-and the Nazis sought to eliminate any governmental opposition by planning a coup d'etat against Mexico City, topple the Camacho regime, and had wanted to do this a month before,

January 1st.

Just north of Magadalena Bay former director of the Union Nacional Sinarquista, the Jesuit zealot Salvador Abascal, continued to establish the Sinarquista – Jesuit colony in the area just north of the bay, at Santo Domingo and Llanos de Irai. He was assisted by Jose de Jesus Sam Lopez; the son of a Japanese father. He had been educated in Japan and two months after the bombing of Pearl Harbor he returned to Mexico thoroughly radicalized. He thus joined the Sinarquista union and Abascal on the Baja Peninsula. A Nazi, German or Dutch, Pieter Theodore Wiegman, was a colonial and an agricultural engineer. His talents were to be utilized in establishing the remote colony. He was married to an American and perhaps was the basis for his middle name being English.

Japan's interest in establishing something at Magdalena Bay was not limited to the fishing industry. Knowing how the former hardliner of the Sinarquista Union was seeking to build this colony in the nigh vicinity of the bay, and of his pro-stance for the Axis Powers, Dr. Tsuru, Japan's Minister to Mexico, had paid 50,000 pesos to Mexican General Felix Ireta to expedite the Sinarquista transfers to Magdalena Bay, to negate any hindrances. The motive for this was that with a 'friendly' colony there assistance would be forthcoming to assist Japanese forces to stage attacks against the United States from the bay, and this lucrative possibility was the reasoning for Japanese submarines appearing in the bay, not only to meet tender ships for provisions but to reconnoiter if the bay could serve as a naval base from which to stage clandestine missions of sabotage.

There continued to be factions within the Union Nacional Sinarquista, of those who still retained the hardline stance of former Union leader Abascal, who opposed those now favoring a more *pious Catholic posture*. They favored Abascal's attempt to establish a Sinarquista-Jesuit colony by Magdalena Bay, and if called for would render assistance to the Axis Powers, and being on the Pacific Coast this would undoubtedly be assistance to Japan. The current leadership favored more of a religious demeanor as promoted by the U.S. Catholics, under the spell of Cardinal

Spellman of New York, and Bishop Fulton Sheen. But too, there were those after Pearl Harbor and Stalingrad who saw reality, that the future was not with the Axis, that an agreement with Roosevelt's Pan-Americanism and adopting his Good Neighbor policy was wiser, rather than following the promotions of 'Hispanidad', that of how the Axis was seeking to foment a crisis between Hispanic Catholics in the Americas against the Anglo-White Protestants of the United States, a divisive posture of the Axis dictators and ultimately for their selfish interests.

The burgeoning colony of Abascal's was begun with confidence but was now on unsure ground, floundering, as supportive UNS (Union Nacional Sinarquista) funds withered. A rift became a chasm as Abascal and his former comrades within the Sinarquista movement were in heated opposition, were even considering a parting of ways. The Catholic influence within the Union was under increasing pressure to restrain the militancy of the membership. Catholic clerics and their influence led to a severance of ties with the Spanish Falange and assumed total control of the Union, making it a religious-secular organization, led by Catholic clerics. Abascal resigned from the Union March 30, 1942, after being arrested for insulting the Mexican army. His arrest insulted the Union's leaders; Truebo and the Olivares brothers, those who had founded and run the Union Nacional Sinarquista with Professor Schreiter's initial help, for the Nazis, departed and now the Union adopted a different tact, of being less confrontive, putting a more pious Catholic seal upon it, conscious of image while seeking revolutionary achievement. The hardliner Salvador Abscal felt betrayed by his own. From thence forward, he and his colony would either sink or swim on their own in remote Baja, unless Japan bolstered them.

News came from the United States that President Roosevelt had signed Executive Order 9066 on February 19th to do as Mexico had done, round up and relocate away from suspect areas the Japanese – Americans, put them into internment camps to safeguard the country. It seemed the same paranoia that had prompted President Camacho to order their internments that a similar order now held fast the minds in Washington D.C. Felipe and Elisabeth sat in the parlor again debating those governmental acts, if founded on sound reasoning or was no more than reactions to inbred racial fears of a war-like race, consumed in the belief that Japan had a divine wind behind them to conquer. Whatever the case, those of Japanese ancestry in North America were being interned *unlike* any others.

April had arrived in the capital. Throughout the month fragrant spring flowers were in full bloom. Felipe and Magaly were enjoying some free time at Josefina's before any of the study group converged. Tacos and jamaica punch quelled any stomach rumbles and thirst. They sat at the large customary table the restaurant faithfully held in reserve for them, in a side room, on their meeting nights. Apart from them, diners throughtout the dining room proper enjoyed their meals and company. Savory dishes in the kitchen sent delectable smells throughout the environs, salivating customers' anticipations. Academic study, however, was not on their mutual minds just then. There was time for that when the others arrived, when they mulled over in a public forum academia they were all engaged with studying, and how it related to the world of now. For the moment, however, they spoke of and shared things of a personal nature, of themselves and their futures.

"Have you and that Commandant had any further talks?" asked Magaly. "You have any idea where they moved those people to?"

"Only that they were moved to some labor farm. Valenzuela was ordered to deny me any more visits; at least that is what he told me when I last saw him and Haru in early March. Even Valenzuela has disappeared. Every one is mum. When that happened it seemed like Providence was telling me to let it all be, to commit my time to studies instead." He rolled his eyes around the room, and out the open doorway to the dining room. "This is the result. But listen! This has merits; studies for the mind and always something for the heart." He held up his glass of jamaica punch and offered Magaly a salute. She smiled warmly with dove's eyes.

"Well, I never met the man. But, I hope this Haru that you so admire and respect will make it through Okay during this painful time, and that his children will not suffer. Maybe when all the madness subsides you and he will meet again, someday, somehow, somewhere." There was a moment, an interlude, before anything else was said. She was about to ask him if he had conferred anymore with Professor Arellano when the first of a dozen fellow students walked in. She held her tongue, knowing that it could wait. They greeted the young man and their conversations catapulted into that evening's topic of debate and discussion. Soon, the others began to filter in by two's and threes's, and an occasional solo person. A couple of waiters were designated to serve them finger foods and drinks for their usual two hour stay.

It was now 10:00 pm and there were remnant crumbs upon the table, even some upon the books and papers that were spread about in front of them. All was indicative to how oblivious they had become while so intently engaging their minds with intelligentsia. There was no complacency. Every one had an opinion, some personal interpretation of their discussion matter, and freely voiced it in animated manners. These were stimulating hours for reason and debate, and from them matured a coming generation of movers and shakers of Mexican society, some even going abroad to make a name for themselves.

"I best be going," admitted Felipe to Magaly. "I enjoy brief visits with Mother and Horacio, have a cookie or two before retiring, share what our respective days have been." He smiled with a mental image of the grinning monk and free hand of mischief.

This had been the normal routine since Haru's disappearing relocation to some rural confinement. It was a routine he had become comfortable with. Yet, there was always an intrusive thought about the Japanese-Mexican plight, even the disturbing mysteries in Guanajuato. He never had peace with what that was all about. But, he had his own calling to fulfill and he had been doing that ever so well with renewed vigor. Meanwhile, in Japan, the bickerings and squabblings within the military had calmed and a two-pronged battle plan had been drawn up to deal the United States a final blow that would make the Americans a non-factor in the Pacific Theatre, that the Pacific and Asia would be all Japan's for the taking.

The next morning Felipe and Elisabeth sat about the fountain in their plaza at home. Floral pedals floated in the pooled waters. A fragrance of floral blooms wafted upon a gentle breeze that bathed the serene setting. They sipped coffee and Felipe enjoyed the monk once more even though a platter of cream-filled churros was on a table before them. The month of May had been pleasant, a bit hot some days, and their personal plaza was a comforting retreat to relax in. The peaceful sound of the running fountain water was soothing, conducive to pensive thoughts, lighter moods.

Horacio stormed in, agitated, angered. "Damn them!" he cried out. "Damn those hellions! I knew it! I knew it was just a matter of time! Damn them all!"

This rude interruption caught Felipe and Elisabeth off guard, completely surprised them. This was so out of character for Horacio. "What are you talking about?" asked a shocked Elisabeth. "What is wrong?"

"I just heard on the radio that a German submarine sank a ship of ours, the *Portero de Llano* off the Florida coast. That happened yesterday, the 14th. Here the Nazis are polluting the minds of our people while they torpedo a ship of ours! What is Camacho going to do now?"

They sat stunned at the news, wondering about what had happened, fearful about what was next. It was a hot topic for discussion everywhere. *Oh, it's just one of those things,* thought many, almost ambivalent, not displaying much national spirit, thinking that if they went beyond their borders in commercial pursuits that that was what was risked. Others were adamant, cried out for Mexico City to do something, restitution for the loss of ship and goods, not to mention the loss of life! They debated what recourse Mexico had for the next three days when on the 17th Horacio stormed in once again, beside himself. "Those damned Nazis! Did it again! They sank another, our *Faja de Oro*. Maybe once can be explained away. Not a second time!"

In his chambers President Avila Camacho raged! He and his advisors debated what actions they could take. What possibly could Mexico do? They had no credible navy to take on the

German U-Boats. They posed no real military threat to the Nazi war machine! Their small army was poorly trained and funded and the navy was a non-factor. Still, there permeated through the halls of government a zeal for retribution in some form. Debates persisted for more than a week. An apprehension over the possibility of further sinkings spiced their deliberations. Finally, it all came to a head on May 28[th.] . President Cammacho had petitioned for a declaration of war against Germany, which was approved by the Chamber of Deputies; the Senate confirmed it on the 30th, but gave the declaration a retroactive date of May 22nd. Mexico now was no longer a neutral country. It was a player in the world war now, linked with the Allies. They were now at war, including with Germany's ally, Japan. Germany claimed they had the right to torpedo the Mexican vessels, carrying oil they claimed that was destined for the United States and its war effort against them. The question now was of what value did Camacho's declaration have. Was it just a piece of paper? It said 'WAR!" But, the president had no constitutional right to send their citizens off to foreign wars. This was a dilemma to be yet resolved in some form or manner, was taking an absurd amount of time.

Among the citizenry of the country there were mixed feelings about the declaration. After all, Mexico was not a country used to international warfare. Now they were allied, in theory, with the United States, the very country that Mexico's Santa Ana had fought against as the Yankees had invaded their country during the period known as the Mexican-American War in the 1840's. The American's Polk Administration had used that war, a ruse, to obtain the spoils of victory, ceded portions of Mexican lands to the United States, basically from Texas to California north of the Rio Grande River. President Polk's aim was to pave the American way for the American cry of *Manifest Destiny,* a belief that the United States was divinely destined to enjoy unhindered ownership of lands from the Atlantic Coast to the Pacific shores. It had been argued the past hundred years that the U.S. had contrived the war merely for the vast land grab. Now, Mexico entered a time of unknown challenges, the nation wondering if the declaration of war meant anything other than a piece of paper and empty rhetoric. For the average citizen it meant not that much, life went on as usual. But, for the learned and politician much was at stake. Like it or not, the Mexican Eagle had to learn to soar with the American's. Both countries had much at stake, indeed the free world had. Mexico's oil and raw materials would bolster the Allies needs, and the Axis Powers coveted all for themselves. The question on every ones' mind was what manpower would be provided for any military operations when the Constitution forbade it? Or, such needs were not in the Mexican budget to field forces worthy of the needs called for. In the wake of the declaration was a time of figuring out what it really meant and in what capacity the country could, would respond to carry it out.

On June 3rd the Japanese Imperial Navy assisted the Imperial Army with their invasion of Alaska's Aleutian Islands, of Amaknak Island. Their aim was the U.S. naval base at Dutch Harbor and the US Army at Fort Mears. In Japan's grand scheme of things this was merely a feint, with their major thrust to be against Midway island far south, a vital outpost of Pearl Harbor. Hopefully this feint would draw US naval forces to the far north, further exposing Midway to an absolute Japanese victory. To this end a task force of two aircraft carriers steamed for the Aleutians. The Battle of Dutch Harbor had commenced on June 3rd (1942) and continued through the 4th. If this feint proved successful, then perhaps enough U.S. warships would have been drawn away for the defense of Dutch Harbor and Ft. Mears, thus weakening US resolve to defend Midway. Before the Aleution expedition concluded the Battle of Midway had erupted, and would persist for four days, concluding the 7th. It ended in a complete disaster for Imperial Japan, as had the expedition in the Aleutians. The losses of four large aircraft carriers and a heavy cruiser at Midway were irreparable. They could not recover from them. The loss of trained pilots and maintaenance crews versus America's industrial might and training capabilities were simply too devastating to recover from, and from the defeat Japan recoiled, seeking to defend its empire rather than expanding it.

A lot of Japan's strategy for the Eastern Pacific had hinged upon the Battle of Midway. They had concluded that upon victory they could carry any future war efforts, to further subjugate and control the United States and negate the American threat, unhindered. Their submarines had crossed the Pacific and had plied the American waters from Oregon south, to the Galapogos Islands off of Ecuador. Finding the Mexican coast ripe for undiscovered stops, Magdalena Bay had proven to be an excellent secluded place to reprovision the subs, as was *La Palma*, the secret land base further south on Mexico's Chiapas Pacific coast.

The previous December Japanese submarines had been sent by the Imperial Navy to cruise America's west coast. They usually arrived off the state of Oregon with a focus on San Francisco to the south. These two secret Mexican bases of call were where these submarines of various classes could put into for refueling and provisions. They had had intentions of doing mischievious attacks along California's coastline, even Oregon. Farfetched considerations were an attack even on the Panama Canal. But, their grand schemes never materialized and the submarines returned to their home base at Kwajalein on the far western side of the Pacific Ocean, closer to home. What drove the final nail into their coffin of strategic planning along the American coastlines was their utter defeat at Midway. After that debacle further submarine adventures in the far Eastern Pacific were greatly curtailed as home defense had become paramount in subsequent planning.

It was study night at Josefina's. Felipe and other young men debated the war abroad consuming so many nations, and now Mexico's role in it, if any. Some felt it would have been best to simply turn their national cheek to the German insult and offense, maintain their national neutrality. Those two sinkings were not like the Americans' Pearl Harbor! The sense of offense slowly boiled in Felipe's mind while most others let it slide away. Thoughts became a rolling boil, a cauldron of anger and frustration. He thought of how he could release such pent up anger. Roosevelt had told the United States that Pearl Harbor would live on in a memory of infamy. Well, for them, Mexico's battle cry was freedom to traverse the seas. But, he knew too that the Nazis, the Spanish fascists, and even the Imperial Japanese had been playing them, all for their personal agendas, not for Mexico's benefit. It was time for the Mexican eagle to flex its wings and talons, but, how? Did their plummed symbol have the wherewithal means to do credible service? What could he do personnaly to feel he was contributing to their national cause? It was a time of much discussion and not much doing. Something had to give!

Chapter 19

"A Declaration of Ambivalence?" "Finally Some Bite!"

Throughout the summer and fall of 1942, and into winter 1943, Felipe assumed the posture of a *hawk,* advocating how Mexico had to fulfill the charges of Camacho's Declaration of War, May 22nd, the past year. It was approaching a year since the government had agreed to his petition. But, in essence nothing had come from it. For those like Felipe this meant frustration and a national embarrassment, a do nothing country when the world was in peril. The study group had had nights when their academic discussions were sidetracked in favor of debating current events, some evenings with heated exchanges. As frustrated as Felipe was President Camacho and the weight he bore was so much more! His hands were tied behind his back. Unless the lawmakers of the land empowered him to send Mexicans into combat of the raging world war, the country would be theoretically at war, but still retaining a neutral's posture. The Mexican psyche had not the mind-set, perhaps even heart, of an international player. In the halls of government the politicos spun their wheels in the muck and mire of debate and procrastination as Camacho's patience endured. What he was asking of them had never been done before in the history of the country. The national compass struggled for a true direction of purpose.

"Our country's politicians are like ostriches!" exclaimed Felipe at the breakfast table one April morning of 1943. "Those imbiciles stick their heads into the ground, thinking problems will go away on their own. They are in denial of what reality is." He fussed and fumed over the dilemma as President Roosevelt of the United States had traveled to Monterry, Mexico to consult President Camacho in person. It was a meeting to sound out each other as to what could be expected from Mexico's alliance in the war effort, if indeed there was a true alliance and commitment. After all, nigh a year had elapsed and as yet, Mexico's declaration had displayed no teeth! Roosevelt encouraged the Mexican President to take some initiative, embark Mexico upon military offenses with them against their mutual enemies. To this, Camacho explained the limitations of his powers and that he was dependent upon what the Mexican Senate would ultimately decide. In the *Land of Mañana* credible things take time to happen and he had been waiting for the country to rally behind his declaration, and that had not happened. That was a truth that President Roosevelt had empathy for. He related to Camacho's dilemma in that he knew all too well how the Republicans in Washington D.C. had tried stonewalling, thwarting him also.

Throughout 1943 the pro-activists in Mexico continued to beseech the government to do something befitting what they had declared in 1942's declaration of war. Yet, business was the same as usual; much talk without the walk. The year came and went without a designated national purpose, the head still buried in the sand. It was as though the country was saying to the allies, 'here are our raw materials. Take and you do the fighting.' Winter of 1943 had just passed and now the spring of 1944 was upon them.

After two years of delays and inaction President Camacho resorted to showmanship as the war continued. He ordered the Mexican Air Force to stage an air show near Mexico City. He reasoned, that if successful it perhaps would inspire the citizenry to build a fire under the lawmakers to get something done, to propel the people to action. One hundred thousand (100,000) *Capitalinos* attended the show, observing their Air Force fly AT-6's and A-24B's on bombing runs on designated targets. The public responded with enthusiasm, enough so that President Camacho was encouraged, that once again he reiterated, implored, that Mexico join the fight, literally!

Inspired by the show's success, the Mexican Air Force

conducted examinations for their Reserves, and interested civilians who exhibited an interest in volunteering for military service, be what it may. Felipe jumped at the chance! He was among scores of others who responded to the opportunity, hoping it would lead to bigger things. From those exams the Air Force compiled a list of names, those who would be put into an elite unit of airmen. Felipe was one of those designees. Elisabeth and Horacio rejoiced for him. Magaly, on the other hand, was concerned where this honor would lead him, take him away for who knows where and for how long, or worse?

The new unit had been designated, *Escuadron 201*. The new recruits mixed freely with one another in the days ahead. A certain *Jaime Cenizo Rojas* Felipe had taken a liking to. There was something about the skinny man of small stature that towered in personality. He had a sense of humor that seemed primed for soliciting laughter from others. He had a levity about him that enlivened others.

"Are you ready for all this?" asked Felipe of Rojas. They were near Mexico City's *Zocalo* enjoying some tacos on a warm day. There was something about fish tacos that Felipe gravitated to regardless of the season, a delicacy from the coast. In the company of some of his fellow recruits, they thought to enjoy the city before they may be too busy to do so, would be far away somewhere.

"Ready? I have been ready since May 22, 1942," replied an emphatic Rojas. "It has been long overdue in my thinking! I guess we'll know soon enough about what we will be doing. This little guy has big things to do yet!"

Another flyboy joined them, *Amadeo Castro Amarillo*. He and Rojas had bonded well, just as they and Felipe had. It was the beginning of a nucleus of comrades that would spend much time together in far off lands.

A month had passed since the formation of their squadron. Not much had happened since. For Felipe and the others it seemed another deadend going nowhere. They all had been in a state of waiting in their respective realms, wondering what next? Out of curiosity he had been poring over a book on aeronautics when Horacio came into the parlor.

"Have a letter for you," he announced. "The mail carrier just brought it. Looks important!" He handed it to Felipe and his heart jumped when he saw who it was from, the Secretary of Defense! He hurriedly opened it up and saw it addressed to him personally, a member of *Escuadron 201.* The Secretary informed him and the others that the squadron would be soon ordered to depart for training in the United States, with some thirty-six pilots and three hundred ground crewmen. The would-be pilots came from the middle and upper classes of society of which Felipe was from.

"I best tell mother this," spoke Felipe. "Orders to report! In a month he says. The Secretary says in a month we leave for training. It looks like we are going up to Texas to be trained there."

"That's a good idea," agreed Horacio, to tell Elisabeth. "I hope the Americans receive you well. No matter which way you look at it, they still have a bias towards us. I hope none of you encounter anything like that!"

"You best tell Magaly about this," responded Elisabeth to his news. "You cannot do something like this and keep her in the dark. I know you two have something, this romance I suppose. Perhaps in the back of your minds you have even considered marriage. If this is so you must be up front about everything. Your days at the university are no more, you've graduated with that coveted degree, and you now are destined for war, if that is what our government decides, if the Senate ever grants Camacho the right to send you overseas. Then again maybe all you are destined for is training and you'll be brought back home. Regardless, you and Magaly need time together. See to it!" Felipe agreed to the need.

It was an off night for Josefina's. The study group was not due that evening, and besides, over the past two years they had become less a part of it until they never attended any more. Felipe and Magaly sat at a table for two, alongside corner windows. It had an ambience for romance; some wine, a breadbasket with cheese. They held hands mid-table and spoke of the unknown days ahead, what lay beyond their view of the many morrows ahead of them. It was a time of sounding out each one's heart.

"Felipe. We have never said in so many words. But, we have always known we love one another," admitted Magaly. "We have assumed that one day we would marry and I think others have known this too. We are not infatuated teenagers. I think friends and family see us as adults with sound reasonings, intelligent, and not ruled by passion. They have let develop and grow our love without intruding. Now we have this before us, when you are about to leave for God knows what. If He wills it, when you return I will marry you if you ask me. I pledge you this."

Felipe absorbed what her heart just coveyed. His was like hers. He had a respect for her that had been nurtured over academics, and when that had encouraged more it blossomed into a healthy love.

"You know I feel the same. When this is over and I am headed home you will be my goal." He reached into a pocket and pulled out a tiny case and handed it to her. She had a premonition what it was, an engagement ring. She opened up his promise unto her and marveled how it sparkled with a hopeful future. He withdrew it and slid it onto her finger with her in delight. She beamed as the moon shone through the windowpane.

"It actually looks nice there," he quipped. "I had worried about the size. But, it seems to fit just fine." He raised her hand and kissed it and the ring.

Josefina witnessed the occasion and came unto them with a hint of tears. "Finally!" she erupted. "We all knew this day was coming and we are honored it happened here! It makes my place special even more! Listen, don't consider tonight's bill. It's my treat! The occasion calls for something special. She summoned a small quartet of mariachis to their table to serenade them in song. It proved to be a memorable occasion that both Magaly and he would carry into the morrows, recalling the evening while they hoped for the day they could wed.

On July 21, 1944 President Camacho addressed the 201st, reassuring them that they should not be worried about matters at home, that if the fortunes of war went bad for them that Mexico would take care of their interests. Three days later, on the 24th, the

201st was preparing to board a train at the *Buena Vista Train Station* in Mexico City. The six, first class rail cars had been reserved for them. Family and friends gathered about them, singing, *Despedidas* (Farewells).

They huddled about on the landing of the station, waiting for the anticipated call to board. Elisabeth stood on one side of Felipe and Magaly on the other with her arm about his waist. Horacio was immediately behind him with Professor Arellano. There was a shrill whistle blown followed by the call to BOARD the train.

"Write me!" instructed his mother. 'We shall be worrying about you every day and night. Letters will help us get through them all. So, write!" She gave her son a strong hug, as if not wanting to let him go. Then she planted a kiss upon his cheek as they parted. It was time, now, for his betrothed. They gazed long into one another's eyes. A sign of a tear was forming in one of Magaly's ready to stain her pretty cheek.

"Here." She handed him a handkerchief, personally monogrammed with her M B initials. "A rembrance in the days ahead. I will be waiting. Always know that. I am yours!" They kissed and only parted when a second call sounded to BOARD. This followed by a long and sincere embrace.

"Come on Romeo" urged a passing, smiling Jaime Rojas. "We have things to do!" They then separated and Felipe said his final good byes to Horacio and the Professor.

"God go with you!" said the Professor as Felipe hurried away. He watched his prize pupil of years past scamper through the mix of people to join his comrades. *Such fine men,* reasoned the professor. They represent a country confused with the realities of today's world he thought. They were summoned from the masses and their few numbers represent the best the country can offer.

The journey to the border had a number of delays. It was taking longer than usual. There were numerous stops along the way to be honored by those well-wishing onlookers. Music and cheers greeted them at each stop.

"Makes me feel like we're heroes even before we've done anything," remarked *Hector Espinoza Galvan* to several others thronged about him, they all staring out the car's window at the crowds of people waving. "Look at all those people cheering us!"

"Seems unreal," responded *Mamerto Albarran Nagera.*

"Get used to it!" commented *Galvan* at his side. "When this war is over there will be more of that when we return."

Return? Felipe wondered about that as he fingered Magaly's handkerchief, overhearing them. He thought to himself maybe they would, maybe not. They had never been to war before and chances are they wouldn't be returning. He watched them continuing to lean towards the window, peering out at the crowds, making comments, Felipe alone in his personal thoughts, sniffing the perfumed cloth.

"Oh my! Did you see that lady?" asked one of them. "There, her in that blue dress, the one waving the flag. I think I'll marry her when we get back," remarked Rojas.

"Marry?" reacted Amarillo. 'You! You're a midget compared to her. She's too much woman for you! Any time she wanted you for something she'd just pull you out of a pocket." Muffled laughter could be heard. Even Felipe had a mental image of that and he chuckled too.

"Go ahead and laugh," responded Rojas. "Sure, I am not that tall. But, look at you! You have the face of a camaron. Who would want to cozy up to you?" More laughter followed as they exchanged humorous barbs.

The last stretch of the ride was coming to an end. It had been more than 35 hours since they set out from Buena Vista Station. And now, only minutes remained before they crossed the border into the United States, into Laredo, Texas.

"You hear that?" asked someone as they railed into the Laredo train station. They listened for something.

"What? I hear nothing," exclaimed another.

"Exactly! There's nothing for we Mexicans on U.S. soil!" There was a stark difference to the cheering send-offs they witnessed in Mexico. It was a completely different experience crossing the border into Laredo, Texas. There was no cheering at all, no warm reception, complete silence. The 201st felt like no-bodies!

"Is this what is in store for us?" asked some one as they were disembarking the train into a world so alien to them. U.S. military buses awaited them, and once aboard they were motored to the *Randolph Army Air Base (Randolph Field)* at San Antonio. Pilot trainees, like Felipe, were transferred to *Foster Field* (Victoria) some two and a half hours southeast of the others at San Antonio.

It had been pre-determined that it would be best that the Mexican squadron would be commanded by Mexicans and would operate apart from the Americans. Command of the squadron was given to *Colonel Antonio Cardenas Rodriguez.* He had credentials to command for he had had combat service in North Africa with the US 97th Bomb Group, and he was personally acquainted with the US Army Air Force's General Jimmy Doolittle. The lead trainer of the 201st was American *Captain Paul Miller.* He was fluent in Spanish having grown up in Peru. He had also served as the assistant air attaché to the US Embassy in Mexico City. His ultimate priority for this training was for pilot safety and their preparation for actual combat. To accomplish this he relied upon a code of strict discipline, agreed to by Colonel Rodriguez.

There were bonds within the 201st of like-souls. Several roomed together in the barracks. Each one had a nickname others had attached to them. *Jaime Cenizo Rojas,* "*El Pato,* "was tabbed so for some thought he had oversized feet and waddled like a 'duck'. *Airman Sanchez* was called "*Sapo*" for being like a 'frog.' *Amadeo Castro Amarillo* was labeled *"El Camaron"* for some considered him to have semblances of a 'shrimp.' Another yet was called "*El Pescado*" for his facial features some jested resembled a 'fish'. Rojas, the perennial clown, wrote a sign in Spanish and hung it outside their room; *Bienvenidos al Acuario,* 'Welcome to the Aquarium'. In the light of humor it became a beacon for others to frequent and socialize. Even Felipe dropped in and as they became better acquainted he earned the name *"El Sabio",* or the 'wise one' as they had learned of his academic background.

Despite all the visible support the 201st had received along the Mexican rails, in general, their nation as a whole exhibited little support at all. In Texas they were sheltered from the realities back home as they trained. The challenges on American soil were daunting; cultural, technical, language, and even racial bias were trials to mature them to the realities of life. They were being trained for war. But, they also were being schooled as to what prejudice was.

To the Anglo-Texans the Mexicans of the 201st were little more than oddities, dreamers that they had something of value to offer. It was a slap in the face for those of the 201st. Perhaps words were never so-expressed to their faces. But, they detected a lot in the facial expressions and demeanors shown them. It was frowned upon by Command that they would fraternize with any of the local señoritas. God have mercy on any one of them if they impregnated one of the white girls. There was this cultural separation of unequaled allies, one that was evident even to a dead man.

"You are here to train and nothing more!" cautioned Captain Miller. "You need to train your eyes upon bombing targets, not rove them about the ladies in town. That can lead only to one thing, TROUBLE! You have been itching to get into this war and prove yourselves. This is your opportunity. Don't louse it up!" Captain Miller did not bear them prejudice. He understood the society they were in and that cautioning the new arrivals was the best course and to have Colonel Rodriguez keep them on a short leash while there.

Pilots at Foster Field (Victoria) were being trained in the P-47 fighter-bomber, to be used as air support for ground troops, wherever. The aircraft had twin turbochargers and could climb to 40,000 feet and in dives could nearly break the soundbarrier. The trainees nicknamed the plane *El Jarro* (the Jug).

The squadron took on the name of the *Aguilas Aztecas* (Aztec Eagles) and in a sense of humor some members were referred to as *Panchito Pistolas,* so-named after a popular cartoon character. While they busied themselves earnestly in training to prove their worth it was not far from their minds that it could all be for naught since their president still had no authority to send them to war. However, word eventually reached them that the Mexican Senate had finally agreed and authorized President Camacho the power to commit them to the cause of war. They would be going into combat! The 201st rejoiced with music and beer. The Aquarium was jubilant! Their room had been a magnet, a favorite gathering place for members. All were celebrating the news from home!

"Well, Colonel, "said Captain Miller to Col. Rodriguez outside by a Jeep. "It looks like you all got what you wanted. Some of those boys in there won't be coming back. You know from your days in North Africa what I mean. Nasty business to write letters home to tell people their son or whoevever was killed. I surely hope your country pays respect to these young men. They have given themselves to this cause and some will pay the ultimate cost for doing so. I hope Mexico will be respective of their service!"

"I hope so, Captain," replied Rodriguez. "We will be going where none of us have been before. Being upon the world's stage with so much at stake many of our people have failed to grasp the entirety of the situation. Maybe the *Aguilas Aztecas* will shake them all up and take notice! Whatever happens, Captain, your ways of greeting us, the training you have supervised, even relating to us in Spanish, have meant so much! We are grateful beyond words. I think the best way to express this is how the squadron performs when called upon, wherever that may be."

"Thank you, sir," replied Miller. "It would be a blessing if this war ended before that is needed. But, I can tell you this. I have not seen any better than what you have shown us here. The only thing you have lacked is opportunity and means. My country is seasoned in war, unfortunately. A great portion of our wealth is being devoted to winning 'this' war for freedom. Since the Battle of Midway we have stymied the Japanese, and in Europe the Nazis are hard pressed after the *Normandy Invasion on D-Day* (June 6, 1944). I have no idea where the 201st may wind up at, Europe or the Pacific. But, wherever, I am confident you and your boys will serve with valor and honor. Mark my words! I have seen no better!"

The two commanders shared a few more minutes together before parting, Col. Rodriguez to pay a visit to the Aquarium and Capt. Miller to his office. They separated to the sounds of celebrations inside the barracks.

Since their initial arrival the squadron had been split up for specialty training sites at either San Antonio or Victoria. But, the day had come for them to be trained as a single unit itself. They were reunited as a whole at Pocatello, Idaho for that purpose. Training now took on a more serious note since they now knew they were cleared by their government for combat service. When they saw dummy targets for practice bombing and strafing runs they envisioned a real enemy now, not mere targets, be they German or Japanese.

All training had come to an end and the 201st was ready as it would ever be to be shipped overseas. On February 25th, 1945, American and Mexican officials gathered together in formalities to send the squadron off to war. Families and hundreds of civilians witnessed the squadron at attention being readied for induction into active service. The 201st was presented with its Battle Flag and two military bands serenaded them as a twenty-one-gun salute resonated through the air. Mexico's Sub-Secretary of War, General Francisco Uruquizo addressed them, saying that they were embarking on a call to defend democracy and humanity and they shall do so with valor and honor. The squadron passed in review, manned their planes, and gave a demonstration of their air skills above. The proceedings were broadcast live on radio across Mexico and Latin America. Elisabeth and Horacio were having coffee on their plaza with Magaly visiting when the broadcast interrupted the music on the radio.

"It has come! The day is here," commented Elisabeth after the broadcast. "Now it is showtime, not like the show the Air Force and Camacho had put on. Now it is for real!" Magaly and Horacio said not a word, thinking the same as all the other families of the 201st were thinking.

February soon ended and spring was once again upon them in Texas. March 27th, 1945. Escuadron 201 was transferred to San Francisco, California. There, they joined 1,500 American soldiers aboard the Liberty Ship, *Fairisle,* bound for the Philippines and the war. It was a month-plus voyage and the Mexicans were confronted with frequent seasickness, threats of Japanese submarine attacks, and the ear- shrieking sirens of constant drills. As Manila Bay neared the squadron was told to write letters home now, just in case they never made it back alive. They had to write in a way so censors could review and thus pass the letters along. Manila Bay was soon to be entered and the Allies supreme commander in the Pacific, General Douglas MacArthur, cabled Mexico's President Avila Camacho.

"The 201st Squadron is about to join this command. I wish to express to you, Mr. President, the inspiration and pleasure this action arouses. It is personally most gratifying because of my long and intimate friendship with your great people."

General George Kenney, acting on behalf of MacArthur, received the 201st upon their arrival May 1st, 1945. He soon had them placed on a train for *Porac Field,* near the more important Clark Field. Their runway was dirt, surrounded by jungled hills. They settled in to their new station, admiring their P-47's, now having their bright tri-color markings of Mexico's red, white, and green flag, alongside the US Star and bar design of red, white, and blue. They were to soar like eagles bearing the insignia of both countries, but eagles of differing natures. One had proven its talons over time and the other had yet to. At night the squadron heard small arms fire about the airfield, and Allied artillery could be heard pounding the retreating Japanese. Liberated American and Filipino prisoners of war shocked them as they observed how starvation in the POW camps had emaciated their bodies. It sobered them fast! They would have renewed vigor as they were ordered up in support of ground troops.

Chapter 20

"A Baptism into War"

The *Aguilas Aztecas,* Mexico's 201st Air Squadron, was assigned to a veteran group, seasoned in the New Guinea Campaign. The 58th Group consisted of three squadrons. The 201st would be the 4th, but unlike the other three would remain apart from the group, operating under Mexican command. For those squadrons of seasoned veterans they eyed with suspicion the new arrivals, the *Johnny-come-latelies* as it were. But, in this case it was the *Juanitos-come-latelies.* They scoured the 201st with critical eyes, wondering why such green recruits they would be saddled with. For the next 2 ½ weeks the new arrivals sought to settle in, tried to feel welcomed. Nothing much happened that included them. But, they commenced on May 17th combat orientation. Although the war was being waged closer and closer to Japan itself, the lingering thoughts of Command of just how costly an actual invasion would be were staggering! The Mexican squadron, even with their small numbers, was to be an integral part of an invasionary force. All their training was about to pay off. Command thought it best to break the new pilots in as individuals, temporarily assigning them to the other squadrons, to prove their worthiness. It did not take long before the Aztec Eagles flew missions as the 201st. When the word came they would be ready, to the hoots and hollers from the other squadrons, more like cheers.

"Give 'em hell, *Juanitos!*" was cried out to them. To this the Mexican flyboys gave a thumbs-up with smiles. It was their being welcomed into the 58th's brotherhood.

East of Manila lies the Marinka Watershed. The U.S. 25th Infantry had bogged down to stiff Japanese resistance slogging through the marshes. The 201st was called upon to render assistance to the ground troops. They attacked with zeal the buildings, vehicles, and artillery positions of the Japanese. For their unit's first combat mission they had played a serious part in putting the enemy to flight, freeing up the ground forces to further pursue them. The *Aguilas* returned to the airfield feeling good about themselves, even with some brogadacio and swagger showing through their 'greeness'. They landed their unscathed P-47's, proud of their *tri-colores* symbols on the borrowed aircraft, and as ground crews serviced their craft the pilots reclined in sought-after shade in the humid heat taking refreshments.

"That didn't seem so bad," Felipe heard someone say.

"It is hard to put up a fight when on the run," observed another. "Just wait! There'll be a time when we meet them head-on. Wait until you see all of that anti-aircraft coming at you! You'll be thinking something else, like changing your pants!"

"Heh! First time out on our own and if you ask me we did well!" commented another. "But, I know things will get tougher. I'm not stupid! As long as we are ordered up and to give support we can expect the Japs will do their best to knock the crap out of us.

"*Sabio!*" called Rojas to Felipe. "You're too quiet. Tell us! What do you think? I saw you make some good moves out there, strafing one of those buildings and those guys running like jackrabbits."

"Small weapons fire I only encountered," replied Felipe. "Not much a rifle can do against a P-47! But, yes I saw those soldiers scamper for cover. It's time they did some running!" He thought of how his country was something that Japan and the others had been playing with, intruding where they never belonged. Yes, he had pleasure in seeing 'them' run for a change, hoping in their flight they caught a glimpse of Mexico's tri-colores emblem as they flew close overhead.

"Way to go!" came some praise from the other squadrons as they heard reports come in from the ground troops, that the 201st freed them up to press on.

Their verbal pat on the back was like a salve soothing them

from all the previous bias and doubts they had encountered, endured, whether in the United States or even here, in the Philippines. If they had known how indifferent and doubtful most of their own, back in Mexico, were they perhaps would be feeling vindicated before their own countrymen. The time had come, thought Felipe, to leave the past behind them, that Mexico had to stop lingering in the shadows of the Revolution, even the vanity of the Cristero War, and pull its head out of the sand, join today's world!

Tragedy first struck the *Aguilas* when on June 1ˢᵗ the youngest pilot in their number, 2ⁿᵈ Lieutenant *Fausto Vega Santander,* was killed when his P-47 rolled and crashed into the sea for unknown reasons. He had been making a run on a target off Luzon's west coast when he appeared to lose control of his craft. The others saw no sign of him taking anti-aircraft fire. The plane just pitched and rolled into sea. What was it? Mechanical failure? Did the ground crews screw up? It was such a needless death they observed. Santander was well liked, the 'baby' of the squadron!

The 201ˢᵗ had little rest in June. Throughout the month they were frequent players in the Luzon Campaign, proving each time they soared above the jungled landscape their mettle. In the central highlands of Luzon the U.S. 6ᵗʰ Army pressed hard into the *Cagayan Valley. General Tomoyuki Yamashita's* 14ᵗʰ Army was dug-in, giving no ground. The rugged, mountainous terrain, terraced rice fields, and mountain passes were dotted by thatch-roofed buildings. It was a horrible terrain to fight in. The Japanese were well hidden underneath the jungle canopy. The 6ᵗʰ was truly reliant on air support to flush the enemy out.

The 201ˢᵗ maneuvered their fighter-bombers deep into the mountains looking for invisible targets. The steep mountains and chasms, and bad weather hampered them. The only thing that met their eyes was incoming anti-aircraft fire erupting from the jungles. The *Aguilas* pulled up and circled, waiting for some sign of prey to dive upon. Below, the 6ᵗʰ Army pinpointed the enemy's locations by firing artillery shells at them that erupted in colored smoke. The 201ˢᵗ focused its attacks upon those points. One by one the pilots plummeted from the skies ignoring in-coming fire and made good their bomb drops. As soon as they released them they accelerated as fast as they could upward to escape the detonation and concussion the one thousand pound bombs exerted. It seemed as soon as they exploded that debris was propelled upward fifteen hundred feet or so. It was a test of their endurance for as they climbed in altitude as fast as the twin-turbo engines would take them, the G-forces threatened blackouts.

The Central Highlands occupied a good deal of time that June. On the 17th a mission over *Payawan* resulted in Lieutenant *Hector Espinoza Galvan* spotting a Japanese convoy. He and seven other planes attacked, strafing the trucks. Flames erupted and the only resistance was a torrent of small arms fire. This was more of a challenege of distance for the P-47's. At six hundred miles from base they were at the extreme limit of their range and fuel was a question. They broke off the attack and returned home.

June had ended for them with a stellar record of sorties. The ground troops had come to depend on their value, and they worked in tandem well. The first few days of July were days of yawning in the shade, and non-stop perspiration. Some of them were grouped under some shade, looked across the runway at the heat waves rise. Their eyes even seemed to sweat. For those of the 'aquarium' thoughts of pistachio ice cream danced through their imaginations.

"Heh 'Sabio'," hailed *El Sapo* Sanchez. "You ever take a girl to Xochimilco and have some of that ice cream there? I don't know what is better, a sweet girl or a cone of that pistachio ice cream. I remember Rosalba. I think she ate a lot of ice cream even before I knew her. When we got into the boat we nearly took on water. I think guys like Rojas here should eat lots of ice cream, put some meat on his bones."

El Pato Rojas reacted, "Listen my friend. That's not meat on your bones, 'gordo'." Laughter erupted.

Xochimilco! Yes, a place of canals and floral covered boats for the romantics. Felipe had never gone there with any particular girl, certainly never Magaly. He never fancied things like that. He did favor books and academic studies and some of his peers had thought him odd in those respects, a bit aloof from them. But,

Felipe had pursuits other than flirtatious in nature. He just smiled at Sanchez's query, let he and Rojas exchange barbs and jests, seeing who could best one another with the funniest lines.

"There's the Colonel," pointed Pilot Carlos Varela Landini. "I wonder what he is talking about with the others?" They all looked that way, seeing Col. Rodriguez talking with the command of the 58th.

"Maybe we're making another run into those highlands," commented Sanchez.

"I don't think so," was heard someone else. "I think things have sort of quieted in there."

He was correct. The discussion was that the first three squadrons of the 58th were departing for Okinawa, and the 201st was ordered to remain at Clark Field for the arrival of new P'47's. In their waiting on July 6th they conducted a flight over Formosa for possible targets but encountered nothing.

July 16th had been a somber one. Lt. Espinoza Galvan had died in a crash into the sea off of Biak, New Guinea. He had been flying on fumes and it was assumed he had run out of fuel. His body was never recovered.

Felipe and the others recalled handsome Galvan on the transport train to Texas from Buena Vista Station; how he led a throng of others to stare out a window at all of the well wishers, hearing their cheers, and saying there would be more when they returned. He would not be returning! There was not even his dead body to return. He was totally gone, food for the sharks. Who was next he pondered, himself even? He looked about his comrades, wondering who else would be dying, who else would not be returning. Then his troubled thoughts found a focus, and they settled when he envisioned Magaly and home. He was not interested in having laurel wreaths about his head and public adulation. No, he was wanting home with his loved ones, private pursuits of merit. His ideals had been undergoing change. He had wanted to go to war, and now that he had seen what it really was, he wanted to retreat into a scene of solitude with loved ones. True, there was a thrill in piloting an aircraft with power and speed. But, he began to think of those at the receiving end of his strafing and bombs. True, they were an enemy. Still, war meant killing and he was growing tired of it. They had not been there that long and already home was longed for. How about these poor souls who had been here for months if not years? They were no longer green recruits. But compared to the Americans and Filipinos and other Allies all around them he was beginning to sense their contribution could never measure up, to what those verterans had endured.

Later that month, the *Aguilas* had been ordered to Biak to commence ferrying new P-47's to Clark Field in the Philippines. Once there they flew the older and weary ones back to Biak for disposal. It was a time of sadness in someways for those they were retiring were the planes they had matured in, had earned respect with. Now, they were bidding adios to what they had had affection for, as they were relegating their 'birds' to recycling or the scrap heap.

As Felipe had wondered in the wake of Galvan's death just who would be next, July 19th came his answer. Captain *Pablo Rivas Martinez* had been weathering a violent thunderstorm. His plane bounced mightily in the throes. His craft disappeared and he was never heard from again. On July 21st Lieutenant *Mario Lopez Portillo*, in the company of an American pilot, crashed into a Luzon mountain due to stormy weather and Portillo was killed.

The 201st now entered a tenuous period of relative inaction. In this downtime they and all others were having a nervous tension build up within, a fear of what everyone knew was coming, an invasion of Japan itself. They heard staggering figures, rumors, of what awaited them. It was of little comfort to know that a huge invasion force was being put together. They and their allies knew that many battles had been won at dear cost, but the war was far from over. The biggest challenge still remained, to bring Japan to its knees in total defeat. The Americans were bound to avenge Pearl Harbor!

Everyone was taking it easy about the barracks late August 6th. There coursed through the ranks of everyone that something big had happened in Japan, but were unsure of what, something about some new kind of bomb. It gave reason to speculate, ask questions of one another. But, no further information was forthcoming. Meanwhile business was as usual.

As the invasion of Japan loomed, was eminent, many felt it was something that they would not survive. They may have escaped death so far, but not this looming time! Felipe took pen and paper to write home, what felt like a death knell.

"Hi Everyone,

We are Okay. We have been bouncing back and forth a bit. I am currently in Okinawa, not that far from Japan. We are expecting a big push to end this war once and for all. We have been beating the enemy everywhere at great cost. But, this coming invasion I just don't know about! We've heard there could be twenty million Japs waiting for us. If they are all fanatics, suicidal like their crazy kamikazes are then we are in for a very tough time. They are committed to die for their emperor god. I have seen pictures of this Hirohito and he doesn't look like someone worthy of that. They are fighting fools with no logic, thinking they have a divine leading to do what they do. I think of the Americans we are with. Pearl Harbor is always on their mind. When we arrived in Manila last May they were skeptical of us. But, we have earned their respect for we have shown we do not run from a fight! We have saved many of them and Filipinos. He paused in thought, thinking what else to say, knowing he had more somewhere in his mind to convey. I still have some things to say but will later. I'm being called.

He set the letter aside with intents to finish it later on. But, one thing or another kept intruding and robbed him of the time to do so.

August 6th was drawing to close rumors persisted that something big had happened in Japan that morning but were not sure what. They all laid upon their cots staring upward into the dark, sleep elusive. What had happened earlier? Just rumor and gossip?

On August 8th the 201st was ordered to fly a mission to Formosa. To avoid radar detection they flew nearly at wave level. It made the pilots nervous, to be nearly clipping the swells with their one thousand pound bombs underneath their right wings and nigh-empty fuel tanks under the left. Near the port of *Karenko* they went in for the kill. The lead plane attacked and the sudden release of the bombs rocked the craft, lurching the plane to the port side as the equilbrium was disturbed. The pilot experiencing this forewarned the others as he had been tossed about in his cockpit. They all returned to base in fine order.

They awoke the morning of August 9th to the news that clarified the rumors of the 6th. There had been a bomb of unbelievable destruction dropped on the port city of *Hiroshima.* They did not know much about that place other than what they heard, that it was a place of much industry and was a port where Japanese troops shipped-out from. This they believed, as they all had, was President Truman's attempt to force Japan to capitulate unconditionally. If they did perhaps millions of more lives could be spared and Japan would avoid complete and utter destruction. It was the Allies prayer that an invasion would not be required to bring an end to the war. It was a wait and see time to see how Japan reacted to this new era of warfare. Their stubbornness risked another display of the power of the United States' arsenal.

Meanwhile operations in the field continued. On the 10th the 201st was ordered to escort a naval convoy from Okinawa. There had been concerns of kamikaze attacks and as the P-47's flew support overhead nothing occurred. They returned to base.

Indeed the United States did drop another bomb. It had been determined previously that five cities would be targeted and each one would be destroyed if the Emperor did not surrender after each one was obliterated. The selected sites were; 1. Kokura (largest munitions plant), 2. Hiroshima (embarkation port and industrial center, plus a major military headquarters), 3. Yokohama (urban center for aircraft production, machine tools, docks, electrical equipment, oil refineries), 4. Nigata (industrial port, steel and aluminum plants, oil refineries). 5. Kyoto (major industrial center). The second city doomed was a substitute target, *Nagasaki.*

Before there was a conclusion to use an atomic bomb conventional and firebombings destroyed sixty-seven cities in Japan. And yet, the Japanese remained defiant with resolve. They knew there was a coming invasion and knew well the geography of their country played well in their defensive plans. They prepared for the Allies with their *Operation Ketsugo.* Four veteran divisions were recalled from Manchuria and another forty-five new ones were assembled. About two and half million army troops were on standby and a mobilized civilian militia tallied twenty-eight million. Emperor Hirohito and his staff estimated twenty million Japanese would die. The U.S. Joint Chiefs of Staff had concluded that a quarter of a million casualties and 46,000 deaths the Allies would suffer. The US Army Chief of Staff, General George Marshall, and the Commander in Chief in the Pacific, General Dougals MacArthur, agreed with the Joint Chiefs' war plans and staggering figures.

An ultra intelligence unit tracked Japan's build up and the figures were drastically altered. It was now figured that the Allies would suffer up to four million casualties, and perhaps 800,000 deaths, and that of Japan perhaps ten million deaths. Such figures staggered the imagination. *General Marshall* even considered using reprehensible poison gases; phosgene, mustard, tear, cyanogen chloride. In the end it was decided to use the nuclear bombs and capitalize on the shock values to bring Japan to its senses. Official orders to go forth with the nuclear bombings had been issued July 25th. President Truman noted.

"This weapon is to be used against Japan between now and August 10th. I have told the Secretary of War, Mr. Stimson, to use it so that military objectives and soldiers and sailors are the target and not women and children. Even if the Japs are savages, ruthless, merciless and fanatic, we as the leader of the world for the common welfare cannot drop that terrible bomb on the old capital (Kyoto) or the new (Tokyo). He and I are in accord. The target will be a purely military one."

It had been suggested to demonstrate to the Japanese the awesome destructive power of the bomb in a non-combat situation. But, it had been decided against because they feared a possible failure of the bomb to detonate, and thus would lose all shock value. There had been sixty-three million leaflets of warning dropped prior the conventional and firebombings. They did not accomplish much. Oppenheimer and his fellow scientists believed that it was wiser to focus on the shock values of using the bomb outright, and cease any thought of a demo explosion or even a special leaflet drop. There should be no warnings to Hiroshima, a city which had signs on its walls saying, *Forget Self! All Out For Your Country!*

While the first bomb was dropped on Agust 6th, President Truman, Prime Minister Winston Churchill, and Josef Stalin of Russia met at Potsdam for a conference. It was there that all three agreed that Japan must surrender 'unconditionally' or risk utter destruction.

They all knew now that a second bomb had been dropped, upon a last minute target change, *Nagasaki,* where the *Mitsubishi Shipyards* were. What was Japan thinking, they wondered? How much more can they take? Will we be forced to invade? The Allies waited to see if the two atomic bombs pounded reason into their heads. If not there were plans to drop more bombs, another on August 19th, three more in September and three more in October.

The very day of Nagasaki's destruction Japan's War Council insisted upon four conditions, which were soundly rejected by the Allies. In the wake of the rejection the council deliberated. On August 12th Emperor Hirohito told the Imperial Family that he had concluded to surrender, something they had never conceived in thought their emperor-god would do. But, he not only had to consider the awesome power of the United States. He also was aware of Stalin's Russian Army poised to invade Japan. On the 14th a recorded announcement of Empero Hirohito was broadcast to the nation over radio. It was the first time that the masses had heard their god's voice.

"Moreover, the enemy now possesses a new and terrible weapon with the power to destroy many innocent lives and do incalculable damage. Should we continue to fight not only would it result in an ultimate collapse and obliteration of the Japanese nation, but also it would lead to the total extinction of human civilization.

Such being the case, how are we to save the millions of our subjects, or to atone Ourselves before the hallowed spirits of Our Imperial Ancestors? This is the reason why We have ordered the acceptance of the provisions of the Joint Declaration of the Powers."

They had only heard of the two bombs that had brought the Empire of Japan down. Just how terrible were they, they wondered? What on earth did the government come up with that could do that! Could only two bombs do what all of the bombs dropped on the Japanese from the beginning could not do? They mulled over in their minds all that had been the Pacific Theatre of War, all across the vast Pacific Ocean and across the United States to the very steps of the U.S. Capital. As word spread around the world of Japan's demise and how it happened a sense of dread gripped all. Indeed just as the first two ironclad warshipships, the Monitor and Merrimack, had done during the American Civil War, making the wooden navies of the world obsolete, the US aresenal had now propelled the world into a new and fragile world of possible nuclear annilhation because of the most lethal bombs imagineable, as if Dante's Inferno had been unleashed. Yes, the war had concluded! The madness of it all had come to a close. The formal ceremonies of Japan's humility and the victorious Allies concluded in Tokyo Bay upon the decks of the battleship, *USS Missouri*. On September 2nd the ship was teeming with crew, guests, spectators to witness the historical event. It had been a somber occasion; no gloating in victory for it had cost so many lives and wreaked unparalleled destruction. Everyone was spent in body and soul. The signed instrument of surrender brought World War ll to a an official close, for Nazi Germany had surrendered the previous May 8th. The atomic bomb age was now upon the world and humanity dared not risk a third world war in a nuclear age! The bombs were now a proven reality. The 'genie' was out of the bottle.

In the aftermath of the surrender Felipe was resting by the desk drawer where he had placed his unfinished letter to home, what he had figured was to be his last communication to loved ones back home. The fortunes of war, however, had turned in their favor. There would be no invasion and his life and many others would be spared. As if by impulse he drew out the letter now of no value to re-read what he had written a month before. He registered no expression, just deeply thought for a while, and then neatly folded the letter along its creased lines and replaced it inside the envelope. He held it in hand for a while, thinking on the lines he had written and had just read again. Then as if on spontaneity he shoved it into his duffle bag with no further thought. I am alive! I will go on living, he thought, and rose up and went outside to breathe in the air of life!

Chapter 21

"A Newfound Identity"

The days following the surrender ceremonies aboard the USS Missouri life for the 201st took on a nature different from combat. They tread through the passing days and weeks expecting word to come that they were returning home, that their service had been fulfilled. It was not until November when they anticipated family and friends at home. They had been in transit across the Pacific and now those thousands of miles were behind them. It had been a vastly different crossing this time compared to months before when they endured seasickness, threats of submarine attacks, and frequent drills on deck as their ship's bow pointed them to Manila, the war, and the perils that awaited them. Now they were returning across the seas as conquering heroes, perhaps due a hero's welcome as Galvan had expected.

It was a sunny November 18th, 1945. Throngs of people crowded Mexico City to hail their returning heroes. President Camacho had greeted them, led a parade down Avenida Madero as thousands of people trailed behind and lined the avenue. Formal ceremonies commenced after the parade had concluded. The Commander of the 201st Air Squadon had returned unto President Camacho the very same battle flag that the Sub-Secretary of War had presented them with as the *Aguilas Aztecas* were being inducted into active service. Training had concluded and they were destined to prove its worth and their mettle. The President received the flag with gratitude and pride. He beamed as he addressed them and the nation.

"General, chiefs, officers, and the troops of the Expeditionary Air Force, I receive with emotion the FLAG that the country has conferred as a symbol of her and those ideas of humanity for which we fight in a common cause. You return with glory, having complied brilliantly with your duty, and in these moments in this historic plaza, you receive the gratitude of our people."

It had been quite the welcome home, something that Galvan and the others they left behind would have thrilled with. The tributes and honors had been paid and all the festivities had concluded. The crowds had dissipated, were headed for home or elsewhere. In the following days the heralded battle flag of the 201st would find a home in the National Historical Museum.

It had seemed that their honors would be lasting, that they would continue to be hailed as heroes. But, that was not to be. The politicians who had wavered for two years to grant President Camacho the right to send them off to a war, which most considered someone else's fight, now felt threatened by the pilots of the 201st. They eyed them with indifference and suspicion. If any one of their number was long-revered as a hero and was encouraged to pursue politics they could very well upset the political establishment. Mexican politicians were usually groomed and handpicked from within their ranks and any outsider could be disruptive. Unlike in the United States where hero worship is commonplace the Mexican political establishment and its machinery of conduct did not exhibit the same national respect for war veterans.

The hoopla and celebrations had waned away long ago and Mexico found itself once again assuming a self-willed posture of semi-isolationism. There was, however, enough gratitude and support to shower the 201st with one lasting honor. In 1947, inside the 1,600 - acre Chapultepec Park of Mexico City, an impressive monument had been erected and was dedicated. It was a tribute to the only Mexican fighting force to ever be sent abroad unto foreign lands to engage in war. The semi-circle structure, cream-colored, is the size of two school buses and a story-plus high. Grand rectangular plates anchor the structure and bear the names of the members of the famed squadron. And yet, despite how impressive the memorial is the 201st's service record in history has faded into oblivion. The nation and culture have remained ambivalent to the worth and sacrifice of these honorable men.

On the day of dedication Felipe and his wife Magaly after the ceremonies stood in silent contemplation before the memorial. Felipe was somber as he read the names of those he had served with. Only when he read the names of those in the "Aquarium" did he offer a hint of a smile. He resumed a somber stance as he read the names of those who had paid with their lives.

Hector Espinoza Galvan
Mario Lopez Portillo
Jose Espinoza Fuentes
Mamerto Albarran Nagera
Crisoforo Salido Grijalva
Faust Vega Santander

"Come dear," said Magaly slightly tugging on him. "It's time to go. They're waiting for us." At home Elisabeth and Horacio had been working long, alongside a kitchen monk, to prepare a special dinner for the special occasion. Yes, concluded Felipe, it was time to step aside and let others around them step up and contemplate the memorial and hopefully they would value the significance of it. It was time to leave that behind and live the moment.

Felipe and Magaly walked the hallway for the dining room. While in the Far Pacific, at night he had invisioned the displayed artwork on the walls, the LLadro figurines on marble tables on either side as they walked by. Such trappings he had taken for granted in his naïve youth. Certainly, he mused, that war will change one's values, or at least heighten those previously nurtured. They passed through and past those memories and entered the dining room. There they found Magaly's mother and father, her sister too. Professor Arellano had honored them again. How they had managed it he had the faintest idea; a couple that he had valued within the study group were there too. If the ornate table of thick hardwood had been any larger there would surely have been some more.

Mother and Horacio had outdone themselves. Their labors of love in the kitchen, overseen by the monk's watchful eye and hand ready to assist, graced the table with delights. There was pavo (turkey) as the main course and too another favorite, Pacific salmon, which Felipe had eagerly savored. Elisabeth had retrieved from the cellar several bottles of aged wine, those that had been valued by her Rodolfo. The day had been a somber one in membrance, and now a jovial one around the table with friends and family together again. Conversations were abuzz about Felipe; many questions about what he had been apart of. But, in his mind he had slipped aside for a moment, briefly considering his past.

He leapfrogged backwards in time, thinking how he had been a naïve student, an idealogue in search of things beyond the classroom, off campus, how that all began with his perceived injustice heaped upon Mexican citizens as the government broke up families, forceably removed them from their homes and relocated them to distant internment camps like criminals destined for prison. They had been guilty of nothing, but for their feared and suspected ancestry. Yes, the image of Haru Yamashita began to come in focus; the man he had not known for long but had befriended in short order. Their brief visits granted through the Commandant had nurtured a healthy respect for one another and Felipe's sense of outrage only heightened for his new-found friend; enough so that it had prompted the journey north to see his wife. The image of Haru dogged him while sitting amongst his family and friends at the table. Where had he gone after they had moved him? Where was he now? Were they together again, Haru, Rocio, the children? Afterall, the war was over!

"Are you Okay?" asked Magaly, aware of his silence. Felipe stirred from his apparent stupor.

"Oh yes! I was just thinking of some things. Don't worry! I am fine."

Professor Arellano sat across from him, noticing the subtle changes in Felipe. He was not as impulsive, rambunctious, was more settled in deep thought. He had known his past prized pupil for being a real thinker. Now he begged to know what his thinking was these days. How had his experiences abroad shapened him now for life at home? His moments of being withdrawn concerned the professor.

"Felipe, when the time is convenient please come see me," prompted Arellano. "I think we have some things we could talk about. I could tell more about those Sinarquistas and what has happened to Schreiter and all his kind. We can even talk about your future if you like. I have some ideas you might like to hear."

Felipe smiled, arched an eyebrown in wonder. Future? He had not given that a whole lot of thought. Yes, he now was married and that meant added responsibilities. "Yes, perhaps next week," replied Felipe. "I have some things to do this week. But, I should be free next week. I'll call you." The professor smiled and raised his glass to Felipe in agreement.

"Excuse me everyone," interrupted Elisabeth. "I think we'd all find it more comfortable in the parlor. If you please, we can remove there."

They pushed themselves away from the table and rose up to go, following Elisabeth's lead. "Leave all," said Horacio to her."I'll clean up." He lingered behind as the others sauntered away and soon was clearing off the dining table and busied himself in the kitchen washing the dishes. In the parlor Elisabeth entertained. The sherry was popular, and so was brandy.

Felipe stood by the portrait of his father, alongside a sizable bookcase. He held in hand a crystal goblet, semi-conscious that he had been twirling it and the brandy within. He raised it to his mouth to savor. He espied over the rim his mother across the floor, engaged in a hearty discussion with Professor Arellano. He looked about the parlor marveling all present, the environs so welcoming. Felipe was silent in self-considerations, as if something was playfully dancing about in his mind, something to debate and analyze, something to question. He had been 'dancing' in his mind when Elisabeth appeared.

"You are far away somewhere," she said approaching his side. "Did you enjoy the meal? Horacio and I spent a lot of time putting it together."

His answer was not immediately forthcoming. His thoughts

had been elsewhere, beyond the parlor, home, even family and friends. She looked into his eyes, waiting for her son to reply with something. Finally he did.

"How would you like to go for a ride, take the train up to Ciudad Juarez again?"

Elisabeth had an incredulous expression. Her mind raced back to when she and he had done so before, and all the intrigue that they had encountered, and how grateful they were to have returned home. She studied his face and demeanor. Was he for real? And just like he had been, long silent before answering, she considered in depth before her own. Then, with an arched eyebrow and smile, she did.

"Only if Magaly comes too!!"

Decades have come and gone since the war had ended, and since the once revered monument unto the 201st was dedicated. In the United States World War ll Veterans are hailed as the *Greatest Generation,* and justifiably so. Many time-honored memorials attest to that. But, in Mexico the memory of *Escuadron 201* and their memorial have faded as the years have, of those gallant young men. The *Aguilas Aztecas* have been relegated to the past as the *Forgotten Warriors!* At home their memory has all but faded. New generations are now present and they know little of their once-honored memorial. But, for they of the *201st* , who had endured their nation's indecision, initial racial bias of the Americans, they finally were given the go ahead for induction into the Allied armed forces that brought Japan down to its knees in unconditional surrender. They gained the respect of their fellow brothers in arms. Both the American Eagle and the Mexican had afterall shown that they share some similar plumage.

THE END

Concluding Remarks:

"Whatever Happened to the National Synarchist Union in Mexico?"

The National Synarchist Union (UNS) of Mexiso underwent changes shortly after the attack upon Pearl Harbor. Seventeen days prior, on November 19, 1941, Mexico signed an agreement with the United States, agreeing with President Roosevelt's proposed *Good Neighbor Policy* of 1932. This paved the way to settle the hotly debated issue of US Oil company losses in Mexico due to Mexico's expropriating those US interests when they nationalized the petroleum industry. In the agreement the United States acknowledged that Mexico has the sovereign rights to all of their subterranean natural resources. 1. It evaluated for compensation the expropriated U.S. properties. 2. Mexico agreed to pay forty million dollars over fourteen years to settle all US claims. 3. There would be a reciprocal trade agreement. 4. The US Treasury would stabilize currency with the buying of Mexican pesos and silver.

5. The US Export-Import Bank would issue credits to Mexico, that the highway network would be expanded from border to border, coast to coast.

October 14, 1941 the Mexican Congress confronted the Union Nacional Sinarquista (UNS) issue. Congress labeled the UNS 'fascist.' Government was committed to resist the 'regressive' agendas of the fascist union. This resolve sprouted from the National Anti-Synarchist Committee for the Defense of Democracy. In the wake of Pearl Harbor, because the United States had acknowledged Mexico's rights to expropriate said oil properties, Mexico completely modified its stance politically. When the United States declared war on Japan December 8, 1941,

Mexico severed relations with Japan the same day, as they did with Germany and Italy on December 12th. This was a major move of Mexico's for they had been dependent upon selling oil to those Axis countries.

Previously, May 1941, the UNS claimed that Roosevelt's Good Neighbor Policy (Pan-Americanism) was no more than a disguised American Imperialism. The UNS embarked upon creating, or at least fostering, an Hispanic-American movement to confront the American 'threat.' However, Pearl Harbor was a wake-up call for the UNS leadership. *Antonio Santacruz,* a chief Synarchist, told membership, "We must agree with the United States. Since Pearl Harbor it is a matter of life and death." Followers of Santacruz fired their hardline chief Salvador Abascal. On December 12, 1941 he was removed from office. Professor Manuel Torres Bueno then took over as the national chief of the UNS.

November 1942, the Mexican Congress being further alarmed at the Nazi-Fascist ways of the UNS and how they followed the lead of the Spanish Falangists, expanded the National Anti-Synarchist Committe to now include an Anti-Nazi, Anti-Fascist Committee.

After Pearl Harbor the Catholic Church in Mexico, an advocate of the Spanish Falange, was pressured to coral the UNS. Under mounting political pressure the Church purposely gave the impression that it was severing relations with the Falange. It even ouright lied that it had had no ties to the Sinarchists or the National Action party (PAN), which in reality the Church controlled via a secret pact with the Falange. A campaign thus commenced to get all Church officials to band together to support and direct the UNS despite its public announcement of no involvement.

Despite its public image the Church had long-issued names of those they recommended for membership in the UNS. The Spanish Falange directed Nazi propaganda in the Union and their secret Accion Nacional Party (PAN). The Falange had a strong relationship with the Archbishop of Mexico and important bishops, and all Church activities involved the Synarchists. In essence the UNS thrived with Catholic Church assistance, grooming the UNS to be similar to Spanish fascism. All the groups were intertwined in one form or another. The Bishop of

Guadalajara, Monsignor Garibi Rivero, however, reiterated that the Church had absolutely nothing to do with the UNS or (PAN).

After the Nazi defeat at Stalingrad, February 2, 1942, the UNS realized the Axis Powers were not good for their Synarchist future. They opted to side with a pro-Franco group in the United States. The Anglo-American faction was anti-Roosevelt and the UNS found this appealing. The Synarchists changed from an anti-Yankee, pro-Axis stance to an anti-Roosevelt, anti-Anglo-American faction led by American Catholics Cardinal Francis J. Spellman and Bishop Fulton Sheen.

These two Church officials worked with the UNS leadership to adopt a platform of "universal' fascism, with a phony perception of being the *New Christian Social Order*. Bishop Sheen went so far as to travel to Mexico City to convince the Synarchists to convert to the new agenda because world conditions were changing. Sheen attended the Eucharist Congress in Tulancingo, Hidalgo and lodged with Father Iglesias, a leader with ties to top UNS officials. Upon his return to Washington D.C. Sheen issued a press release November 1943.

"What Mexico needs is a revolution; no revolution has been less revolutionary than that of Mexico; the corruption in this country is scandalous and total, Only the religious faith of the people and their Catholic tradition can save Mexico."

This was a scandalous announcement in itself for Mexico was now an ally with the United States in the war effort against the Axis Powers. However, Bishop Sheen's appraisal is what the UNS and PAN held true.

Through corrupt Spellman and Sheen the U.S. Catholic Church was now deeper involved with the UNS than ever. They had encouraged Mexican Catholics to wage the Cristero War (1926-29). They were also supporters of Franco in fascist Spain and were now opting to promote a universal form of fascism in the aftermath of the World War for a *new world order, and of course with their Church directing the New Christian Social Order.*

As 1943 drew to a close the world had undergone substantial change, even fascism in Europe was declining. The UNS had to modify. The once pro-Fascist Bishop Sheen intervened. He directed changes and found new sources of funding. After Sheen had left Mexico UNS Director Torres Bueno began receiving large caches of money from anti-Roosevelt groups in the United States. The Mexican Synarchists were further inspired to adopt these changes from Argentina's anti-Semitic priest, Julio Meinvielle, a fascist.

Post War

Former chief of the UNS, Salvador Abascal, and present chief Torres Bueno had serious disagree-ments, verbally fought and in general had a terrible relationship. Historically the UNS demonized President Benito Juarez for stripping the Church of her rights and property and disbursing to the people. In April 1944 Abascal seethed, condemned Bueno for getting the UNS to exonerate Juarez even posthumously. Abascal further vented. He railed on Bueno for equating Mexican Catholics with America's Protestants. *Our destiny was in our Hispanic culture and the ideological battle against Yankee imperialism.* In 1944 Abascal, the former hardline leader of the UNS was expelled from membership and others of his persuasion were to follow.

The Synarchist union now had to convince membership and others that they had not sold out to the Americans and the push for a new social order. The UNS ceased their miliant ways of opposition to the Mexican Constitution of 1917, which evolved from the 1910 Revolution. The deputy leader of the UNS, Juan Ignacio Padilla stated in the *El Sinarquista* publication, "*This is no government. Sinarquismo appeals to the Army!*" Padilla claimed that President Camacho was trying to emulate the Soviets and he appealed to the Army to step in and prevent a Communist take-over. "*We have raised an army of 500,000 soldiers who are resolved to give Mexico a government of real authority.*" This prompted the government to shut down the publication and banned Synarchist meetings in twenty-eight states. Padilla was arrested and charged with treason and other offenses.

October of 1944 saw an upheaval within the UNS, going through revisions, even new affiliations. Bueno had been charged with embezzlement and being too subservient to the government. He broke away from the UNS and in his place a new leader was installed; Gonzalez Sanchez for the UNS-MTB. In February 1945 the UNS-CAC appointed Carlos Athie Carrasco; the UNS-MTB legally registerd a political party, the *Popular Force Party*. But, January 28, 1949 its registration was terminated. "The unpatriotic activities of the Popular Force Party, its confessional nature, its campaign of proselytism based upon stirring up religious feelings, its ardent desire to modify the political organization of the country by means of violence, longing for times that have definitely gone, and the resemblance of its structure to fascism" were reasonings for the termination.

1954, The Synarchists attempted to legally form another political party, *Party of National Unity*. But its application was denied for lack of membership. May 23, 1954 the UNS celebrated their seventeenth anniversary of founding, named Padilla's successor, Martinez Aguayo, who himself was followed in succsession by Ignacio Gonzalez, David Lomeli Contreras, David Orozco Romo. With new leadership and tact the UNS reorganized, embarked upon establishing institutions, military and confessional antiquated types, with purposes of returning to its founding principles and force a *clerical-fascism* upon membership.

More Recently

The official publication of the UNS today is the *ORDEN*. In 1971 the Union promoted the *Democratic Party of Mexico*. In the 1982 Presidential Election their candidate, Ignacio Gonzalez Gallo, received 500,000 votes; in 1988, Magana

Negrete 700,000. Carlos Salinas Gortari won in 1988, but terminated that party's legal status since they would not accept his election. From 1992-96 corruption within the UNS brought on a crisis. Since the Democratic Party of Mexico was no more, those of that defunct party renounced the UNS and formed the *Party of Social Alliance* (PAS).

In 1996 Leonardo Andraca Hernandez now the new chief of the UNS, tried to restore the Union's nationalistic and popular visions of the past. In 2000 the UNS decided that election politics was not for the UNS and the new focus was to reconstruct itself within, return to its roots at founding.

2002 marked intense social change in the UNS under Lic. Magdaleno Hernadez Yanez. His goals were to restore the Christian Social Order based upon Catholic doctrine, to reject liberal politics and theology, to regard the Mexican Revolution as 'satanic', to transform Mexico's detested liberal institutions into organizations in harmony with Catholic social doctrine, and to establish a Christian Social Order. Claims were made against the government for failure to be faithful to Hispanic Catholic culture, turning away from Mexico's *Virgin of Guadalupe*.

Contrary to UNS claims, promoting the ideas of a clash of cultures between the United States and Hispanic America, nothing proved out. The New Christian Order as promoted by the Synarchists is actually non-Christian. They have tried qualifying their Nazi-racist origins and persistent fascist tendencies and agendas by quoting the Popes' pronouncements.

Collaborations of Roosevelt (Good Neighbor Policy) and Mexican Presidents Lazaro Cardenas and Avila Camacho in the end brought the Mexican Synarchist movement down, ending that threat, and in the broader scope of things helped defeat elements of synarchism globally during World War ll. It is evident, that without President Franklin Delano Roosevelt, Winston Churchill, and those like-minded in whatever degree of contribution, the Berlin-Rome-Madrid-Tokyo - connection would most likely have succeeded trampling further asunder the free peoples of the world. But, it must be acknowledged too in the years since World War ll such radicals have continued attempts to resurface, mutated into grotesque nations and splinter groups in a digital age of mischief and mayhem. Synarchism, politics, religion! A proven trio of strange bedfellows that wreak havoc!

MEMBERS of MEXICO'S EXPEDITIONARY AIR FORCE

201 st AIR SQUADRON

"AZTEC EAGLES"

Commanding: Colonel Antonio Cardenas Rodriguez

Carlos Garduno Nunez
Gracio Ramirez Garrido
Fernando Hernadez Vega
Carlos Varela Landini
Angel Sanchez Rebollo
Miguel Moreno Arreola
Praxedis Lopez Ramos
Raul Garcia Mercado
Miguel Uriarte Aguilar
Hector Espinoza Galvan
Mario Lopez Portillo
Radames Gaxiola Andrade
Jose Luis Pratt Ramos
Joaquin Ramirez Vilchis
Carlos Rodriguez Corona
Roberto Legorreta Sicilia
Jacobo Estrada Luna
Pedro Martinez Perez
Jaime Zenizo Rojas

Jose Espinoza Fuentes
Mamerto Albarran Nagera
Julio Cal y Mayor Sauz
David Ceron Bedolla
Audberto Gutierrez Ramirez
Justino reyes Retana
Manuel Farias Rodriguez
Reynaldo Urias Aveleyra
Crisoforo Salido Grijalva *
Faust Vega Santander
Javier Martinez Valle **
Guillermo Garcia Ramos
Jose Gutierrez Gallegos
Note: Bold Print / Died
Killed in training / Army Air Base/ Abilene, Texas
** Killed in training / Army Air Base / Harlingen, Texas

Birds of a Feather Flock Together, Threatened by the Winds of Change

eagles of a different feather

BIBLIOGRAPHY

1. Los Angeles Times, July 25, 2004
2. Wikipedia.html
3. Wikipedia.org / Cristero_ War
4. Welcome to the Mexican Expeditionary Air Force 201st Fighter Squadron.html
5. The Nazi-Instigation of the National Synarchist Union of Mexico. html

6. Executive Intelligence Review, July 9 & 16, 2004

7. The Scholar Works , San Jose State University
Re-Imagining Collectives; The Mexican-Japanese During World War ll and Selfa Chew of the Department of Languages and Linguistics, University of Texas at El Paso
8. Secret Japanese Submarine Bases on the Pacific Coast
"The Wandering" Desktop.com
9. "The Land Where Time Stands Still", Max Miller (1945) and Feb. 8, 2018 / Sagwan Press
10. Collective Hearts: Texans in World War ll, Joyce Gibson
"Night of the Yaqui Moon", Jane Pattie (1996)
11. "A Maritime History of Baja California" series, Edward Vernon , Jan. 15, 2010, Ashwin Pubns.

About the Author:

JOAQUIN ANDRE HAWKINS

Joaquin Andre Hawkins resides near San Juan Tecomatlan, above Lake Chapala in Jalisco, Mexico. Originally from Tacoma, Washington in the USA he has been associated with lakeside since 1982, and has been in full residency since early 2007.

Mr. Hawkins has had long-standing interests in history. He had been for many years a re-enactor of the American Civil War; portraying both Union and Confederate soldiers before the enthralled eyes of a viewing public, even before cinema and television cameras. His wife was a teacher in a public school classroom and he was a teacher in the field as a living-history re-enactor.

He is retired from the federal government in the United States and today is a permanent resident in Mexico. His interests in history, writing about that which stirs his imagination, will have him embark upon research online and literally traveling to historical sites to further his knowledge and insights of any given subject matter. Historical novels will slowly take form in his imagination, taking him on a journey and concludes only when he types THE END.

Other such journeys have resulted in two other published novels:

Calamity's Children: Civil War / Post War novel

Enza: the Spanish Lady: How the 1918 Spanish Flu arrived in Seattle and Puget Sound

* * *

Made in the USA
Middletown, DE
23 September 2018